RUTHLESS MONSTERS

RUTHLESS MONSTERS

GAME OF PSYCHOS
BOOK TWO

MIA HARTSON

ISBN: 978-0-6457298-5-6
First printing edition 2024 in United States
Cover design by Trif Book Design

Mia Hartson
PO BOX 1052, Golden Grove Village, SA 5125
www.miahartson.com

You really are mine, aren't you gorgeous?
~ Nate

For you, dear reader. This is your excuse to put down the dishes, ignore the unfolded washing, and escape into another world where the men are gorgeous protective assholes who smell like chocolate. I hope you enjoy the read. xx

For a list of trigger warnings, please visit
www.miahartson.com/triggerwarnings

~ Nate ~

Damp earth. Sweat. Sulphur. The pungent smell of rotting eggs combined with the stench of unwashed bodies thickens the air, and for a moment, I think I'm in the dungeons of Kanzepes, the beast realm. The sense of familiarity is shattered when a musky scent I can't place reaches my nose, the unusual odor mixed with the distinct smells of oil, blood, and something nutty. My instincts shout a warning at me, and when my eyes fly open, I find a strange creature towering over my form.

The being's bottom half is that of a winged stallion, with four muscular legs and massive feathery wings folded at its sides, but its top half is that of a man with long, dirty-brown hair, and an array of weapons secured in a belt around his waist. Grimy plates of battered armor cover the male's otherwise bare chest, and he glares down at me with disgust. The shape of his face already gives it a squashed look, and the curl of his top lip only highlights those features.

"Well, you're the fuckin' ugliest demon I've ever seen," I comment with a grin, even though it's obvious we never made it to Seral, the demon realm. Princess Blake isn't anywhere around me, a fact I'm certain of seein' as her honey and cinnamon scent is absent from my nose, and while knowing this has my anger rising, I maintain my focus on the immediate threat in front of me. I'll be useless to her if I'm dead. I've never heard of beasts with half-animal forms, so somehow, when we stepped through the portal and tried to return to Seral, we ended up somewhere else entirely. Prince Callan and Dante are still unconscious nearby, and going by the throbbing in my skull, we'd been knocked out by something strong. *Which is just fuckin' great.* It had already been a journey making it through the demon king's competition, and I'd been lookin' forward to a nice bed and some proper food. *Looks like I'm gonna have to wait a while longer.*

As expected, the creature's face flares with anger at my comment, and he rears up on his hind legs, his large hooves rising into the air. Before he can strike, I attempt to shift, knowing I'll easily be able to gut this beast while in my agile jaguar form, but when I try to bring on the change, a sharp, searing pain shoots up my right leg. I'm caught off guard, and I snarl in surprise, struggling to my feet. I only just manage to glimpse the silver enchanted cuff around my ankle before the beast's front hooves slam hard into my chest. I'm sent crashing back to the ground, the air violently stolen from my lungs, and before I can lift to my feet again, a large pickaxe lands heavily on my chest.

Cursing, I glare up at the male creature. "What the fuck is this?"

I'm referring to the cuff that's stifling my magic, but the male replies, "A mining tool. Get to work or I'll report your refusal to the king." His voice is rough and scratched like something damaged his vocal cords, and he sneers down at me like I'm nothing more than the dirt beneath his hooves. "Something tells me he's just looking for an excuse to end your miserable life."

The king? I wrack my brain, wondering if any of the rulers from the allied realms could be responsible for this, but it's too early to tell. Lowering my brows, I finally let myself assess the vast cavern I'm in. The space is connected to a network of narrow tunnels, and I assume these lead to more caves and caverns. The structure reminds me of an ant nest, but of course, it's much larger in size. The only light I can detect comes from a few sparse glowing crystals embedded in the rocky ceiling high above, and going by the thick, stale air, I'm guessing I'm far underground.

Around me, dozens of figures mine the cavern I'm in, but unlike the creature before me, they appear almost human. Standing on two legs, some of them are around my height, except their filthy bodies are wiry and gaunt, and their backs are arched as they continue to hack at the stone, making them appear smaller. The steady *tink! tink!* of metal colliding with rock echoes in my ears, and aside from a few furtive glances, the other prisoners ignore me completely.

That's right, *prisoners*. Because given where I am and the cuff on my ankle, it's the only conclusion that makes sense. Somehow, I've been captured, but by whom and why, I have no idea. Given his armor and commanding attitude, it's obvious now that the half-horse creature in front of me is some kind of guard, and more guards like him are spread throughout the space, watching over the other prisoners with matching stern expressions.

A female prisoner collapses on the other side of the cavern, the pickaxe slipping from her grip as she falls hard to the ground, and a guard steps forward, shouting obscenities at her. Pulling out his whip, he uses it on her bony back, not stopping until the female crawls forward, struggling again to her feet, blood dripping through her torn clothing. Pain shines in her murky eyes, but she doesn't cry. Her gaze briefly finds another prisoner before she hastily starts mining again, her thin arms straining as she lifts her pickaxe.

Well, fuck me.

"Move it, or you'll get the same treatment," my guard growls with a cruel twist of his lips.

I eye the whip tied to his belt, but I'm not dumb enough to test him. Not when my magic has been barred from me, and I have no idea what the fuck he's capable of, magically and physically. Begrudgingly, I find my feet, grabbing the wooden handle of the pickaxe and turning to the wall of rock behind me.

That's when I notice Alaric is already there, chipping away with his own pickaxe. I should have scented him, but I was too distracted by whatever fucked up place this is. Raising a brow, I give him an incredulous look. *Bastard could have shouted a warnin'.* The Drozac assassin ignores me, but I notice his left cheek is red and swollen like he's just been smashed in the face. *Well, that makes me feel a little better.*

"What are we minin' for?" I ask the guard, my muscles bunching as I swing the axe and drive the steel pick into stone. The rock cracks, and a small section pulls away from the cave wall, stones tumbling near my feet.

"Crystals go in there," the guard points to a metal cart on wheels not too far away. "Make sure it's full before the end of the day, or you'll learn the hard way that dead weight doesn't survive in this place."

I glance up at the glowing crystals high above before bringing my pickaxe down again. "And how will we know when it's time?"

"Because I'll tell you," the guard replies with a

yellow-toothed smile, and he laughs like he's just said something funny. His laughing soon turns to coughing, and he spits on the ground beside me, leaving a glob of yellow phlegm. I narrow my eyes, but otherwise, I don't react. He's not the first disgruntled guard I've had to deal with, and until I can get this cuff off me, I'm better off spending my energy working out how this place runs. Prisons, like most places, have their own systems and hierarchies of power at play. Once you can figure it out, you can find a way to make it work in your favor. At least, that's how it was in the prisons I've had the pleasure of visiting in the past.

Groaning sounds to my left, and I turn my head as Prince Callan and Dante both regain consciousness. Our guard gives them the same treatment he gave me, and Prince Callan is livid when he realizes he can't use his power. Dante's tail flicks in agitation as he repeatedly asks about Blake, but the guard only shouts at him, dropping a pickaxe at the demon's feet. Leaning down, Dante grabs hold of the axe, and just when I think he's going to attack the guard again, he turns, slamming the pick into rock rather than the guard's body.

Glowering at us, the guard watches from close by, but aside from a few shared glances, the four of us find a steady rhythm, excavating crystals. Keeping silent, we add to the echoes of clanging steel and grunts.

Time blurs as we work, but I'm sure hours have passed when a commotion starts up some distance to our right. "I said keep your eyes to yourself you bastard," snarls a guard with a bald head and small eyes that look too close together. Careful not to slow my pace, I keep working as I snatch glances at the unfortunate prisoner who was caught staring in our direction. Our guard leaves his post, joining the other guard as they berate the prisoner.

"Where's Blake?" Dante asks in a low voice now that our guard's attention is finally elsewhere. The demon's words are steady, but there's a dark gleam in his eyes that betrays his emotions.

"Your guess is as good as mine," I reply, instinctively scanning the cavern again, even though I already know she's not here. The cuff around my ankle might be blocking my ability to shift, but my heightened senses remain, and I still can't detect my mate's delicious honey and cinnamon scent. I try not to think about how it's making me want to tear the limbs from the guards as they scream in agony.

"They took her," Alaric growls under his breath, his massive muscles bulging as he slams his pickaxe into rock again.

Prince Callan's eyes are as cold as ice. "Who did?"

Alaric's muscles tighten. "A foreign king. It's all they've given away."

My nostrils flare as I think of my unbonded mate, and the urge to shift and hunt her down has my skin itching uncomfortably. Without thinking, I try to change into my animal, and I snarl under my breath when pain radiates up my leg, spreading from the cuff. *Fuckin' thing.* Steeling myself, I check that our guard is still busy, then I peer at my cuff and take aim with my pickaxe.

"Don't," Alaric warns, but it's too late. As the steel pick connects with the metal cuff, an intense wave of pain crackles through me. I hiss through the agony, only managing to keep my pained howl contained as my muscles contract and then release again. My breathing becomes labored, and I sag against the rocky wall to keep myself standing.

The three assholes stare at me in amusement.

"Could have warned me earlier," I grumble to Alaric.

The assassin doesn't look the least bit remorseful. "You wouldn't have listened," he replies bluntly, and the matter-of-fact way he says it has me flashing him a grin.

Prince Callan works at prying a crystal from the rock in front of him, and he holds up a green crystal that sparkles in the dim light. Had we been in a different situation, I would have attempted to rescue some of these crystals for myself, but even I'm not a big enough fool to try anything right now.

"So, Blake's not here, and we've been imprisoned and neutralized by an unknown magic," Dante comments, his expression hard as he continues to mine. "Could this be the work of the witches?"

"These beings ain't witches," I point out, my gaze flicking to our guard who still hasn't returned.

"They could be working with them," Prince Callan

says. "Like the giants we fought in the ruins of Perstalia."

Alaric's brows lower, and we're all silent for a moment as we contemplate this.

"Whoever's behind it, we have to find her," Dante says, his dark eyes fixed on the rock in front of him.

None of us argue with that, and it's obvious we're all thinking the same thing. That we aren't going to be able to rest until we know the demon princess is safe.

I tell myself that her disappearance shouldn't bother me. After all, my goal when I attended the ball in Seral had been to hunt down the treasure in the demon castle and head back to Kanzepes. But the princess has gotten under my skin, and now my every instinct is telling me to find my mate. If I don't find her soon, I'm going to lose my absolute fuckin' mind.

"The guards have been paying extra attention to that prisoner," Prince Callan says, his head cocked as he listens to the guards still shouting insults.

The archangel's comment jolts me from my thoughts, and I turn my attention to the guards and the prisoner not far from us. Torn strips of clothing barely cover the prisoner's scarred back, and thick layers of dirt and crystal dust coat his tattooed brown skin. His hair is a tangled mess of black knots, and his face is sunken and pale, but even as the guards hurl obscenities at him, he doesn't cower. I've been in enough prisons to know how hard it is not to break when you've been there for long enough and every day is designed to test your will to live, so a trickle of respect goes through me at his defiance.

"You're a bloody disgrace," our guard spits out as the prisoner continues to work like this is an ordinary day for him. "Defender of the realm? You couldn't save any of us when they came."

I frown, my curiosity piqued by the guard's comments. Nearby prisoners continue to mine, but a few of them cringe, their backs curling over more when the second guard detaches the whip from his belt.

"You think the newcomers are going to change things, don't you?" our guard mocks. "No, when they're gone, you'll still be here. Even when I'm the one in the king's crystal palace, enjoying the life he's promised us. Oh yes, you'll still be toiling in your own filth where you belong."

The prisoner's face remains passive as he uses his fingers to clear away the crumbling rock, and he leans down, blowing the dust from a cluster of crystals. It's not until the other guard unfurls his whip that the prisoner speaks. "You've been here as long as I have, Javier. Tell me, who's the bigger fool? The prince who knows exactly why he was betrayed, or the guard who, even after all these years, still doesn't realize he's been forgotten?" The prisoner glances our way then, and there's a spark in his glowing blue eyes that doesn't fade, even when the other guard snarls and brings the whip down on his back. The crack is loud enough that it makes me wince, but the prisoner doesn't cry out.

Not even when the force of the strike makes him fall against the stone. He clutches at the mound of rock, his gaze never straying from the four of us.

"He's a fuckin' prince," I comment to the others.

"And he could be our way out of here," Alaric growls. "We need to find a way to speak with him."

I keep watching, unable to take my gaze from the prince as another crack of the whip rings in my ears.

CHAPTER

TWO

~ Princess Blake ~

Crack! I slam my shoulder against the bedpost for what feels like the hundredth time, and I'm rewarded with a resounding crack as the wood splinters. I'm making enough noise that the guards stationed outside my room must hear, but no one comes to check on me. When the Perstalian ruler, King Celzar, dropped the news of who he is and how he'd kidnapped me, I'd been disorientated, but after he left the room, I wasted little time in setting about my escape. It helps that I heard his command to the guards before he left. No one is allowed to enter my room without having direct orders to do so. Which is perfect. *Because now they won't enter, not even when I'm destroying things.*

If it weren't for the cuff around my ankle blocking my magic, I could have easily done this with one blow, but now, sweat beads on my forehead and my limbs shake from exertion as I try to free myself from the bed. "Finally," I huff, feeling accomplished that the wood of the thick post has cracked, though I'm sure Dad would be appalled by my efforts if he could see me now. *Then again, it's his fault I'm even here.* It was Dad's stupid competition to find my fated mates that led to this. At the thought of the four males I'm destined to bond with, my stomach twists, everything inside me rebelling at the idea that we're apart. Anger heats my blood, and I force myself to take a deep breath and remind myself that they're alive. At least, they are for now. If they were dead, I would feel the hollowing pain that comes when a demon loses her fated. But despite knowing they're alive, fear slides down my spine. I have no idea how much time they have left. Days? Hours? King Celzar's words from not too long ago float into my head: *You won't have to worry about them any longer. From what I've seen, you should be thanking me.*

Gritting my teeth, I slam into the post again. My mates might be complete assholes, but they're *my* assholes, and I'm not about to let them die at the hands of an unhinged king. "I mean, sure, not all of them want to bond yet, and truthfully, considering I accidentally killed my last lover, Kai, I'm a little afraid to even try, but we'll get there. Right?" I say that last bit out loud and look over to where my best friend, a crow named Shade, is perched in her cage. She squawks, staring back at me, but she doesn't reply in my head. Without my magic, my mind is as quiet as it was before I met her. And I hate it.

Grunting, I drive my shoulder into the bedpost again, and this time the wooden support snaps into two. Shade squawks a warning, and I twist out of the way as the top half of the wooden beam falls onto the mattress along with the bed canopy. Balancing on one leg, I lift my cuffed ankle, sliding the chain free of the post, and I grin as I plant both feet onto the floor.

"Well, I can't do much about the cuff, but at least I'm no longer chained to the bed," I say triumphantly.

Shade flutters her feathers to show her happiness at this tiny bit of progress, but there's no disguising the anxiety that shines in her beady black eyes. I move toward her gilded cage, ignoring the way the chain connected to my ankle drags on the floor as I walk.

She shuffles along her perch, closer to the bars, and I poke my fingers through, stroking her black feathers. "Sorry, girl," I tell her. "I'll get us out of this." Of course, I still have no idea *how* I'm actually going to free us, or even where we are. King Celzar said we're in The Haven, which sounds a little pretentious if you ask me, and it doesn't actually explain our location. All I know is that we're not in the allied realms. *One problem at a time, Blake. One problem at a damn time.*

Turning, I scour the room we're in. There isn't much here besides the beautiful wooden dresser on my left with a chair encrusted with crystals, and a narrow door which leads to a simple washroom. I'm busy running through my extremely limited escape options in my mind when the door to my room opens.

Swivelling around, I tense as two guards in royal armor march into the space. Their eyes widen when they take in the destroyed bed and my position in the middle of the room, but they don't say anything. Like the king, they have a half horse form with wings tucked at their sides, and I wonder what the full extent of their power is. Not that it's going to stop me. Dropping low into a fighting stance, I mentally prepare myself to fight, but just as I'm about to lunge forward, and most likely get my ass kicked, I notice the female standing behind them. She's small and thin, and she stands meekly with her head down and one hand wrapped around the handle of a thick silver case. From her size, I'd have thought she was a human if it weren't for the cuff visible around her ankle. A cuff that looks identical to my own.

"Do your job," barks one of the guards. "We'll be outside." Then, giving me one last wary look, the guards both march out of the room as quickly as they came.

I tilt my head to the side, staring at the female and her silver case. "If you're here to torture me, you should know I'm not in the mood," I say, still in a defensive stance. She doesn't look like much, but I know more than anyone how looks can be deceiving.

It's not until the room door clicks shut that the female lifts her head. Her gaze travels over the black wings folded behind my back, and then she peers over at the broken bed. I'm sure I'm imagining it, but I swear the hint of a smile teases her lips.

Starting forward, she doesn't speak as she makes her way to the dresser and places her case down. With a click, she opens the lid and rifles through the contents, taking out colored bottles and brushes, and arranging them in a specific order on the dresser.

I groan, unable to believe what I'm seeing. "You can't be serious," I comment, relaxing my stance.

She finally turns to look at me again, her pale blue eyes fixing on my face as she beckons to the chair with slender fingers. "His highness has requested that you be made presentable for the party this evening. Please sit."

I don't move because getting ready for a party is the last thing on my list of my priorities. Oh, who am I kidding, it's not even on the list. I cross my arms in front of my chest, jutting out my hip, but the servant holds my gaze. "If you are not ready by the allocated time, we will both be punished. Please." She indicates to the chair again. "Sit."

That softens me up a little, but I still hesitate, and it's not until Shade squawks that I start moving. "Fine," I mutter, reassuring myself that if nothing else, I might be able to get information out of the servant while she works.

She styles my hair first, detangling the knots and arranging my black waves into a loose bun with white crystals pinned amongst the strands. When she appears satisfied with my hair, she focuses her attention on my face, adding color to my cheeks and lining my eyes with kohl.

"So...what is this party?" I ask as she brushes powder over my eyes. "Is this something to do with the, uh, wedding?" I'm still in disbelief that King Celzar plans to make me his bride, something that I'm definitely *not* going to let happen. Just saying the word 'wedding' makes me scrunch my face, and the servant clicks her tongue showing her disapproval. I smooth my features, not wanting to piss her off in case it makes her less likely to talk.

When moments pass and she still doesn't speak, I sigh heavily. "You do realize I could kill you, right? Your king doesn't care very much for you if he's willing to leave you in here without the guards." I expect that to get a reaction, but she doesn't look fazed by my comment, continuing on with her work. To be honest, I'm a little impressed.

She finishes my face, and I'm about to press her harder for information, when she says softly, "Actually, I'm the one who requested the guards wait outside." Instant regret flashes on her face the moment the words are out, and she presses her lips tightly together.

My brows lift. "What? Why?"

She gestures for me to look in the mirror again, clearly trying to distract me, but I'm too focused on what she's said. My only guess to explain her response is that she's excited she's able to tend to the new queen-to-be, and she didn't want the guards hovering over her while she worked. But perhaps, she was supposed to let the guards stay. "You know, I'd make a horrible queen for your kind," I tell her. "I don't know what your king has told you, but I'm not meant to be here. I already have my own kingdom to run."

She goes to fix a stray strand of hair that's dropped near my eyes, but I jerk my head back.

"Are you listening to a word I'm saying?" I ask her. "This is all a mistake. Whatever this party is. This place."

Ignoring me, she forgets about the hair and starts packing up her powders, stacking them neatly in her case. I clench my jaw in frustration, and the gleam of something silver in her boot catches my eye. In a swift motion, I lean down, snatching out the small dagger she'd had concealed there, the metal hilt only just visible.

A surprised noise escapes her throat, and there's expectation in her eyes, like she expects me to drive the dagger into her chest, but I turn from her, slamming the hilt of the blade hard onto my cuff. I'd hoped to weaken the metal. I'd thought perhaps a blade that's forged in this land might not be affected by the magic. Or maybe, I just wasn't thinking clearly. Either way, pain races up my body, and I gasp as agony tears through me.

Breathing rapidly, I lift my hand, and the servant must think I'm about to do it again, because her pale blue eyes widen, and her fingers wrap around my wrist, stopping me.

"That won't work," she says softly. "Many have tried before you."

I blink as I absorb her words. *Many have tried?* "Are you...?" I think about the cuff around her ankle. The one that looks nearly identical to mine. "You're a prisoner, just as I am, aren't you?" It's more of a statement than a question, but she dips her head once.

Her gaze goes follows mine, going to her own cuff. "We didn't realize what they were at first. But then again, we didn't realize a lot of things." She blows out a breath, and I'm still processing this bit of information when she reaches down. By the time I realize what she's doing, it's too late to stop her. Appearing from seemingly nowhere, she holds a white crystal in her fingers. As she taps the stone against my own cuff, bursts of color appear in the crystal, and I brace waiting for the pain. To my surprise, this time when a jolt shoots up my leg, the feeling is dulled, and the skin under the cuff warms accompanied by a prickling sensation. A faint burst of power goes through me, and I latch onto it, startled when a familiar voice enters my mind.

"Hurt her and you'll be added to my shit list, right after the king, and the guards outside of this room!"

For a second, I can't breathe. *"Shade?"* The word in my head is weak and tentative, but when small beady black eyes find me from across the room, I know she's heard me. Nothing can stop the smile that spreads across my face.

"Blake? Oh god, Blake, is that you?" Shade flaps her wings in excitement, almost falling off her perch, and relieved laughter bubbles out of my chest.

"Merciful Lady, I've missed your voice," I reply, because finally after hours of having a craptastic time, something good has happened. *"Tell me you're doing okay in there."*

"Better than you by the looks of it," Shade teases. *"Girl, have you seen yourself in the mirror?"*

Grinning, I turn my attention to my reflection. My bright pink cheeks and the vibrant color on my eyes is a different look for me, especially accompanied by the white velvet dress I'm wearing, and I know my bestie is never going to let me live it down.

"Glad to have you back," I say to Shade, and I mean it, too. The hours I just had to endure without her felt like some of the longest in my life. If I have my way, I'll never let it happen again.

"I can't take the cuff off," the servant says, pulling my attention back to her as she pockets the crystal. "But we have found ways to return small traces of our power. If nothing else, but for our own...mental wellbeing. The king shouldn't be able to detect it, but it's best to be wary when using your power around him."

"Thank you," I say genuinely as I smile at her. "But why did you do that?" In Seral, demons don't usually go out of their way to help others. Not unless they're expecting something in return, or unless they've been given a specific order to carry out.

Her lips curve upward, and I get the feeling I'm about to discover this servant's motivations. "You were right, you know," she says, returning my smile. "You could have killed me. When I was told you were a foreigner, a creature from a demon realm, I knew it was a high possibility." Her gaze goes again to my wings, and the next time her pale eyes find my face, her gaze is intense. Unsettling. "But it was worth the risk to see."

I frown. "To see what?"

"To see whether you can finally be the bride we need."

Ah, so this is all about her wanting me to be their next queen. I shake my head, not liking where the conversation is going. "I've already told you, I'm not—"

"We're all winged centaurs," she says, cutting me off. "Most of us have the same powers. Enhanced strength and healing. Super speed, agility, and endurance. Some are able to do more. Or at least, they would be able to if it weren't for these cuffs."

"And you can harness the power of crystals?" I ask, thinking of the crystal in her pocket.

"That was a gift," she replies, not giving anything else away.

"Okay," I say slowly. "And when you say *we're all winged centaurs*, you're referring to?"

"My kind and the inhabitants of this place," she

says grimly. "Those who are left, anyway. But we can't change into our centaur forms with the cuffs blocking our magic," she adds, indicating to her lack of wings and two legs. "The only ones without cuffs are those favored by the king, or his warriors. He wants his soldiers strong so they can keep everyone else in line."

"The guards," I mutter, thinking of their half-animal forms. "So, given your two legs now, does that mean your kind are like shifters? That ordinarily you would be able to change your form at will?"

"Shifters? I've never heard of that term before, but yes, normally we can all change forms," she replies.

I nod my head. *Interesting.* "Okay, but I'm still not going to be your queen," I say. "I'm grateful for what you did to my cuff, but I still don't see—"

"He's had many brides over the years," she forges on. "But none of them survive. When the king proposes marriage, there is no refusing him. Usually, the brides are females of our own kind who he has selected, but sometimes, a female will volunteer. After what we've been through, some will do anything to taste the full power of their magic again, even if the moment is fleeting."

My heart misses a beat as an important part of what she's just said jumps out at me. "Wait. So King Celzar removes the cuffs from his brides?" I don't care much for the vows of marriage. For demons, marriage is simply a piece of paper to divide assets. It's the fated mates bond that holds real meaning. "Okay, so I marry your king, and I get my power back?"

She watches me carefully. "Yes, you'll get your magic."

I'm about to celebrate with a fist bump to the air, because I hadn't thought it would be this easy, when she adds, "And then, you'll have seconds to kill him before he has you."

It takes me a moment to realize what she's said. *Seconds?*

"I'm sorry, but what the hell did she just say?" Shade squawks in my head, her panic coming through.

"Kill him?" I clarify, darting a glance at the door, because surely, she's risking death by suggesting this. If someone was saying this about me in Seral, I'd have to make an example of them. A bloody one.

"Yes," she replies matter-of-factly and, like she didn't just drop a bombshell, she goes back to packing up her things, carefully placing the different makeup brushes into her case. "That's if you want to get out of here alive. And just maybe, the rest of us can be freed as well."

"Well, that's just great," I send to Shade.

"And now we know why she helped you," Shade replies blandly. *"She thinks you're going to save them. She thinks you'll be the first bride to best the king. I knew she had an ulterior motive."*

"As is tradition," the servant says, neatly arranging her items, "over the next two days, you will participate in certain activities before the wedding. Once they're complete, there will be a big wedding ceremony held, with a lot of fanfare, I'm sure. When you say your vows, the king will remove your cuff."

I shake my head. "But you said I only have seconds. What if it's not enough time? I don't even know what the king can do."

Her lips thin. "It's all the time you have."

I frown, thinking about how I still haven't bonded with my fated mates. "You don't understand, I'm still not that strong. I'm not the *bride* you're looking for. Can't you find someone else? If you know how the king removes the cuffs, let's find a way to steal whatever it is that he uses before the wedding?"

"None of us know how he removes them," she replies. "We only see the cuff falling to the ground. This is the only way. You have a better chance than the rest of us. Even if we had our power, none of us can match him. There's a reason he's the king now." Her eyes darken, making me wonder just what she's seen over the years.

"You don't even know me. How can you think I have a better chance?" I say. "And what's to stop me from telling him about you?" I mean, of course I wouldn't, but I'm interested to see how she reacts. She went from hardly speaking to me at all, to spilling all of this.

She stands a little straighter. "It's unusual for the king to bring someone down from the surface. If you're here, he must think you're special. He must think you're powerful."

"It's still a big risk," I point out.

The servant doesn't look the least bit cowed by my comments, and I can't help but respect her a little for that.

"I have nothing to lose," she replies.

I examine her carefully and pass back her knife that I've been holding onto until now. She doesn't hesitate to take it from me and slide it back into her boot.

"Then it looks like I'm going to have to hope those seconds are enough," I comment with a tight smile. Because right now, I don't have a better plan.

"What? Blake that's crazy," Shade protests in my mind. *"What if this is all a lie, and she's setting you up?"*

"She could be, but if she's being truthful, I'll have the element of surprise when the king takes the cuff off."

"We'll all hope," the servant replies. "Please know that if you do this, there are many who would follow you."

I don't know what's more unsettling, the idea that by killing the king I could make myself queen of a realm I want nothing to do with, or the fact that this servant makes it sound like the subjects here are so desperate they'd worship a stranger for killing their king.

She takes a pair of pearly white heels out of the case and hands them to me, then she snaps the lid closed. Realizing she's about to leave, I blurt, "There were four males with me when I arrived here. Do you know where they are?"

Her expression is sympathetic. "If they're not

already dead, I'd guess they've been taken to the mines."

"The mines? I don't like the sound of that, either," Shade comments.

The servant lifts her case.

"And these mines," I ask, lifting to my feet and blocking her way, "how do we get there?"

Her expression is grim, and she purses her lips. "You don't. If these individuals are important to you, the king isn't going to let you near them. Even if you could break out of this palace, you'll never get past the guards that patrol the prison. Like I said earlier, many have tried before you and failed."

This time I don't stop her when she steps around me and heads for the door. "I can't linger," she says when she's still halfway across the room. "The king will be here soon to take you to the announcement party. Smile and agree to anything he says."

"Agree to anything he says? Wow, she really doesn't know you," Shade snarks.

I keep my eyes trained on the servant. "Thank you, uh..."

"Sassia," she replies. "Good luck. We will all be watching you." Before I can say anything more, she wraps her knuckles on the door. The door swings open barely a second later, like the guard was waiting with his hand on the doorknob, and Sassia leaves the room before the door clicks shut again.

"And here I thought Seral had problems," Shade says. *"I still think this plan is a horrible one, and we should just*

escape from here and go find Dante and the others. You guys are stronger together, remember?"

"*We're stronger if we're bonded,*" I reply as I walk over to her cage. "*And the last time when I saw them, not all of my mates wanted to bond. Besides, they're imprisoned, and I can only assume they've been cuffed as well. We need our powers.*"

Shade looks me up and down, observing the white velvet dress clinging to my form. "*Some of your mates might not want to bond, but I'm pretty sure they'd be pissed if they knew you were intending to marry someone else.*"

I stroke her feathers through the bars. "*By the time they find out, the king will be long dead. Something tells me they won't mind.*" But even as I say it, I have a feeling that I'm wrong.

CHAPTER
THREE

~ Princess Blake ~

King Celzar arrives not long after Sassia leaves. Two guards escort me from my room, and I tense when I see the king standing in the hallway. He's in his non-centaur form, standing on two legs and dressed in a pressed silver suit with a blue silk tie. His dark hair has been slicked away from his angular face, and his sharp gaze shines with approval as he takes in my appearance.

"Very good," he murmurs under his breath. "Now, one last thing." He lifts his hand into the air, sending out a burst of power, and I'm surprised when pain lashes my back, my muscles convulsing as fire ignites on my skin. I grit my teeth, refusing to cry out and give him that satisfaction, but I bend over, breathing heavily. When the pain subsides seconds later, I straighten and peer over my shoulder in horror.

"My wings," I choke out, and my hate-filled glare goes to the king. "What have you done?" Panic flutters in my chest, but I work on steadying my heartbeat. The king has already suppressed my power. I shouldn't be so surprised that he's taken my wings from me, too. It's simply another thing I'm going to have to fix when the time comes.

"Blake? What's happening?" Shade asks from back in the room, clearly sensing my distress through our connection.

"I'm fine," I tell her quickly, and I block her from my mind. I haven't forgotten Sassia's warning to be wary when using my power around the king, and the last thing I want is for him to take that small win away from me now.

I don't need to worry. King Celzar is too busy beaming at me like he's proud of his handiwork. "The existence of other realms isn't a secret, but this way there will be less...questions," he says primly, replying to my earlier question. "I don't need the high lords and ladies of The Haven knowing there are outsiders here. Now come, my beloved." He gestures with his head and holds out the crook of his arm like he expects me to take it.

My eyes narrow to slits, and I can't believe the audacity of this guy. Forcing the thought of my missing wings from my mind, I lift my chin and stride forward, ignoring his arm as I stand beside him. I might be in another realm, but I assume the rules here are the same. *Never show weakness.* I'm not about to let the king think he's already broken me.

On the other hand, I know he might retaliate at my show of defiance, but his grin only grows wider. He lowers his arm and turns to the two guards closest to us. "We'd best not forget our other new friend, as well," he tells them, and I watch in confusion as the guards nod their heads and disappear into my room.

There's a squawk, and my heart sinks. "What are you doing?" I hiss at King Celzar, but I'm pretty sure I already know. It turns out I'm right, because the guards reappear shortly after with Shade's cage held between them, and my friend clinging onto the perch for dear life. *Fuck.*

Something sinister enters King Celzar's eyes as he watches me. "Behave tonight, and no harm will come to your precious pet," he warns me, his lips quirking upward into a smile like he thinks this is all a game.

"Behave? And what exactly are you expecting from me?" I say, glaring at him. I should know better than to give him the reaction he wants. Years of growing up while having to deal with the demon king's games should have prepared me better, but I'm overwhelmed in this strange place, and I'm on edge without my mates, so I can't help but ask.

King Celzar leans closer to me, and his overpowering scent of roses makes my nose twitch. "The announcement celebration we're about to attend will solidify our engagement. The high lords and ladies of The Haven will want to meet their future queen and offer their congratulations." He flashes his perfect teeth when he smiles. "All you have to do is play along and mind your tongue. I trust that's not too hard a task for you to accomplish."

Mind my tongue? The fact he's just said that shows he *really* doesn't know me, and I give him a forced smile. "And if I don't?"

His smile turns cruel, his thin lips twitching as his gaze slides to Shade before finding me again. "If you don't, let's just say our guests will get to witness a different kind of spectacle tonight."

A chill races down my spine. "Hurt Shade, and you'll wish you never kidnapped me." It's a promise, but the king doesn't look bothered by my threat.

"Shade? Is that what you call her?" He smiles, tapping his chin with his finger. "Now, why is that name so appropriate?" There's something about the way he says his last comment that has unease going through me, but he starts forward, his heeled boots clicking on the floor as he strolls away from me and up the hallway. I snatch another glance at Shade before I begrudgingly follow him. The moment I move, six guards flank us, two of them carrying Shade's cage between them.

King Celzar walks slowly, clearly waiting for me to catch up to him, and I maintain a healthy distance as I keep pace with the male. The slit in the white gown I'm wearing reveals a generous portion of my left leg as I walk, but otherwise, the stroll through the palace is mostly uneventful. You know, aside from the fact that the palace is absolutely huge, and much more extravagant than the demon castle back at home.

Despite the shitty situation, for a short while, I find myself distracted by hallways filled with incredible murals that are expertly crafted, crystal sculptures that are so detailed they almost appear lifelike, and intricate paintings that are embedded with enough crystals that it starts to feel as though we're walking past stars. Larger crystals extend from the walls, bathing the hallways in glowing white light, and my heels sink into the plush silver and blue patterned carpet beneath our feet. Unlike the demon castle which has been designed for war, this palace screams luxury, and it's hard not to get swept up by the stunning artwork.

We turn down another hallway, and it's filled with at least a hundred mirrors of different sizes, all with frames made of white crystal. The mirrors are arranged together like some kind of mosaic artwork, and I can't help but roll my eyes when the king tilts his head to the side, admiring his reflection. He is attractive, I have to admit, with his sleek features and sharp jawline, but he always seems to have a pinched expression, and I still think he'd look better with my hands wrapped around his neck.

Not thinking, I unblock Shade, unable to help myself. *"I don't see why he needs another bride when he's obviously already in love with himself."* Of course, going by what the servant, Sassia, said, the real reason he's chosen me is because of my power, but why go through all the effort of a wedding ceremony? Why not just kill me now?

Shade's laughter trills in my head, and just the sound of it is enough to ease some of my tension. *"All he needs is his hand and a mirror, and he's set for life. Do you think he calls out his own name when he comes? That would be weird, right? Like, ohhh Celzar."*

Her comment makes me snort with amusement as that unwelcome image works its way into my head, but then her laughter abruptly stops, and she hisses a warning in my mind. *"Crap, Blake! Look out!"*

I lift my gaze to find King Celzar scrutinizing me. He's stopped before a set of double doors made from white crystal, and I quickly squash my magic again, re-blocking Shade from my mind.

As I move to stand beside the king, I feign innocence, and he examines the side of my face. "You, my darling, smell...different," he muses suspiciously.

I give him a sweet smile. "It must be all the excitement," I reply, fighting hard to keep my sarcasm contained.

His gaze lingers on me for a moment longer, and then his attention goes to Shade in her cage.

Oh, fuck. "Well, what are we waiting for?" I blurt, indicating to the doors in front of us with my head. "Is this where the announcement party is being held? The guests must be getting antsy." Truthfully, I have no idea if we're late to the party or not, but King Celzar turns his attention from Shade, so thankfully, it looks like my distraction tactic works.

The king levels me with a stare, and when he finally speaks, his voice is deathly calm. "Don't embarrass me, my betrothed. When we enter, you will be on your best behavior. I will not be laughed at."

So clearly, I must have done a terrible job at hiding my sarcasm, and my instinct is to respond with something offensive, but I'm smart enough to keep my mouth closed. I simply nod once, and it must be enough to satisfy him, because he turns forward again. Lifting himself higher, he puffs out his chest.

"Open," he commands, and the guards standing sentry near us, pull the doors wide. My mouth drops open. *Whoa.* Despite my reluctance to be here, I can't help but look on with surprise as I peer into the enchanting space beyond. Like the rest of the palace, everything sparkles and gleams, and white crystals are embedded into every surface, even arranged in intricate patterns along the walls. Three large chandeliers hang from the ceiling, comprised entirely of crystals shaped into perfect roses, and they glow brightly, bathing the room in bright, white light. Guards wearing royal armor stand sentry along the walls, their centaur forms tall and imposing, and the large room is filled with hundreds of guests dressed in lavish, glittering clothes. Unlike the guards, the guests all stand on two legs, and now that I know to look for them, I notice the cuffs visible around their ankles.

Unlike the king, they don't have the option to change into their centaur forms at will.

Gasps erupt around me when I enter the room, walking beside the king, but the high born of The Haven are quick to bow their heads, showing their respect as we make our way through the center of the ballroom. All the while, King Celzar beams proudly, keeping his nose high in the air as we stroll past the guests toward the raised dais at the other end of the room. There, the king stops before a long table and turns to face the guests.

Following his lead, I force a smile as Shade's cage is carried over and placed on a pedestal close by. The king holds out his hand, and a servant hurries forward, passing him a crystalline glass filled with bubbling liquid. When I'm given one as well, I wrap my fingers tightly around the glass, hoping there's at least something alcoholic inside.

Music starts up as a band that's to one side of the dais begins to play a sweet tune, and when the melody ends shortly after, the king clears his throat. "My high lords and ladies of The Haven," King Celzar's melodic voice rings out, and he raises his drink into the air. "For many years we have had peace here in our new home, and for as long as I rule, this peace will continue." There's polite applause, and the king grins widely, waiting for the room to quiet down before continuing. "However, as you know, my late queen, Desmer, passed away years ago, and I feel as though the time is right for me to take another wife." He pauses and his eyes crinkle, glowing with warmth as he stares at me, and if it wasn't for the fact that I know he's completely full of shit, even I might have thought his expression of endearment was convincing. As it is, it takes all my effort not to roll my eyes. *Behave Blake. Let's not start the party by getting Shade killed.*

"Tonight, I urge you to celebrate a new royal union," he continues. "One between me, and my new betrothed. Many of you will not have seen her as she is not a high born like you, but she brings me happiness, and I have no doubt she will make a fine queen."

It doesn't surprise me that the king wants to pretend I'm one of them. Considering he's already hidden my wings, it makes sense that pretending I'm a nobody from their kingdom will result in less questions. But going from what Sassia said, it's no secret that the king kills his brides. So why pretend this is going to be a happy union?

The room erupts with applause, and I stare again at the cuffs on the lords and ladies around me. I think about everything Sassia has said about her kind, and the idea that these high-born citizens are prisoners just like me is unsettling. *Remember, this isn't your fight, Blake. You just need to get this cuff off and rescue your mates.* It sounds simple when I say it like that, but I can't seem to forget about Sassia's plea for me to free them.

Over the next few hours, I sit beside the king as a banquet of food is brought to us and the lords and ladies come forward in turn, offering gifts of gold, crystals, and other treasures to show their support of the new royal union. *The new royal sacrifice.* Clearly everyone is on board with the fucked up situation I'm in, and a sickening feeling churns in my gut as I stare at the growing pile of gifts.

"Congratulations, your highness," a shrill voice has me looking up, and my attention goes to a tall, plump female with a hawkish nose and short blond hair. Bird designs adorn the waist of her vibrant red dress, tiny crystals decorating the eyes of the animals and outlining their wings. The lady studies me carefully before turning her gaze back to the king, and I don't miss the fact that she's the first guest to stand straight as she addresses him. "I am glad to hear this union will bring peace. I truly do hope our new queen will help to bring you the happiness you deserve. Nothing could mean more to us." Her lips curve into a smile, and I'm not sure if I'm misreading the undertone of sarcasm, or if I'm just projecting, but I could swear her words are less than genuine. Then again, it makes sense considering the guests are all prisoners just as I am. Sassia had said that many have tried to remove the cuffs before me, and I wonder just how many citizens would be glad of the king's death.

King Celzar doesn't seem to pick up on anything, and he thanks the lady in red for her kind words, as she offers him a silver pouch filled with diamonds. Most of the other high lords and ladies hardly glance my way when they bring their offerings to the king, and the ones that do only stare at me with pity, though they hide the expression behind their carefully maintained smiles.

As the night goes on, nothing eventful happens. Unlike in Seral, where the demon leaders from the different clans are constantly at each other's throats, everyone here just gets along. It's seriously creepy, and I have to wonder if it's because of the cuffs. I mean, what happened to make everyone like this? And why the cuffs in the first place? Is it simply so the king can have control, or is there another reason?

I'm deep in thought when King Celzar leans close, his unpleasant floral scent shattering the calm bubble I'd created. His lips come close to my ear, and I have to stop myself from acting on instinct and smashing my fist into his face. Instead, I sit there letting him move in uncomfortably close. *Behave, Blake,* I remind myself.

"It is time, my beloved," the king tells me, his voice smooth but a little slurred, likely from the multiple glasses of that bubbly liquid he's consumed.

"Time? For what?" So far, I think I've been doing a pretty stellar job at handling myself during this party, but truthfully, all I've had to do was sit here and keep my mouth shut.

"As is tradition, it is time for us to partake in the dance of the *falina*," he says, his voice taking on a strange accent as he says the last word. "The dance that signifies a new commitment," he explains.

A dance? I have to stop myself from groaning. It's not like I hate dancing or anything, it's just that I'm not very good at it. When Dad organized my lessons as a child, training and classes on war always took precedence over the less meaningful arts such as dancing. Though I learned the basics, something tells me my mediocre skills aren't going to cut it tonight.

"You sure?" I ask him. "Because I can barely pull off the dances we have back at home. Trust me, you do not want me on the floor."

The king looks less than enthused about my admission, and ignoring my warning, he lifts to his feet and holds out his hand.

Dancing it is, then.

I place my hand in his, and the moment we're standing, he signals to the band. The music quietens, and the nobles move to the side, clearing a space on the ballroom floor. I let the king lead me forward, and when we're in the center of the cleared space, the music starts up again as the band plays a lively, but passionate song. It's like nothing I've heard before, the musicians playing low, soulful notes before their fingers move on their instruments and the melody reaches up high again, but I don't have time to appreciate the music because the king pulls me in way too damn close for my liking. It feels so wrong to have his hands on me, but I grit my teeth, forcing myself not to do anything stupid as he starts moving us in time to the song.

To my surprise, while the king is clearly a terrible leader of his kind, he has a knack for dancing, and I find it takes little effort for me to follow his lead. Of course, his scent of roses still makes me want to step away from him, but for a moment, I don't find myself hating it as I'm swept up in the song, feeling the notes vibrate through me as I move my body. *Well, who knew dancing could be so...* I pause, mid-thought. 'Fun' isn't the right word. Relaxing, maybe?

We've been dancing for a while when some of the lords and ladies move on to the floor around us, each of them dancing in perfect synchronization as they join us. And when I say synchronized, I mean *perfect*, down to the placement of their arms and the wide and somewhat creepy smiles on their faces. It's a practiced kind of beauty, and it makes me wonder how many times they've danced this before tonight.

I'm almost tempted to ask the king about it, when I feel his hand lower, sliding down from the curve of my back to my ass. That's right, my freaking *ass*. Repulsion rises in me, because this male is definitely *not* my mate, and I grind my teeth as I try to stop myself from reacting. *Behave, Blake. Behave.* But the warning isn't helping, because this is not okay, and I'm about three seconds away from breaking his wrist. King Celzar smirks, a hint of lust in his eyes as his hand tightens on my ass, and before I lose my shit, I decide to give him the curtesy of a warning.

"Move your hand, King Celzar," I say quietly through gritted teeth. "Or you're about to lose it."

I figure that shouldn't get me into too much trouble, but a high lord and lady gliding past us must hear me, because the female loses her balance and trips, twisting her ankle and tumbling down, pulling her partner with her.

The music stops, the room growing quiet as King Celzar glowers at me, his eyes turning into cruel dark orbs. "Never when I have danced the *falina*, has a dancer fallen," he seethes, and going by the anger rolling off him, I'm starting to get the feeling that this is a bigger deal than I first thought.

His head twists to the side, addressing the closest guard. "Take her."

At first, I think he's referring to me, but then two guards march forward, grabbing the fallen dancer under her arms. They force her to her feet, ignoring her cries when they make her place her weight on her sore ankle. I expect her dance partner to protest, but he only watches in grim silence as they start leading her away, presumably to be punished. *What the fuck?*

"Stop," I say. "She only fell because I distracted her." I don't hold any loyalty to the Perstalians around me, but it doesn't sit right that this female should be punished because of me.

"Yes," King Celzar replies, his eyes still dark. "She *let* you distract her, when nothing should have broken her focus."

"You can't be seri—"

"As for you," he says, his grip tightening on me as he stops me from finishing. His head lowers, and he breathes in as he drops his head beside mine. "You do not tell me if I can or cannot touch you. I own you now, my beloved, and you'll learn to love my hands on you, or at least, endure it." To prove his point, he squeezes his hand that's still on my ass, and I swear to Lady Fate there's only so much control you can expect a demon to have. My knee is up and in his groin before I can think about what I'm doing, and King Celzar grunts, bending over as he stumbles back from me.

Fucker.

Shocked gasps fill the air around us, and I curse, realizing what I've done. Shade hops in her cage, her feathers ruffled, and panic shoots through my system. The guards along the walls start to draw their blades, but King Celzar gives a hand signal, and they relax their stances again.

Opening my mouth, I go to hastily squeeze out an apology, but King Celzar's makes another hand signal, and the words die in my throat as the guard closest to Shade unlocks her cage door. He reaches in, grabbing my friend, and Shade squawks, trying to wiggle herself free. This only makes the guard squeeze his hand tighter, and her feathers spill between his fingers until she stops moving. *"Blake,"* Shade whimpers in my mind when I let her back in. I don't care anymore that I'm using the shred of magic I have.

"Stop!" I shout at the king, my heart thrashing wildly in my chest, but King Celzar only cocks his head, glaring at me.

"Please," I plead when the guard keeps holding onto Shade. "It was just a reflex. It won't happen again." It's a blatant lie, because I will gouge out the king's eyes before I let him touch me in that way, but I'll say anything to save my friend.

King Celzar blinks at me, obviously not believing a word of my lie, and I hold my breath, waiting to see what will happen. If I had my magic, he'd be halfway across the room by now, broken and bloody, but with the cuff, all I can do is wait.

I'm relieved when his lips twist, and he laughs. "A reflex, she says. She's certainly more spritely than my Desmer."

I smile awkwardly, staring around me as the guests start laughing along with him. It doesn't escape my notice that the lady in red with the hawkish nose is the only one of the guests with her lips still pressed together, and a serious expression on her face. *Yep, she's definitely not on his side.*

King Celzar moves into my space again, and this time I stay perfectly still, not reacting to his close proximity. "I told you if you misbehaved, darling, your pet would be the one to suffer," he tells me, his voice so soft I only just hear him. "Maybe if I break every bone in the bird's body, you'll start taking me more seriously."

I breathe heavily, struggling to control my anger. "Harm her and we'll see who's the one making mistakes," I seethe. "The moment I have this cuff off, you'll regret ever taking me. I've dealt with worse than you."

His eye twitches at my threat, and I think this is it. This is the moment I accidentally get my friend killed.

My heart is beating so hard my chest aches, but I don't take my gaze from the king's face.

Seconds pass, and I ready myself to attack. I might not have my magic, but I can still do damage. I'm ready to drive my palm into the king's nose when his expression softens, and he gestures with his hand. The guard holding Shade releases her and steps away from the cage again, and my shoulders sag. *Thank the lady.*

"Embarrass me again, and you won't get another warning," King Celzar whispers, and I know he means it. He reaches down, his finger tracing along the side of my face, but unlike the other times when he's touched me, this time his skin is ice cold. At his touch, a burst of energy rushes into me, and I gasp. There's a crawling sensation inside me, like ants are burrowing under my skin, and then my energy starts draining from me, my body weakening at his touch. It's like his magic is *stealing* a part of me. *Fuck.* This must be what Sassia was talking about. She'd said the king could steal power, and I should have seen this coming... except I didn't.

My heart thunders, and I try to move away, but my body is paralyzed, like his magic is holding me hostage. Shade squawks, clearly panicked, but I can't hear her in my head anymore. Just when I think this might be it, King Celzar pulls back, releasing me. I fall to my knees, my breathing ragged as the king watches me in satisfaction. "Better," he murmurs.

My vision swims, and I blink rapidly, but the faces

of the guests around me remain blurry, a smear of color.

"What did you do?" I croak, though I already know. This was just a little taste of the king's power.

King Celzar ignores me and addresses the guards who escorted us to the party. "Take her and the bird back to their room," he orders.

There's the rattling of armor, and rough hands grab under my arms, lifting me to my feet. I'm too weak to fight, and it's clear I underestimated the king's power. What had Sassia said? That once the king removes the cuff following our wedding ceremony, I'll have seconds to kill him before his power has me?

Well, fuck. We're in trouble.

CHAPTER
FOUR

~ Dante ~

We finish filling our cart with crystals just before a bell rings from somewhere in the cavern, and the prisoners start putting down their pickaxes. Sweat streams past my eyes, and I wipe it away angrily with my arm, focusing on the burn of my muscles. My princess, my *mate*, has been taken from me, and diverting my energy to collecting crystals is the only thing that's gotten me through the last few hours without doing something I regret. There's no point in getting myself killed before I can find her.

Fuck. When we'd entered the portal to Seral, I'd

been looking forward to having Blake in my arms… finally warming my bed… and riding my…

"Get in line!" our guard shouts, snapping me back to reality.

I fight down my irritation and give him a devilish smile. His face blanches a little, but his scowl doesn't fade. I'm going to kill him first when I get the cuff off me. I'm willing to wager he knows it, too. In fact, the moment I get the chance I intend to kill everyone who played a part in taking my delectable princess from me.

Starting forward, I follow Nate and the others as we form an orderly line with the prisoners, then as a group we move toward a tunnel on our left. The prisoner who had been whipped mercilessly, the *prince*, according to what we'd heard, staggers on his feet a few places in front of Alaric. His back is ruined, a display of torn flesh and blood, but even now defiance still shines in his eyes. He's tough, that one, and I eye the male curiously wondering how long he's been imprisoned here.

Wherever 'here' is. In any case, I'm guessing the guards expected their treatment of him to serve as a warning to the prisoners, but they failed miserably. Whenever the prince looks in the direction of the other prisoners, they try and straighten their curved backs and lift their chins a little higher. No, despite what the guards were attempting, it was becoming obvious that the prisoners respected this fallen prince, and respect could be a dangerous thing in a place like this. At that thought, my mind goes back to my formidable, winged princess, and her fiery tongue. I smirk, thinking of how she's probably giving her captors a hard time, if she hasn't escaped already, but then I remember the cuffs and my smile falls. *If anyone has harmed her...* I don't let myself think about it. Instead, I focus my attention on the prince, because something tells me he's going to be our way out of this.

It's not long before the guards stop us, and Alaric, Nate, Prince Callan, and I are forced into an empty cell. I pretend not to notice that our fallen prince sneaks into the cell next to ours. *Crafty prince,* I muse internally.

Turning, I assess our new surroundings. The cell is painfully small with a single narrow cot against the back wall, a bucket in the corner, and the iron bars at the front which seal us in. I eye the single bed and raise a brow.

"Not uncommon in prisons," Nate comments, striding past me.

"What is?" I ask.

"Testin' prisoners like this. They'll give less portions of food, beddin', water, you name it. The idea is to get us fightin' with each other, so we have no energy to fight our captors," the shifter explains.

"And here I thought the guards were unable to count," I drawl with a smile.

Alaric settles on the floor, resting his back against the wall, and Prince Callan paces the room, his wings folded behind his back as he tests for weak spots in the bars, looking even more annoyed than I am. Nate pounces onto the cot, and he stretches out in an entirely feline gesture, folding his hands behind his head.

"I thought the bed was some kind of test?" I point out, not entirely pleased that he beat me to the cot.

"Oh, it is," Nate agrees with a mischievous glint in his eyes. "But I deserve this."

"And how do you figure that?" Prince Callan asks coldly, looking like he's contemplating pulling Nate's ass from the bed just to piss the shifter off.

"Well, because for once I'm not in prison because of somethin' I did, so I figure I at least deserve a cat nap," Nate replies, yawning and closing his eyes like he intends to do just that. "Actually, this would be the second time," he corrects. "But who's counting?"

I find a spot on the floor, not in the mood to argue with the shifter. Had the cot been wider, I would have suggested that we share.

"None of us signed up for this," Prince Callan retorts, and Alaric grunts in agreement.

"And neither did Blake," I drawl, my body tightening and my tail flicking as I say her name out loud. The name of *my princess*. The others all tense as well, and Prince Callan scowls, clenching his fists like just saying her name has physically hurt him.

"So, we'd better find a way to get out of this shithole so we can rescue her," I go on. "Before we all have to live the rest of our miserable lives without our mate."

No one replies for a long moment, and I exhale loudly, running a hand over my horns. "You all might be intent on pretending she's not ours, but I've tasted my princess, and I don't intend to let her be imprisoned by whoever rules this place."

"From what I saw, the princess can look after herself," Alaric growls, though from the giant's rigid body I know he's as affected by our mate's kidnapping as I am. As we *all* are.

The thought of the four of us bonding with Blake makes my cock harden, and I push away the delicious images working into my mind. Even if those delectable images are the only thing currently keeping my desire for violence at bay.

"And what do you suggest?" Prince Callan asks, his keen gaze on me. "We're disadvantaged with these cuffs and without our power."

I turn to Nate who's lounging on the cot like he's content to sleep for the next few hours. When I'd visited the beast realm in the past, I'd heard talk of a renowned thief nicknamed, Nine Lives. I hadn't realized that's who Nate was when I'd first met him in Perstalia. "From what I've heard, you're supposed to be an expert at getting out of places like this," I say to him, genuinely curious at his relaxed demeanor.

He cracks his eyes open, and his slitted gaze slides to a scowling Prince Callan before he focuses on me. "It takes time," he replies cryptically.

"That's his way of saying he doesn't know a fucking thing," Alaric snarls.

Nate fixes the assassin with a stare. "Now, I didn't say that."

"Then tell us, shifter," I drawl. "What *are* you saying, exactly?"

A playful gleam shines in Nate's eyes as he props himself up on his elbows. "For starters, I know the guards here each have an assigned cluster of prisoners they watch over, and if I'm right, replacement guards will be here soon for the night watch."

As if on cue, there's chatter in the tunnel beyond the cell, and I peer out, watching as the day guards swap with fresh guards. The new guards take their places standing sentry against the wall opposite the cells.

"We could all deduce that," Prince Callan says coldly.

"And while they're intent on makin' us suffer," Nate goes on, ignoring the prince, "it's obvious they genuinely need the crystals we mine. This means two things. First, there must be some system in place to ferry the stones out of here. Second, it means that while they'll weaken us, they'll want to keep us strong enough to lift our pickaxes."

I frown. "Tell that to some of the prisoners we saw today. Some of them are no more than walking bones."

"My point is," Nate says, "they're goin' to want to feed us, and unless they have a kitchen here in the mines, that food is goin' to come from outside."

"Hmmm," I muse, contemplating this. It's an interesting point, because back in Seral if you were sent to the dungeons beneath the castle, according to the rumors, food was the last thing you could expect to receive during your likely brief stay. Demons could live without food, but if enough time passed, the lack of sustenance would take its toll.

As if Lady Fate herself is keen to prove Nate's point, it's at that moment that a trolley appears outside our cell. A male servant crouches, sliding up the bars at the bottom of our door to reveal a small opening. Carefully, he pushes four trays of food inside our cell, then he closes the opening and moves on, wheeling his trolley away.

Nate jumps up from the cot, and he grabs one of the trays before getting comfortable on the bed again. I can't say the food looks appetizing, but I grab one of the trays for myself, and Prince Callan does the same. Alaric doesn't move from where he sits.

I find my position on the floor again, and I stir the plate of gray mush with my wooden spoon, unable to bring myself to put any of it into my mouth.

"Tastes like wood shavin's," Nate says through a mouthful of food. "You're gonna want to eat. We'll need our strength."

"Unless it's poison," Alaric warns gruffly.

Nate shrugs. "Could be. But I doubt it. If they'd wanted us dead, they would've ended us when we first came through that portal and were unconscious."

I still can't convince myself to bring the disgusting gloop to my lips.

"He's right," an unfamiliar masculine voice says.

"It's not poisoned." It takes me a moment to realize the sound is coming from a small grate on the bottom right wall beneath the cot. Laughter comes from the guards across the tunnel, and I share a look with Nate before moving closer to the right wall of the cell.

"Who is this, and why should we believe you?" I ask.

There's a dry chuckle. "You shouldn't," the voice replies, only answering my second question.

Nate places his tray of food down and frowns. "Fuck, now even I've lost my appetite."

The chuckle comes again, raspy and weak.

"I'm going to go out on a limb here and guess you're the prince we saw today?" I drawl, assuming that we must be talking to the male prisoner who was whipped mercilessly by the guards.

There's a beat of silence, but then our new friend replies. "I was."

"And I'm also going to presume that you shouldn't be talking to us," I add.

"Correct, again," the prince replies. "But provided you don't call the guards over, we should be just fine."

None of us ask why he's risking talking to us. We could use all the information we can get. Even if we can't trust it.

"So, prince of what, exactly?" Prince Callan asks coldly. "Or, *where*, I should say."

There's another pause before the prince finally replies, "You're in The Haven."

"Sorry, but did you say haven? I think that word

must have a different meanin' for our kind, because this doesn't look like a haven to me," Nate jokes.

"Trust me, it doesn't look like this everywhere," the prince replies. "While it can't compare to the old city, even I have to admit that what he created is beautiful."

I feel a little relieved to hear that. If that's the case, then maybe my princess is being held somewhere nicer than this prison.

"You said 'he' created," Alaric growls. "Who is this creator?"

"Hmm don't let him hear you call him 'the creator,'" the stranger replies. "He'd like that too much. But I'm referring to King Celzar. Ruler of The Haven and monarch to the remaining inhabitants of Perstalia."

Nate lets out a low whistle. "Perstalia? So, some of you survived the blast?"

"Some of us survived," the prince agrees. "Others, thrived." There's bitterness in his tone when he says the last part.

"And where exactly are we in comparison to the old Perstalia?" Prince Callan asks. "Are we in a new realm?"

The prince chuckles again. "Celzar likes to think of it that way, but no. We're simply far below the surface of our old city."

Fuck.

We're all silent as we process that information.

Nate is the first to speak again. "Underground,

huh? We can work with that," he comments, going back to eating his food. "We just need to find a way to return to the surface."

"It's not that simple," our new friend says. "The only way to travel there is by using the portal key. The king wears the ring at all times."

Nate places his tray onto the cot and cracks his knuckles. "That doesn't sound too bad. Get me close to the king, and I'll have that key in no time."

"Don't forget about our cuffs," I remind him, gesturing to the cuff around his ankle.

"Yes, about that. Any information for us?" Nate says to the Perstalian prince.

"No," is the curt reply.

I curse again, and so do the others.

"You haven't told us why you're risking speaking to us," Prince Callan says.

Nate flexes. "I'm guessin' this king guy is a piece of shit, considering you're in here. What are you, the rightful ruler to the throne or somethin', and he threw you in here so he could rule in your place?"

"It's complicated," the prince replies.

"But you think we can help you get out of here," I say, and when the prince doesn't reply I know I'm right.

Nate claps his hands together. "So we simply need to break you out so you can take the king's place, somehow remove these cuffs, and use the portal key to return to the surface. Any great escape plan you want to share with the group?"

"Not really," the prince admits, but then he adds, "But for Celzar to even bring you here, he must have plans for you, and that means opportunities."

I cross my arms in front of my chest. "Well, we'd better figure out something, because if we don't find Blake soon, I'm going to start killing people, consequences be dammed."

"Blake?" the prince asks.

"Our mate," I drawl, and it feels so good every time I admit that out loud. For years, I'd kept it to myself, not declaring it to the world, and now satisfaction goes through me at being able to publicly voice the claim.

"Who is this, Blake?" the male asks.

"She's the future queen of Seral, realm of the demons," I reply proudly.

"Our fated mate, so it happens," Nate adds.

"And a pain in my ass," Prince Callan grumbles.

Alaric doesn't say anything, but I note the way his body reacts to hearing the sound of our princess's name again. His muscles grow tight, and his gaze is sharp.

"...If she's the future queen, I take it she's powerful?" the prince asks.

I grow wary. "You could say that. Why?"

There's another pause before the prince speaks. "That explains why he wants her."

"What do you mean?" Alaric speaks up, his voice gruff.

"Celzar steals power from others," the prince

explains. "It's how he was able to take over the throne. He's as strong as the power he feeds on, and it's been a long time since his last big meal."

My expression hardens as I think of this Celzar and how he's probably holding Blake captive. "So, what you're saying is…"

"He's planning to take your princess's power," the prince says bluntly.

Rage flows through me at the idea of some king taking what belongs to my demon mate. Before I can ask more, the bars at the front of our cell rattle as the door swings open. Javier, the guard who had been watching us all day strides inside, flanked by three other guards.

"Funny, I don't remember ordering night-time entertainment," I drawl, though my eye twitches at the sudden intrusion.

Javier bares his teeth, smiling cruelly at us. "Couldn't leave for the night without singin' you all a lullaby, now could I?"

I smile back at him, because this is precisely what I need. I'm on my feet and my hand is jabbing into the guard's throat before he can utter another word. He splutters, jerking back as his mouth opens and closes like he's a fish starving for air. Before I can deliver another blow, the other guards step forward. One of them slams their steel baton onto my cuff, while another delivers a punch to my nose. Pain ricochets through me as I'm forced to my knees, and I smile as blood trails from my nose.

"And here I was hopin' we might escape the obligatory beatin' for new arrivals that's common in prisons," Nate mutters, finally moving from his relaxed position on the cot. "All right," the shifter says, facing the guards as Prince Callan and Alaric tense. "Let's get this over with."

~ Prince Callan ~

My Ahalian Touizda has been taken from me. My mate. Rage makes my blood heat as my soul demands vengeance. I think about finding those who have taken her from me, and making them suffer unimaginable pain. Instinctively, I try to access my power, digging for that energy inside me, but pain rushes up my leg, making my muscles contract. Not having my magic is an incredible inconvenience, but right now the agony is like a breath of fresh air, and I breathe through the pain like I have done since I discovered the demon princess was gone.

When we were in the ruins of Perstalia, I'd thought I could handle not being with her. I'd deluded myself into thinking I could reject the bond and return to

Toralyn alone, but now that lie has been shattered. Whether I want the bond or not, the demon princess is my fated, and I don't know what the fuck I'm going to do about it. The pain from the cuff helps me focus my mind, and I close my eyes, surrendering myself to it. I think about the promise I made all those years ago. I need to get back to Toralyn, but it looks like I'm going to have to find a way to take my mate with me. Because she is...*mine.*

I open my eyes in time to see one of the prison guards slam his fist into Nate's face. The shifter is thrown backward, and he laughs as he picks himself up from the floor. This angers the guards more, and they start dealing out blow after blow, attacking him mercilessly. The demon, Dante, gets the same treatment, the two of them sharing the punishment, but I don't move from my position. It's nothing Nine Lives doesn't deserve, and the image of him bleeding on the floor of a prison cell reminds me of the first time I saw him in Toralyn...

"Ah, this must be your generous hospitality I've heard so much about," the prisoner laughs, lifting his head from the filthy floor that's smeared with his blood. Three angels watch on, and one of them flicks his hand sending out another wave of power. The prisoner curls up on his side, clenching his teeth as he hisses in pain.

"That'll do," I say, striding into the cell. *"Leave us."*

The prisoner's head slumps to the stone floor, and he lays there breathing heavily as the guards file out. When the door to the cell closes again, the prisoner peers up at me through bloodshot eyes. Claws peek from his fingertips, but the magical barrier around the cell stops him from shifting entirely. His lips twist into a crooked smile. "An audience with an archangel prince. Now what did I do to deserve this honor?"

I ignore his question and watch as he sits up and props his back against the cell wall. "Your execution has been planned for the end of the week to correlate with the queen's birthday," I say. "I hear, it'll be quite the spectacle to have Nine Lives tortured and killed as the opening act of her party. The infamous shifter thief caught in Toralyn. It's all anyone is talking about."

The prisoner chuckles dryly. "The openin' act? Had I known the angels loved me this much, I would've visited years ago."

My brow wrinkles as I stare at him. I'm not sure whether he understands the gravity of his situation. "I don't know exactly what the queen has planned, but I can assure you it will be unpleasant. Likely, you'll wish for death long before the moment comes. I find it curious that you would even contemplate trying to steal our most sacred artifact, considering this palace is the most secure place in Toralyn."

He smiles. "What can I say? The greater the challenge, the bigger the reward."

My lips quirk up at the sides, and I cross my arms in front of my chest, surprised by the male's casual demeanor.

I'd prepared myself to converse with a savage thief, but had we lived different lives, I could imagine myself sharing a drink with the male across from me. It's an odd thought that leaves me unsettled.

I lift my gaze to the camera in the left corner of the room. The red light is still not blinking, but I know I don't have much time. When I turn my attention back to the prisoner, his slitted gaze is clear and calculating, and there's something in his eyes that makes me think he already noticed the camera isn't recording.

"Nine prisons," I say. "I'm told you've escaped from nine prisons in the past, and nine death sentences, hence the name, Nine Lives. Can I ask, did you come up with the nickname yourself?"

He grins. "Actually, I've escaped more times than that, but Eleven Lives doesn't have the same ring to it, does it?"

"Well, unfortunately for you, this isn't a prison you're going to be able to break out of. The moment the queen realized who she'd captured, she took extra measures to ensure your...secure incarceration. Not even someone with your reputation could make it past the multiple security layers she's put into place."

He narrows his eyes at me. "If that's the case, and I am fucked, then do me a favor and leave me in peace to enjoy my last moments, will you?"

His lack of fear intrigues me, and had this been a different situation, I would have walked away just so I could see if he is as great at escaping prisons as I've been told.

I glance at the camera again. Still no red light. "I'll

admit, I do regret stopping you from enjoying your time with the guards," I say, smirking. "You're somewhat of a celebrity around here, and I know they're keen to get to know you."

He lounges back against the wall. "In that case, if you're done gloating." He gestures to the door, but I don't move.

My lips flatten. "I didn't come here to watch you squirm, shifter."

There's a gleam in his reddish-gold eyes as he watches me. "Then why are you here, prince?"

I take the time to choose my words carefully. "It's not possible for you to escape this place," I say, hesitating before continuing. "But with a little assistance it could potentially be achievable."

He stares at me warily, and though the movement is subtle, I note the way he sits up a little straighter. "Assistance?" he questions, speaking slowly. "And what would this assistance cost?"

I check the camera again. "I need to get someone out of Toralyn. If I can get you out of the prison, you must take them with you to the beast realm."

His brows slam down. "I'm no smuggler."

"Either you take her with you, or you suffer at the hands of the queen. The choice is yours, thief."

"Her?" He leans back against the wall again, and a moment passes before he asks. "Who do you want me to get out of Toralyn?"

"Someone I've made a promise to," I reply. "Now, if we're agreed, I'll arrange for there to be lighter security *measures around your cell on the night before your execution. The palace will be a hive of activity as the servants prepare for the party. I trust you know the layout of the palace well? Meet me in the portal room one hour before sunrise." It's a risk to trust the shifter thief to meet me there, but moving throughout the palace without detection is near impossible. It'll be easier for him to achieve without an escort.*

There's a knock on the cell door, and I know my time is almost up.

"When I get your friend to the beast realm, what then?" he asks. "I'm not in the babysittin' business."

"While the city recovers from the celebration, I'll be able to leave Toralyn and meet you there the following day," I drawl. "All you need to do is make sure you remain in Genzen City, and that you leave enough crumbs for me to follow."

His expression becomes thoughtful. "You must be desperate if you're askin' me to do this."

"Then I guess right now we're one and the same," I reply. "If this is the part where you ask for money, I don't have time for it. Get her there or suffer your execution."

Leaning forward, he rubs the stubble on his chin. "Well, when you put it like that, how could I refuse?"

"I need to hear the words, shifter. Say you agree."

He stares at me like he thinks I'm joking, but my gaze is unwavering.

"Yes, I agree oh merciful one," he finally mocks, but the serious edge in his gaze is enough to satisfy me.

"Good." I reach the door in a few strides before turning

back. "Oh, and if you cross me, rest assured I'll stop at nothing until I've found you, and your execution will be even grander than what the queen would have you endure." I don't wait for him to reply. I exit the room, because I have plans to put into motion.

Over the following days, I bribe multiple guards, weaken wards, and run through various scenarios in my mind. I don't advise my sister, Sen, on what's going to happen. If she knows, she might let something slip when talking to her maids. Between my duties and my plans, my days are absorbed quickly, but every night I visit the shifter. I tell myself I'm simply there to check that he's still in his cell. As impossible as escape sounds, the stories surrounding the infamous Nine Lives thief have me questioning whether he would be able to find some weakness I'm not aware of on his own. But every night, he remains, and by the third night, I realize I look forward to our chats. His responses are always entertaining. He tells me amusing tales involving some of his more outlandish exploits, stories of which I'm certain must be grossly embellished, and I tell him tales of battles in Toralyn, and the great games held in the grand ampitheater. Shifters rarely come to our realm, and it's refreshing to hear his different views on the realms and those within them.

It's the fourth night when he finally asks me about Sen, though there were multiple times when I thought he'd ask.

"Why her?" he questions as he takes the flask of wine I

offer him. "Why risk freeing me for a female? Is she your forbidden mistress or somethin'?"

I study him, calculating how to respond. I shouldn't say anything, but the wine I've consumed makes my lips loosen. "I think of her as a little sister," I say, twisting the truth as I take another swig from my own flask. Unbeknownst to the shifter, our flasks contain one of the finest wines in Toralyn from the vineyards on the floating hills in the north. The smooth liquid warms my throat, and nothing could dampen my mood in this moment. "She's in a bad position, and if she doesn't leave, her life is in danger. I need to get her away from here." I lift my head higher. "No matter the cost."

Nine Lives doesn't speak for a moment, and his eyes lose focus like he's lost in his own memories. Eventually, he nods and takes another drink of his wine. "And what if this whole plan of yours doesn't work. What if I'm captured and slaughtered like a squealin' pig, and your little friend never sees the beast realm. What then?"

I contemplate before answering, "Then I stay to make sure she doesn't die."

I know he doesn't truly understand the gravity of what I'm telling him. How could he when I've only shared a taste of the truth? But at my words, he lifts his flask in salute and takes another swig. "Then I guess we'd better make this fuckin' work."

My lips twitch, and I take a drink as well. "I guess so." Blowing out a breath, I pocket my flask and walk toward the cell door. "See you in the portal room tomorrow, shifter. Remember, your life depends upon it."

"It's Nate."

My brow furrows, and I turn my head to the side.

"My name's Nate," he clarifies, not moving from where he's sitting next to the wall.

I pause thoughtfully. "Well, it's not quite as mysterious as Nine Lives, is it?"

He chuckles. "No, I s'pose not."

"Until tomorrow night, Nate."

~

The night before the execution...

I can scarcely remember the last time my heart pounded this furiously. When I was a child, perhaps? It's a risk. A big one. But using the shifter thief is too good of an opportunity to pass up. He's exactly what I need. Someone who's a master at staying in the shadows. At keeping hidden. If anyone can get Sen away, it'll be him.

I'm not worried that the shifter will harm her in any way. Even though she's a child, with her power, he'd be dead before he managed to do anything that would cause her to lose sleep. A part of me feels guilty I didn't warn him of this, but he'll figure it out the moment he sees her.

No, as long as he can get her to Genzen City, that's all I need. No matter what happens, I can find her after that. I think of the promise I made to her as I lead her through the palace and toward the portal room, toward *her escape from this place. I won't let the queen use her. I won't let her become another pawn to be abused by our court.*

Sen is silent as we dart down the corridors, neither of us speaking, not even when we reach the portal room, our hoods pulled low. The guards outside the room are loyal to me, and they start opening the doors the moment they see me. I don't bother asking them if they've seen Nate. If he's as good as they say, undoubtedly the shifter has found a way inside without alerting them. I usher Sen inside and follow after her.

There's a brief moment, when I fear Nate won't be there. When I imagine the room to be empty, and the entire plan to be a failure. It's possible the shifter could have simply escaped into the city with plans to find another route home, but then I spot the shifter's broad form.

He stands before the empty portal gates and turns, grinning at me. "Thought I'd be gone, didn' ya? Gettin' here wasn't the easiest task, but nothin' I couldn't handle." His relaxed smile fades when he sees who I'm with.

When he spots her ashen face beneath her hood, his playful expression darkens. "You didn't tell me that's who I was takin'," he says. "Is that—"

"My sister, the Princess Mirelle," I confirm. "And if I had, would you have agreed?"

"Not fuckin' likely," he admits, scrubbing a hand over his face. Then he winces as if he only just remembers that she can hear him. "Look I appreciate that I'm not in the cells anymore, but had I known this is what you were askin'..."

"You'd have what?" I retort, giving him a deadpan look. "Waited for your execution?"

"I'd have found another way," he replies, running a hand through his hair. "I can't have the whole of Toralyn after me, prince."

I frown, my patience wearing thin. "We don't have time for this, Nate. Given the tales of your exploits, this doesn't seem like too big a task for you. Now, let's see." I pause, pulling a thin object from my robes. The turquoise ring glitters as I rub the crystal and whisper a few words. Magic hums through me, and energy crackles around the gateway before the center floods with silver light that shimmers and ripples, moving like liquid metal. Smiling in satisfaction, I tell him. "Believe me, you will be rewarded for this."

"You say rewarded, but you mean 'hunted,' brother," he replies, but I ignore him, turning to Sen.

Crouching down, I open my mouth to speak to my sister when the doors of the room swing open. Varek, my mother's prized general, storms into the room with four soldiers marching behind him. "What is the meaning of this?" he shouts, his temples pulsing with anger as he takes in the scene.

The guards fan out at his sides, but I lift my hand, sending out a burst of wind that sends them flying backward. All of them, that is, except Varek. His wings are spread wide, and he braces, his enchanted shield protecting him from my onslaught.

"You'll be punished for this," the general snarls.

"Get her out of here!" I shout at Nate, but when I turn

my head, the shifter is gone. The silver fire of the portal burns brighter, the only indication of where Nine Lives has disappeared, but Sen still stands behind me, her hood pulled back to reveal the markings all over her face. Her eyes are round and frightened as she watches me.

"Damn it!" I curse as panic makes my heart rate spike. "Go, Sen! Before the portal closes!" I shout, but as I take a step toward my sister, Varek's illusion power rushes at me. In seconds, multiple Varek's materialize around me, blocking my view of her. I hear the portal close, the crackling energy silencing, right before someone crashes into me from behind.

No!

My mind snaps back to the present, and I'm still staring at Nate's bloodied face. It's because of him that my sister never made it out that day. He left without her, and it's because of him she's still in Toralyn suffering the fate I'd hoped to save her from. I clench my jaw, and it's not until the shifter is on the ground unconscious next to Dante that I lift to my feet. Alaric still hasn't moved from his spot against the cell bars.

The guards turn their gazes to me, and I give them an emotionless smile. "My turn."

CHAPTER

SIX

~ Princess Blake ~

The guards march me back to my room, and by the time they leave, locking the door behind them, some of my energy has returned and I can connect with Shade again. I rush over to her cage. *"Tell me you're all right."*

She comes closer to the bars of the cage, her black feathers still ruffled and sticking out at odd angles. *"I am,"* she replies, though I can tell she's rattled as I smooth her feathers.

I swallow down the lump in my throat as my body trembles with anger. I hate this. I hate *them.* My body still feels drained, almost like I've been drugged, and I curse the king. For the first time in years, I feel weak, and it's fucking terrifying. I think of Dad's rules for demon royalty. "Rule number one, never show weakness," I mutter, and I feel like such a joke right now. Closing my eyes, I lean against the cage as my head swims.

"What did he do to you?" Shade asks.

Blowing out a breath, I fight against the sudden bout of nausea that grips me. *"I've never felt anything like it,"* I reply. *"I feel...wrong."*

"We need to get out of here, Blake. This place... These people... It's all wrong here."

I take another deep breath and wait until the pounding in my head starts to subside. Slowly, more of my energy is returning, and I force my eyes open. This isn't me. Whatever this King Celzar is trying to turn me into, it's not going to happen. *And he's not getting Shade either.*

My gaze falls to the metal chair before the dresser, and I walk over, flipping the chair upside down. When Sassia had been doing my makeup, I'd felt there was something off. Now, I find the wobbly chair leg and start working on the loose bolt. Gritting my teeth, I work at twisting the small bit of metal free, not caring when my fingers are raw and bloody. Thankfully, my body still heals despite the cuff, though it's working at a slower rate. *Come on, dammit.* My grip feels pathetic, but I keep at it, wiping away my blood so the steel isn't so slippery.

"Got you!" I shout, not caring how loud I'm being when the leg finally detaches. I figure, if the guards are dumb enough to enter now, I'll probably damn the consequences and end them before they realize what's happening. Well, I'd try to, anyway.

Shade hops on one leg. *"Geeze, Blake, you're lookin' a little..."*

"A little what?" I ask, swinging toward her holding the chair leg like it's my newest prized possession.

"Uh... nothing," she comments sheepishly. *"So, what are you planning to do with that?"*

I place the chair leg down and tear a strip of fabric from my dress. Then I wrap the cloth around the chair leg, and stride over to her cage. *"This,"* I say, and I slam the wrapped metal leg against the hinges of the cage door. The metal shudders from the force, but it doesn't give way.

"What is this thing made with?" I grunt out when I slam it into the bars for the tenth time, and I'm panting and sweating. "It's like this damn metal is indestructible. It's like—"

A click sounds, and Shade lets out a startled noise as the small metal door of the birdcage swings open, the metal bent and twisted.

"Y–you did it!" she squawks.

"You don't need to sound so sur—" I don't finish the thought because Shade hops out of the cage so fast, and then she's flying into me, a blur of silky black feathers.

"You did it, Blake!" she says again, and there's such relief in her voice at being out of the cage, that all I can do is grin stupidly and stroke her feathers as she nuzzles into me. It feels like we spend hours like that,

but I'm sure only a minute has passed when Shade says quietly, *"I can't get back in the cage, Blake. I just... can't."*

I continue stroking her feathers. *"I'd never ask you to."*

"But the king. When he sees I'm out—"

"You'll be long gone by then," I tell her.

She jerks back, tilting her head to the side and fluttering her feathers as she stares at me. *"What? I'm not leaving you."*

"Yes, you are," I say with a small smile, because finally I feel like I've *done* something.

"I'm not leaving you with that monster," she insists. *"What happens when he realizes I'm gone?"*

I shrug. *"I can handle the king's attention, but we both know it's you who he'll hurt first, and I won't allow that."* Truthfully, after his last energy-sucking trick, I'm not sure if I can handle the king myself, but Shade knows better than to argue with me. *"Besides,"* I add before she can protest further. *"The cage door is all bent now, anyway. One look and if he doesn't kill you, he'll put you somewhere I can't get you out. This is your chance."*

"Blake—"

"Find the guys," I tell her. *"We all need to get out of here, and that includes them. Do you think you can do that?"*

She snaps her beak shut like she's trying to hold in more protests, but the next time she speaks in my head, her voice is dull with resignation. *"Fine, but I hope you know I'm not happy about leaving you."*

I grin. *"Noted. Now let's get your feathered butt out of here while we still can."*

She looks at the door, no doubt imagining the guards on the other side, and then she peers back at me. *"And how are we going to do that?"*

I point up.

"Ahhh, right," she says nodding as she stares at the small grate positioned high up on the wall.

"I'm guessing it's some kind of filtration system," I explain. *"Maybe you can use the vents until you find a better way of getting around. Luckily for us, the vent coverings aren't screwed shut. They're also even easier to open from the inside. Sassia said Dante and the others are likely in the mines. Maybe if you listen in on the guards and servants you can find out where they are. Someone will slip out with something useful."* It's a risk letting Shade go up there, but at this point, I'm willing to bet those vents are safer than her being in the cage.

"Okay. I can do that," she says like she's trying to pump herself up. Then she turns to me. *"You know your mates aren't going to be happy when I lead them back here and they find out about the king."*

I smirk, thinking about my four lethal mates. *"I'm counting on it."* I won't go so far as to say that I need my poorly matched mates, but I'm not going to be upset if they find a way to get here and cause some havoc. If nothing else, it would cause a big distraction, and I'm hoping I'll find a way to get my cuff off by then. *"But you'd better go."*

Shade nuzzles against me one last time, then she

lifts off my lap. I use my piece of broken chair to carefully lever open the vent cover, and she flaps her wings, landing just inside the vent.

"I won't put the cover back on until you've walked away," I tell her, not wanting her to feel like I've taken her from one cage, just to put her into another. *"Remember, there are no screws on these things, so you just have to push against it hard enough and it'll open."*

"Got it," she says, not at all sounding confident. *"Easy as pie."*

~

~ Shade ~

Okay, Shade, you can do this. It's not a cage. No, it's just a tunnel. I inhale and exhale slowly, trying not to focus on the four walls encasing me. *Yep, it's a wide, innocent tunnel. No one's trying to hold you against your will or torturing you. It's just a tunnel that leads to freedom. Or, you know, it leads through a dazzling palace where there's a king waiting to squish you like a bug.* I swallow hard. Turns out, I suck at pep talks.

"You okay up there?" Blake asks me, and god, it's so good to hear her voice. Being in the cage was bad. *Real* bad, but it was even worse not being able to speak with my bestie.

"Never been better," I chirp back, and even though I

feel like I'm a few seconds away from collapsing into a feathered heap, I mean it. Being in the cage I'd felt helpless. Even worse than that, I'd felt *useless*. Now I have the chance to actually help Blake and find the guys.

I can hear the concern in her voice when she replies, *"You don't have to do this if you don't want to. If you'd rather hide—"*

"Do what?" I say, cutting her off, because there's absolutely no way I'm just hiding in the vents while she faces off with the king. *"Find four assholes who absolutely don't deserve you?"*

I hear her laughter in my head.

"Then again," I amend, *"now that I've seen King Celzar, maybe I've been judging them too harshly."* I pause, thinking about Prince Callan and the damn assassin, then I say, *"I guess I'm willing to give them another shot, though they've already lost points in the rescue department seeing as I'm the one going to them."*

Blake chuckles again, but there's a vulnerability in her voice when she says, *"Find them, Shade. Make sure they're okay."*

I swallow again as my heart squeezes. *"I will, girl."* It feels wrong to leave her with the king, and I don't like my chances of finding the guys. And even if I do find them, I'm not sure if I'll be able to remember the way back. Still, I don't remind Blake of the fact that unlike other birds, I have horrible navigational skills. I'm pretty sure she's just relieved she's managed to get me away from the king's clutches. *If only I was a pigeon,*

I muse to myself. *They always have an incredible sense of direction.*

I move slowly, careful so my feet don't scratch too loudly in the vents, and it's not long until I'm following a vent down a long corridor. As I near the end, I take a bend to the left and accidentally trip over my feet. A thud echoes along the steel tube, and my heart practically stops. *Oh, crappity crap!*

"You hear that?" a male voice sounds from below, and I shuffle over to peer through a grate and see two guards standing in the corridor below.

"Hear what?" the other guard says, sounding bored.

The first guard scratches his forehead. "Thought I heard something." He peers up, and I hold my breath, freezing in place as he stares straight at the grate. *Oh, please, please let it be dark enough that he doesn't see me.* My tiny heart beats furiously as he frowns, and I wait for him to shout that he's seen me. I don't know if there are many crows in this place, but I'm sure the guards know about the king's new caged pet. *Please,* I think again.

"*Where are you now?*" Blake asks, and I almost jump at the sound of her voice in my head.

"*Uh, just moving along a corridor,*" I tell her. The last thing I want her to do is worry.

The guard tilts his head, and just as I think he's about to damn me and alert everyone to my position, his partner nudges his arm. "Probably just a rat. Koran told me they killed one in the kitchens a few days ago. Said the furry bastard was the size of a cat."

The first guard looks away from the ventilation shaft and peers at his comrade. "Sounds fucking disgusting. You serious? I hate rats."

I blow out a relieved breath, though my gaze darts to the path ahead of me. *You and me both, buddy,* I think, shuddering at the thought of encountering a rat up here.

I'm not brave enough to move for a while, just in case these guards take it upon themselves to try and capture the, uh, *rat* that they think is in the shafts. Instead, I wait until they have a change over, and while they're distracted, I hurry away, trying to make as little noise as possible.

Minutes pass, and I make my way through the palace, keeping an ear out in case I hear any chatter about prisoners. I'm close to another grate, but as I pass it, a familiar chilling voice draws my attention. *Keep moving,* I tell myself, but curiosity grips me, and I shuffle closer to the opening and peer down.

Whoa. I blink as I stare into the room below. I'm looking over some kind of garden, but instead of greenery, the eerily still plants, trees, and animals are made from crystals. White crystal rose bushes are scattered around tall trees, the leaves delicately carved so they almost look lifelike. Nestled among the branches are birds of all kinds, the statues so real-looking it's as if the animals had been in the middle of singing a morning song when they were frozen like that. Everything sparkles and glitters in the dim lighting, and even the stream is made from crystal that's been shaped and smoothed to mimic flowing water. *Well, that's seriously creepy.*

"Aren't you happy for me, sister? It's not every day your brother gets engaged." King Celzar's voice is unmistakable, and instantly, my feathers puff up.

"I found the king," I hiss to Blake. *"He's in some kind of weird garden."*

"The king?" Blake sounds pissed. *"You're supposed to be finding my mates and getting away from the king. Not searching for him!"*

"I wasn't searching for him," I defend. *"He just happens to be in the room I'm passing. Now, shh. Do you want to know what he's saying or not?"*

She huffs. *"Just don't get caught."* Of course, I know the extended version of that statement. What she means is, don't get caught or she'll have to risk everything including her own life to come and save me.

"So, what's happening?" she prompts.

I crouch closer to the grate. Standing near the stream is a tall female with obsidian-colored hair that reaches her waist, smooth tan skin, and a long gossamer gown adorned with crystals. She stands with her back to me, so I can't see her face, but I note the thick silver cuffs around each of her ankles. "Our kind aren't blind, Celzar. If you think they're oblivious to what you've continued to do to them all these years, then you're a bigger fool than they are." Her voice is feminine and soft, but I don't detect any hint of fear.

Not far away, King Celzar stares at her. "It doesn't matter what they think," he replies harshly. "They can't challenge me. And neither can you."

"There's a female here," I tell Blake. *"He called her his sister. I think he's keeping her in this garden against her will."*

"You must know your arrogance will be your downfall," the female replies. "Even I didn't think you'd be daft enough to bring outsiders here. You say you created this place to keep us safe from the witches, but by now, even your most loyal followers must see it for the prison that it is. If outsiders are visiting our land, it stands to reason that the witches are gone. And your power is fading, brother. Before long, our kind will realize they don't have to stay under your control."

"If it weren't for my power, we'd all be dead by now," King Celzar snarls back.

"So, you say," the female replies bitterly. "Yet, it seems strange that the witches would find our lands and attack us mercilessly on the same day you violated your banishment and returned home." She pauses before continuing. "I hope your new bride sees you for the snake you are. For once, I don't think this will be the wedding you intend. From what I hear, your new prisoner isn't quite as willing as your last brides."

King Celzar doesn't look bothered by her last comment. "She's as willing as she needs to be."

"Is that so?" the female replies. "Because from what I hear, you've imprisoned four males, her fated mates. Are you so far removed from reality that you forget the lengths some might go to in order to protect their mate?"

"Fated mates don't exist," King Celzar retorts. "And in any case, they won't be a problem. For now, the males are insurance. When I have her power, they'll be of no use to me, and I'll have no trouble keeping order in The Haven."

I relay this information to Blake, and she curses, her rage flowing into my head.

The female in the room below tenses, and she turns, subtly gazing in the direction of the grate I'm peeking through. I'm sure I've been caught, but she turns away quickly, directing her attention elsewhere.

"The prison isn't far from here," she says to the king, making her voice a little louder. "When the food rations are brought to the prisoners, it only takes them a half hour to walk there. What makes you think your new captives can't sense your betrothed even from that distance?"

Food rations? Excitement goes through me at the information the queen has given away. It's too useful, and for a moment, I wonder whether she was really speaking for my benefit. But then I tell myself I'm being ridiculous, and I shake that notion away.

King Celzar lets out a humorless laugh. "Oh, I do so love our little chats, Nerelia. I truly don't know what I would do without our entertaining conversations. Rest assured, the cuffs are as effective as ever, and even if they could sense her, they can't escape the mines." He straightens the collar of his shirt. "Now, I'm afraid I must leave you to take care of matters. Try not to worry yourself with such absurd thoughts."

It's not until the king has left the room that I step back from the vent and relay all the information I've gleaned to Blake. *"I think I know how to get to Nate and the others,"* I tell her eagerly. *"I need to find my way to the kitchens."*

"Be careful," Blake tells me, and I start making my way through the palace again, moving slowly to minimize the noise. The vents are an absolute maze, but I keep walking until the scent of freshly baked bread guides me down to a room that's bustling with activity. In the large kitchen, servants cook over large fires, while others busy themselves kneading dough, measuring ingredients, and chopping an array of vegetables.

"Hurry up! This is the last cart, and if I'm late to the mines for the morning meal, I'll be the one who gets punished," an older male snaps at the young servant piling trays onto the cart beside him.

The mines! Crap, I can't miss that cart! Thankfully, between the chatter, crackling of the fire, chopping noises, and the scrape of various cooking utensils, no one notices as I pick up speed, scurrying along the vent until I reach a grate that's lower to the floor. Careful to pick a time when everyone is distracted, I bust out of the grate and run over to the cart, darting onto the bottom level. As I move further into the middle of the cart, I have to hold in my squawk when my feet sink into a portion of strange warm mush. Scurrying out of the food quickly, I move forward only to find myself stepping into another sticky pile. The food has a gritty texture, and I cringe as it slides between my toes. Before I can move out of it again, the cart starts rolling forward, and I fall back, completely sitting in the mush. *Ugh. Gross.* I groan inwardly as the unpleasant smell of some kind of mashed vegetable fills my nose. But then I remember that I made it!

I keep silent as the cart is pushed from the kitchens down a service entrance, and then we're outside of the palace. A rush of warm air reaches me. Ducking low, I keep still as we pass the guards patrolling the palace, and then the trolley is being wheeled down a paved road.

"Holy crap! I made it outside the palace, Blake!" I send to my demon friend. *"This cart should take me straight to the mines."*

Blake's voice sounds distant when she replies, *"Try not to get into trouble."*

Like the female in the garden specified, it feels like it takes a half hour of traveling down a series of tunnels before the air changes, and I detect a rancid smell that grows consistently stronger as the cart moves forward. *Well, I can't say I'm loving this,* I grumble internally, though I have a new appreciation for the mush I'm squished in, because the food is helping to mask the smells around me.

"About time," a gruff voice sounds from somewhere overhead. "You know the boss hates it when you're late."

The servant pushing the trolley doesn't reply. He simply waits for a series of gates to open, and then he wheels the trolley forward, the steady screech of the wheels sounding in my ears. The guard moves in behind us, escorting us down a dimly lit tunnel, and when the trolley stops at the first cell, I peek my head out. Guant, hungry eyes stare back at me from behind the bars of the cell, and I recoil as black eyes lock onto me and cracked lips widen to form a yellow-toothed smile.

"What do we have for dinner tonight, aye? Fresh bird for a change?" the prisoner says.

The guard slams his baton onto the bars, and the prisoner reels back. "Stop your nonsense. You get the same as always." The guard reaches down, grabbing a tray and sliding it through a hole at the bottom of the bars.

The prisoner looks back at where I'm trying to hide amongst the trays, and once again, I'm left wondering if this is it. *Oh crap. Please look away. Look away, buddy.* I wait for the prisoner to point and shout at me, but the guard bangs his baton against the bars again, and the prisoner takes a step back. The grubby-looking male winks at me. "Prefer this anyways," he says to the guard. "Wouldn't wanna ruin a good thing I've got goin'."

I personally think that whatever mushy gruel they've been given looks like vomit, but hey, who am I to judge? If it's keeping his mouth shut about me, then I'm happy.

We visit one cell after another, and I'm starting to get worried that I'll be discovered when I see them. The cell they're in is much like all the others, but Blake's four mates are unmistakeable. I'm so relieved I almost collapse back into the mush I'm standing in, but I don't.

As the guard slides four trays of food through the opening at the bottom of the bars, I dart from the bottom of the cart, quickly squeezing through the bars and hiding behind Alaric's large form. The giant's expression slackens when he sees me, but he hides his surprise and pivots his body, concealing me even more.

"I've found them," I send to Blake.

"What? How do they look?" she asks me. *"Are they hurt?"*

"Well, they've looked better," I say slowly.

"What does that mean?" she asks, her voice tinged with worry.

I peer at where Nate is sprawled on a metal cot with a nasty gash across his forehead. Prince Callan is standing, peppered with bruises, and Dante has dried blood crusted on his chin. Even Alaric looks rough. His clothes are ripped and bloody in places.

"They're fine, I promise. But let's just say it's obvious they're missing you," I send back.

Blake doesn't reply for a few seconds, but then she says, *"Thank you, Shade. Get them back here if you can."*

"You can count on me, girl." Honestly, I'm not actually sure if she can count on me for this. I'd been so distracted at the idea of being caught while I'd been on the trolley, that I forgot to memorize all the turns we took through the tunnels to get here. I try not to stress about it, though, and instead, I tell myself I'll figure it out when the time comes.

The trolley moves on to the next cell, and none of the guys go to collect their food. Nate lifts from the cot, his nostrils flaring as he breathes in deep. His slitted gaze focuses on me as the others all turn as well, and I stand there feeling completely exposed. Nervously, I hop from one leg to the other.

Nice kitty, I think as Nate's gaze turns predatory. *Remember, you wouldn't dare eat your mate's friend. Right?*

The shifter blinks, and just when I think he might pounce for me, his lips stretch into the biggest crooked smile. "Well, I'll be damned. Thought I smelled you," he mutters.

I sway on my feet. I'm not sure if it's because I really thought he was going to eat me, because I still can't believe I made it to their cell without being captured, or because the way his smile lights up his face is enough to make any female weak at the knees. *Holy hell, I have no idea how Blake has managed to resist any of these guys.* Sure, it's not great being told that I stink, but they're sweaty and covered in dirt, and they're still gorgeous. If I was her, I'd be banging them in a heartbeat, but then again, I take in Prince Callan's icy expression, and I remind myself what an asshole he is.

"Is that who I think it is?" Dante asks, coming closer.

I puff out my chest. *Yep. Blake's almighty bestie to the rescue.*

"Well, aren't you a sight for sore eyes," Dante says like he's responding to my comment, though obviously, he can't hear me. The demon's seductive lips curl upward, and it almost makes me want to preen, but I'm distracted when Alaric scoops me into his massive hands.

"It's good to see you, little one," the assassin tells me, and normally, I'd be annoyed at being manhandled, but right now, I just peer dumbly up at him admiring his stupidly chiseled face.

"So, I'm goin' to hope that the fact that you're here is a good sign rather than a bad one," Nate comments.

At that, Dante's expression grows more serious than I've ever seen it. I stare at the dried blood on his chin and the dirt smeared over the demon's clothes, wondering just what these guys have been through since we exited the portal. "Tell us Blake is all right," he tells me.

Of course, I can't actually speak to them, so there's no way to tell them of the danger Blake is in and the king, but I nod my head once, copying the gestures they're used to.

All four guys relax, their shoulders dropping. Dante leans his back against the wall and closes his eyes for a few seconds before opening them again.

"If we get out of here," Alaric asks, his voice rough. "Can you take us to her?"

I nod again, even though I'm still doubtful that I can. Surely, a giant palace will be easy enough to find. Right?

"Does she know about the king's plans to take her power?" Prince Callan asks, and this time I nod vigorously.

"They know about the king," I send to Blake. *"And his plan to steal your power."*

"Then they must be talking to someone in the prison," she muses.

"Good," the assassin grumbles. "Maybe she can kill him already, and we can get out of here."

I shake my head, using my beak to point to the cuffs around their ankles. They look the same as the one Blake has, and I don't think I need to guess what they're for.

"They have cuffs as well. Just like yours," I send to Blake. *"Explains why they haven't been able to escape."*

Blake lets out a stream of curses in my head.

"If she has a cuff, she's as vulnerable as we are," Prince Callan comments, and it's confusing as hell having two conversations going on at once.

"What do you think their chances of escaping the

prison are?" Blake asks me, and I peer at the guys, contemplating my answer.

"They're crafty," I tell her. *"I mean, there's the guards, and cuffs, and layers of security, but they seem pretty determined to find you."*

To add to the confusion, someone else speaks up then, a strange masculine voice coming from the other side of the cell wall. "Who are you speaking to?" the voice asks.

Nate leans closer to the wall, stretching out on the cot again. "A friend."

SEVEN

~ Masón ~

Letting my head hang down, I sit slumped with one shoulder leaning against the cell wall. The guard has just brought the morning meals, and though it's been hours since I was whipped, pain thrums along my back, my body slow to heal with the cuff around my ankle blocking my power. It's a stinging, searing agony that I've become accustomed to ignoring over the years, but the guards gave me a rougher treatment than they usually do. It was probably so I'd serve as a warning to the newcomers, though I don't think it has had the effect they intended.

"Here, your high—" My cell mate, Jaiq's, words cut off when I crack my eyes open.

He dips his head, peering at me sheepishly. "I mean, Mason," he corrects. "Here, take mine." He slides his tray of food toward me, and I peer at the grainy gray mush. It's the same meal they've been feeding us for the entire forsaken time I've been in this prison. Thorak—the roots of Thoran plants. It's a delicacy when prepared differently, but I hated it as a child, and I hate it even more when it's boiled and mashed like this. Which is exactly why Celzar has been serving this as the prison dish. It's simply another reminder that I'm here because of him. Though, when I made it clear I'd eat it without complaint, my brother started ordering the guards to skip my meals all together. Either I starve, or one of my followers does. *Bastard.*

I want to refuse the food, but instead, I give Jaiq a grateful nod. He moves back, finding a place on the grimy floor, and I force myself to bring a spoonful of mush to my mouth. On another day, I would have refused. Jaiq needs this as badly as I do, but the chattering from the cell next door is enough to spur me on. The food tastes like nothing in my mouth. It's simply sustenance to give me the energy to heal and keep going, and I choke it down.

When I'm done, I already feel a little better, but that could be because of my new neighbors. I haven't felt hope like this in a long time. Not since just before the last uprising. Many of the warriors in this prison are in here because of me. Because they were loyal to me, including Jaiq. But the day of the last uprising, we'd finally been able to get many of us out. There had been a severe loss of life on both sides, but my most loyal ex-commanders had made it beyond security and into the tunnels. With the help of a few cityfolk sympathizers who had discovered uninhabited tunnels, my friends had escaped. But Celzar had arrived before the rest of us could make it.

Anger pulses through me at the thought of my older brother, but it doesn't squash the buzzing energy inside me. Because for the first time in years, I finally feel like we have another opportunity.

The new arrivals are still talking in the cell next to me, and I lean my head closer to the wall, concentrating on their conversation. They're talking to someone new, though I can't imagine who. Since the last uprising, Celzar increased the number of guards, and visitors are prohibited from ever entering the prison. I know I should keep quiet and glean what information I can, but I'm in too much pain to think clearly, and curiosity has me speaking up. "Who are you speaking to?" I ask, unable to hold my tongue.

"A friend," one of the male's replies.

A friend? They haven't been in the prison long enough for me to think this friend might be imaginary, and I sit up a little straighter, not caring when the pain along my back intensifies.

"And who is this friend?" I ask, my heart beating a little faster.

"Let's just say she's a sign our mate, Blake, is still alive," another male voice replies.

Mate? It's so strange hearing them use the term so casually. Finding your fated mate was a rare occurrence in Perstalia, and an even rarer possibility in The Haven with the cuffs on, but I don't let myself dwell on it. A thousand other questions fire through my mind, and I focus on the most important questions that could help with our escape. "And this friend found their way in here? Past security? How is that possible?"

There's a beat of silence, but then the same voice replies, "When we say 'friend' we don't mean someone like us. Shade here, is a crow."

"A crow?" I repeat in confusion. I think of the black birds I sometimes saw flying around Perstalia before the city was destroyed. There aren't any crows down here in The Haven, but from what I'd been taught as a child, crows are clever birds with surprising memories. A thread of something sharp and thrilling goes through me, despite my best efforts to push the feeling away. A stronger explosion of hope warms my chest, but I remind myself that crows can't follow directions. Maybe one that had been trained to follow a specific route, similar to a homing pigeon, but not a crow in a strange land.

"You heard us. And now that she's here, we need to discuss our plan to get out of this shithole. As much as I don't want to sound ungrateful for the hospitality, I was kinda hopin' you might have some ideas."

My gaze darts to my three other cellmates. Jaiq was one of the youngest recruits to join the army before the battle with the witches, and he's proven his loyalty on countless occasions. The two females had once been the ladies-in-waiting for my older sister, Nerelia. They'd been thrown in here when Celzar had locked Nerelia away, and they'd started asking about her wellbeing in the palace. I'm confident that none of them would divulge any escape plans. One of the females lies in a crumpled heap, her breathing ragged, while the other, Renee, stares at me with a hopeful spark in her hollow eyes.

I wet my lips, and I check that none of the guards outside the cell are within listening distance before I go on to say, "How can I be sure that freeing you won't be a mistake?" From what I've gathered, these outsiders are from the surface and from a world we're far removed from. The last thing I want is to accidentally release an even bigger threat. Celzar might be cruel, but our kind has survived this long.

"You'll just have to trust us," a rough voice growls in response.

I pause, considering.

"If we can get word to the others, it could work," Jaiq whispers, coming up beside me. I clench my jaw. We might only get one more chance. A single chance to try again for the tunnels, and if we fail, we could be locked in this place forever. Or at least, until Celzar finally tires of leaving me alive.

"Look, I wouldn't trust us either if I were in your position," a different voice drawls. "But it's obvious you see that we present an opportunity, and I'm guessing you don't want to spend the rest of your days in here. Let us out, and we'll leave and take our princess with us. This king of yours can't take her power if we've disappeared from here."

I think of this 'Blake' they've been talking about. She's obviously important to them, though sometimes with the way they talk, it's a little hard to decipher their true feelings for the female. Either way, she must be a formidable figure to be stirring such emotion from all four of them, and from the sounds of it, she's powerful. It would be good to get her away from Celzar.

"I have an idea," I say carefully.

"Now, that's just what we like to hear," one of the males replies eagerly. "What are we talkin' about here? Do you have a secret weapon hidden somewhere? A secret tunnel? An 'in' with one of the guards?"

I clear my dry throat. "I have warriors waiting in the tunnels."

"Rebels?" someone asks.

"If we can get a message to them, I can advise them of the weak point in the security. If we coordinate so they know exactly where and when to attack, they could give us the opening we need to escape."

"Nice. Rebels aidin' a breakout," one of the male's replies. "So how do we get word to them?"

"And now you know why we're still here," I reply. "We have no way of getting word to them, and because we can't organize ourselves, any efforts they've made to free me have all been thwarted."

I hear cursing from the cell next door.

"I have a few loyalists in the palace, but visitation to the prison was cut off years ago. Now, unless it's a worker or the king, no one goes in or out." I pause. "No one, except your crow friend, I guess."

There's another stretch of silence.

"Ah, well that's not exactly what I was hopin' to hear," one of the males replies less enthusiastically.

I hear quiet squawking then, and I furrow my brow, still surprised to hear the noise even though they'd said there was a crow with them.

"And what if our crow can get back out of the prisons? Could she carry a message to your rebels?" a gruff voice says.

Jaiq lifts his brows, and shuffles closer to the wall like he's desperate to hear every word they have to say.

I rub my chin thoughtfully. "Unless she's able to follow instructions and memorize a map of the tunnels, I don't see how that would work."

There's another stretch of silence followed by a faint squawk. Then I hear, "Ready to be brave, little one?"

CHAPTER
EIGHT

~ Shade ~

You know, when Blake asked me to find her mates, I didn't realize this was where I'd end up, I complain in my head as I walk cautiously along a dark tunnel. I would be mad at the four males who suggested I do this, if it weren't for the fact that they'd called me 'their crow.' Hearing it had given me the warm fuzzies, and I get the feeling that just because I'm Blake's friend, they'd do anything for me. *Best friend,* I correct myself, puffing my chest out a little, though no one is around to see it.

Shortly after Alaric had volunteered me for the job as messenger, the prisoner on the other side of the wall had passed a strip of rolled fabric through a small hole. As the males had worked at tying the message to my neck, they'd fussed over me, and it reminded me of how human dads sometimes fussed over their daughters. *Except these daddies are sexy as sin.*

Amusement goes through me, and I'm quick to amend, *no, not daddies, they're more like brothers.* I think of how for a long time, it was mostly Blake and I on our own. I'd do anything for my girl, but it was nice to know she had others looking out for her now. *Even if I'm still the one doing all the work.*

I kick a tiny pebble as I walk in the pitch black, and I stumble a little before correcting myself. *I just wish this escape plan of theirs didn't rely solely on me.* Even after the message was strapped to my neck, the stranger from the cell next to us had spent a long while describing the route I needed to take to get to the rebels. Once again, I was left wanting to explain about my terrible navigational skills, but from the sounds of things, I'm all they have. Once I was out of the prison, it had gone reasonably well. The instructions had been mostly straightforward, and I was able to fly through the tunnels for a while, but now the way is completely dark. Aside from a few random bursts of flight, I stumble around blindly, and worry has my heart beating rapidly in my chest.

To make matters worse, not long ago my connection with Blake had cut off. Earlier, I'd explained about the rebels and the whole being a messenger thing, and despite her obvious concerns, she'd mostly been on board. But I'd been relying on having her in my head for advice. Now, there is only the silence of the tunnel, and the scrape of my feet on the ground.

It's not so scary, I tell myself. *It's just a hole made out of rock. A long, dark, freezing hole that probably leads to rebels who might murder you on sight.*

I think of what Alaric had said to me before I'd hopped through the bars of their cell. "Remember that the rebels are not your friends. Don't let your guard down around them. Living in the tunnels has likely hardened them into something cold. Something dangerous. Just make sure that the message you're holding gets into the hands of the rebel leader, Eliza."

Yep, the assassin is as bad at giving pep talks as I am. Still, I appreciated his confidence in me because I sure as hell didn't have any. Neither did Prince Callan, it turns out.

"You know we're fucked right?" Prince Callan had said dryly as I'd almost tripped while hopping through the bars of their cell.

"Give the bird a chance," Alaric had growled. "Some battles have been won by the most underestimated of opponents."

"And many more have been lost," Prince Callan countered coldly. "We'd better devise a plan B."

I'd taken that opportune moment to dart across the tunnel while the guards weren't looking and take the bend around the next corner, because I didn't need that negativity in my life. If I let those thoughts in, I wouldn't make it, and I'd never get the help they needed. And I wasn't about to let Blake down.

Swallowing, I blink in the dark, bringing my thoughts back to the present. *Just keep walking. Just keep walking. Just keep walking, walking, walkiiiiing,* I think the words to the tune of a song I once heard when my humans watched a movie about a blue fish with a horrendous memory. If I was that fish, no doubt I'd still be lost in the endless black of the deep sea. As it is, I'm a crow stuck in the endless black of the caves instead.

Hours. That's how long it feels like I've been down here. Freaking hours. A scratching noise sounds somewhere to my left, and I skitter sideways, banging against the rocky wall I've been following. *Ouch!* I shake myself off, starting forward again, and forcing myself not to start running like a lunatic. I can't fly because I can't see where I'm going, but if I run, I'll probably break one of my twig legs and get stuck here. *Not a pigeon,* I think, remembering how I'd wished I was a pigeon earlier. *No, right now, I wish I was an owl. Then at least I'd be able to see in the dark.* I force myself to take more steps. *Keep calm, Shade, and just keep wallllking.* My heart is pounding hard enough that I'm worried I won't hear if something comes up behind me, but thankfully, the next time I hear a scratching noise, it sounds like it's further away down the tunnel.

Still, I don't let myself celebrate. Not when there could be something else stalking me. I think about how the guards had talked about rats in the palace. *Please, please don't let there be any rats here.* I imagine a family of the huge rodents living their best life in these tunnels, and just waiting for me to walk into their territory. My thoughts start spiralling, and I force myself to take a breath. *Quit it, Shade. There aren't any rats. Okay, so the dead end the prisoner talked about should be right around... Oof!* I walk beak first into a rocky wall and topple down. I've definitely bruised something, but I'm back on my feet shortly after. *Crap. It definitely would be better if I was an owl.*

According to the stranger in the prison, this is actually a secret entrance to the rebel camp. I feel around, pecking the rock until I find a small opening on the bottom right. The hole is just large enough for me to wiggle my feathered butt through, and I slither past the rock, emerging on the other side.

There's more rocky walls and stone underneath my feet over here, but a white glow emanates from somewhere up ahead. The further I walk, the more light bleeds into the space. I follow the twisting tunnel as it curves around, and...

"What the fuck is that?" someone comments as I bump into something hard. Before I have time to register what I've walked into, large, sweaty hands clamp onto me, lifting me into the air.

Ahhhh! You'll never take me aliveeee! I panic, pecking my attacker's hand furiously like a chicken with an adrenaline rush.

"Ouch! Stop! It's a fucking bird!" That same deep masculine voice says, squashing me even more.

Come on, Shade. Deep breaths. He's not going to drop dead from a few pecks, so just take a breath, will you?

The male stops tightening his hold on me when I stop pecking him, and my chest heaves as I force myself to maintain a ceasefire.

"Well, don't kill it," a feminine voice reprimands. "Hold it like that and you're going to squeeze it to death. Show me."

The hands around me loosen even more and open enough that I look up to see a female with a freckled face peering down at me.

"It's a crow," she says in surprise. "I didn't know Celzar saved any of those?"

"It's a bad omen, that's what it is," the male holding me says with a frown. Weapons are strapped to a leather belt across his chest, and my face blanches at the small throwing knives I can only just make out. "What are the odds that soon after we hear the news about the king's upcoming weddin', that a black crow finds its way to our camp."

I sigh internally. It doesn't matter if it's humans, demons, or now apparently these rebels, crows always seem to get a bad rap. I want to point out that since I've been around, Blake's luck has actually improved, but then I think of her dysfunctional mates and the fact that she's currently locked up by a foreign king, and I start to doubt myself.

"We'll take it to, Eliza. She can decide what to do with it," the female says.

The male holding me grumbles, and for a moment I think he's going to crush me anyway, but then he starts lumbering on, jostling me about in his large hands as he walks.

By the time I hear voices again, I'm almost convinced he's given me a concussion, but I quickly manage to pull myself together when I hear, "Where is it?" This female's voice is sure and commanding, and when the male opens his hands this time, I'm about ready to wing it out of there.

Or I would, if I wasn't frozen to the spot as the male removes his top hand and stretches his bottom palm flat, exposing me to three more individuals who gawk at me. Two more males and one female stare straight at me, their gazes shrewd and hard, but it's the new female with long dark braids and piercing black eyes who moves in close. I'm still frozen to the spot when she reaches over and...strokes my feathers. Her fingers glide down my back, and despite her serious expression, her touch is kind. Warmth seeps out from her fingertips, soothing my anxiety, and I can't tell if I'm imagining it or not.

"You were right to bring her to me," the female says. "I can confirm there aren't any crows in the city, so she must be from above."

One of the other females steps closer. "Above?"

"And I think..." the female says, her fingers finding the strip of cloth fastened around my neck, "that a crow finding its way down here right to us in these tunnels can't be an accident." Her ebony gaze meets mine as she pulls off the strip of cloth, and I hope this girl can make out the squiggles and lines the prisoner splodged on there. Otherwise, I'm screwed.

CHAPTER

NINE

~ Princess Blake ~

I pace the room, unable to sit still as I think about Shade in the tunnels trying to find the rebels. Our connection had cut off some time ago, and the silence is driving me crazy. It was one thing not hearing her voice when I could still see her, but now worry has me second-guessing my decision to send her out there. I scrub a hand over my face. *Pull it together, Blake. She's fine and your mates are, too.*

My body warms at the thought of the four males in the prison. Shade had said they were okay, and I relax a little even though everything in me is telling me to go to them. I'm clearing the destroyed bed just to give myself a distraction when Sassia enters my room. I pivot toward her, and she takes one look at my innocent smile and peers at Shade's empty cage. I don't give her an explanation, and thankfully, she doesn't ask for one.

I'm aware she could alert the guards to Shade's escape but considering her plea for me to kill their king, I'm hopeful she'll keep it to herself.

"The servants are talking about what happened at the party," she tells me, turning from the empty cage like it's of no consequence.

"Yeah? And what are they saying?"

She purses her lips, and my expression flattens.

"That good, huh?" I ask her.

Striding forward, she places her silver case on the bed and gestures for me to sit on the mattress. I perch on one corner, and she gets to work, cleansing my face.

"You must have upset him," Sassia says as she finishes cleaning my face, and then works on powdering my cheeks, only applying a thin amount of makeup this time. "He normally doesn't treat his soon-to-be-brides like that. At least, not in front of the high lords and ladies. Not until the wedding ceremony is complete."

"Why do I get the feeling this is your way of saying it's my fault?" I reply dryly. "He's the one with terrible taste in brides. If he wanted a demure sacrifice, he should have chosen better."

Sassia's lips quirk upward, and I narrow my eyes at her.

"And why do I feel like you're happy about all this?" I ask.

She flicks her brush, finishing the touch of color on my cheeks. "Because his little temper tantrum shows that you're exactly who we need you to be. He's trying to scare you because he knows you're powerful."

I grimace. "Yeah, and it also means he'll be even more powerful if I can't stop him from draining me."

Sassia doesn't seem bothered by this comment, and she smiles as she moves on to brushing my hair. Her confidence that I'm going to free her and her kind has me feeling guilty, but I decide I don't need to tell Sassia that it's not my main priority. Truthfully, I'll kill the king if I get the chance, so it might still work out, and she's the only friend I have in the palace right now. I don't want to risk upsetting her.

"So, do you think he'll notice?" I ask, tipping my head toward the cage.

She looks over at the mangled bars and a small smile teases her lips. "Luckily for you, King Celzar has given me strict orders to get you ready for the day, and then the guards are to escort you to him."

"And what is on the agenda today? Another party?"

She makes a face. "Not exactly…" she trails off as she finishes my hair and rifles in her case. A moment later, she holds up what looks like a white silk bra and some kind of skimpy underwear covered in crystals.

"Uh, what the fuck is that?" I ask, pointing to the clothes.

"This is your outfit for today."

I furrow my brow in confusion. "Wait, so I'm going stripping?"

She snorts and rifles in her case again. "No. Look, the bright side is you'll also get to wear this for most of the time." She holds up an almost sheer white gown, and I peer at her incredulously.

"You can't be serious."

She gives me a sympathetic look. "You'll be joining the king at the sacred waters. There, you'll both be cleansed. It's a tradition meant to signify new beginnings."

"Right," I say, pointing at what I now realize is a tiny swimsuit. "But why do I have to do it wearing that?"

"Would you rather be naked?" she teases with a laugh. "Because the last bride went full commando."

I press my lips together. Honestly, I don't really care about others seeing me naked, but it's the vulnerability of not being clothed that's bothering me. You're more likely to sustain an injury with such minimal protection. I want to protest and request that the royal tailor bring me a dress with inbuilt armor and pockets for weapons, but then I remind myself that I have no weapons, and the king isn't going to try to kill me. Or at least, he's not going to do it by running a sword into me.

Begrudgingly, I dress in the bathing suit, and when I look at my reflection in the mirror, I can't help but grin. I'm pretty sure my mates would be livid if they saw me dressing for the king like this, but then I remind myself that some of them probably wouldn't even care, and I scowl. *Stupid dud mates.*

"Ready?" Sassia prompts, watching me.

"Do I have a choice?"

Her brows lower, and when she speaks her voice is quieter. "Choices for most of us are few and far between these days."

I'm taken aback by her words. "Okay, so I'm going to take that as a 'no.'"

Someone raps their knuckles hard on the door, and Sassia jerks at the sound. "You'd better go. The guards are waiting to take you to him." She packs up her case and strides toward the door.

I follow after her, tightening the straps of my white gown as I walk. *Looks like it's time for a swim.*

The guards look annoyed when I emerge from the room, so I'm guessing we're late. I smile at them sweetly and let them lead me through the palace. Twice I catch the guards staring at my ass, but as soon as I question whether the king would appreciate having his guards staring at his betrothed like that, the males stiffen, and their expressions turn sour as they escort me the rest of the way.

The hallways of the palace seem never-ending, but eventually, I'm led down to some kind of large stable. The air smells of oil, grain, and straw, and massive wooden stalls line the space. We stop, and one of the guards rests his hands on his hips.

"Lets go, Wendel," the guard calls out impatiently.

"I-I'll be right there!" a male replies from somewhere out of sight, and the guard mutters something under his breath.

We aren't waiting long when a large bird-like creature walks into view, and my mouth drops open. The creature stands taller than the winged centaur guards beside me, and while it has a curved beak and beady eyes like that of a chicken, rainbow scales cover its body instead of feathers, the colors seemingly always changing in the light. The creature pulls a crystal carriage with an open top, and as it comes closer, it takes me a moment to realize its fiery tail is made of fur rather than flames.

Whoa. I wish Shade could see this.

A male coachman sits at the front of the carriage, presumably the individual named Wendel, and with his hooked nose and bushy hair he almost looks comically like the creature. He smiles kindly at me, and I grin back, feeling the tiniest bit happier about this whole situation.

That is, until one of guards opens his mouth. "Get in," barks the one who'd called out to Wendel, and I try not to let his bad attitude ruin the moment. It's a strange sensation being called the future queen while also being treated as if you're less than dirt. Then again, I guess they think I'm going to die soon anyway. I would dwell on that morbid thought if I actually thought it was going to come to that. For now, I ignore the grouchy male and open the carriage door, sliding onto the plush leather seat.

"Welcome, welcome," Wendel says, still smiling at me, but the guard barks another impatient order, and Wendel quickly closes his mouth, facing the front.

Wendel says a few soothing words to the bird creature, and as the animal starts forward, the two guards move to either side of the carriage, matching the steady pace. We approach two wide crystal doors, which open automatically when we draw near, and then we're exiting the stable and moving beyond the palace walls.

What the—? I knew we were underground given what Shade had said about the tunnels, but I'm really not prepared for the city of The Haven. Craning my neck, I gape at the massive concave ceiling that's far above us and lined with white crystals. The stones are arranged in a pattern that reminds me of scales, and they glow, giving off warm, luminescent light. Around us, the road is also made from crystals, though these have been shaped and arranged together like a mosaic artwork. The small houses up ahead have been constructed in a similar fashion, the oddly shaped crystals neatly stacked together to form the walls and roofs, leaving no house appearing the same.

We're not far from the palace when the streets become thick with citizens walking about, all of them in their non-centaur forms with cuffs around their ankles. Some turn and bow to me as we pass, but most avoid looking in my direction like they're determined to pretend I don't exist. Had we been back in Seral, this would have been seen as an insult, but here, the guards act like it's expected behavior. Not that it bothers me. If anything, I feel less obligated to smile back at people, and I'm happy to spend more time marveling at my surroundings. King Celzar might be cruel, but his city is magnificent.

Another cart pulled by a bird creature starts to pass us, and I'm admiring the rainbow scales of the animal when a lively voice chirps in my head. *"Hullo!"* I blink, turning to my side in surprise, only to find my trusty guard still staring sternly straight ahead.

Frowning, I convince myself I must have imagined it, and it's not until I hear the voice again that I realize it's the bird-creature pulling my carriage who's speaking in my mind. *"Yes, yes. Here we are, another day. More walking. Always walking."* I notice the slight tingling sensation in my mind now that I'm aware of what's happening, and excitement makes me sit up in my chair. We leave the other carriage behind us, and everything is silent for a short while until we go to pass another carriage, and I hear, *"Hullo friend!"*

I watch in fascination as both bird creatures subtly dip their heads to one another as they pass by, and it's not until the other creature is some distance away that I say, *"Hello?"* like I'm the one who's responding to the bird's greeting.

The carriage jerks to a halt, and the creature

swivels its head, peering back and staring at me with beady eyes.

I lift my hand and give him a little wave. *"Nice to meet you, friend."*

The bird cocks its head in surprise. *"She speaks. How does she speak?"* the creature rambles.

Unaware of what's happening, Wendel nervously pats the bird's neck. "C-come now. Can't keep the king waiting." At that, the creature starts walking again, but it leaves its head to the side like its determined to keep an eye on me. *"Strange. So strange,"* the bird mumbles.

"Yes, I speak," I say when the creature has a steady gait again, and this time aside from a misstep, the bird doesn't stop walking. *"It's nice to meet you,"* I say, politely. *"I'm Blake."*

"Blake? Blake?" the creature repeats. *"Must not talk to the Blake."*

"No, Blake is my name," I explain. *"Do you have one? A name, I mean?"* This is honestly one of the most exciting things to happen to me since I was kidnapped, and I can't help but keep talking.

There's silence for a moment, but then the creature replies, *"Pask. Pask is my name."*

"Pask," I say with a nod. *"I like it."*

"Who are you, Blake? You are a stranger, new queen-to-be. You shouldn't be here."

I frown. *"You've heard about the wedding, huh?"*

"Oh yes, we all talk. The king just does not listen. But Wendel does. Yes, he does."

He reaches back to nudge the driver with his beak, and I grin when Wendel smiles and rubs the bird's neck affectionately.

"So...you're happy here?" I ask Pask, still trying to figure this place out.

"Happy? Strong word that. Very strong word. No, we're stuck. We're all stuck." He pauses for a moment then goes on. "No wind. No sky. No sun." He ruffles his huge wings, before tucking them in tighter against his back. "No, I would not say happy, but safe from the witches, yes. No witches. Horrible witches."

I think about the ruins of Perstalia and stare around at the life bustling around us. "But this place is incredible," I say.

"It does not matter," Pask replies thoughtfully. "We are not free. Not even my Wendel." He lowers his beak and sends me an image of the large cuff around his right leg.

I sigh. "So you, too, huh?"

"Yes, yes, all of us. This is his plan. We all know it."

"His plan?"

"He must have control. Magic is chaos of the best kind. He does not want chaos except within himself. He wants order. And now he wants you. The king gets what he wants."

I think about this as I stare at another group of citizens that we pass, all of them with cuffs around their ankles. "Do you think he'll be upset when I say 'no' to him?"

Pask's laughter is warm and genuine in my head.

"He will not allow you to say no to him, little bird. He will not allow it. Even the fish know this. But I will be rooting for you." He falls silent then, and as the tingling sensation fades, I realize Pask has severed our mental connection. It's not hard for me to figure out why when I see who's standing up ahead. As we pass another row of houses, a vast lake emerges before us, shimmering at the city's edge. The water sparkles in vibrant shades of blue, illuminated by the light of the crystals high above. A semicircle of elegantly dressed citizens stands nearby, their gazes fixed on me in the carriage, and at the riverbank, the king watches intently, flanked by a contingent of guards. He's dressed in a silver t-shirt and three-quarter-length trousers that reveal his calves. He beams when my gaze locks with his, though the light doesn't reach his eyes.

I move from the carriage, and Pask gives me a reassuring nudge with his beak, propelling me forward.

"Stunning," the king says as I approach, though the compliment is empty.

I smile, pretending his comment was sincere, though I get the feeling that all the extravagant outfits are more for show than anything else. "Anything to please my king," I say with a sickly-sweet voice, and he narrows his eyes at me.

A male with long plaited red hair comes up to the king's side, his elegant robes flapping as he moves. "Shall we begin, your highness?" he asks King Celzar, his gaze roving over me and no doubt seeing straight through the sheer robe I have on. *Hope you're enjoying the view.*

Like he realizes what he's doing, he looks away quickly, turning his attention back to the king.

King Celzar doesn't seem to notice. "Yes, now that my betrothed has finally arrived, let us proceed."

"Very good, sire," the other male says and steps forward, pulling the gathered crowd's attention to him. He clears his throat. "Today we continue to celebrate the impending union between our benevolent king and his new bride-to-be. As is tradition, the king and his betrothed will enter the waters at the same time, and while they are submerged the water will both connect and cleanse them, washing away their impurities in preparation for their coming union."

Connect them? I curse under my breath. Sassia never mentioned anything about being connected to the king, and the idea of it has alarm bells going off in my head. I think about the way he'd drained power from me the last time we'd touched, and my gaze slides to the royal.

He's busy smiling at the citizens who are clapping politely, but when his gaze connects with mine, there's a dark eagerness in his eyes that has me wishing I had a weapon. I remind myself that he's not going to drain my full power until we're married.

"Come, my beloved," he says, and music starts up from somewhere in the crowd. A strange burst of color shines ahead in the water, and I think I spot one of the rainbow fish we'd encountered back in the baths in Perstalia, but then it's gone again a second later.

King Celzar holds out his arm for me, and I arch a brow. "Such chivalry," I mutter sarcastically. Ignoring him, I take off my robe, and when no one comes forward to grab it, I throw it at the closest guard. He's too busy staring at my sparkling bra that the robe catches him in the face, the fabric smacking him in the eyes. He curses, reeling back as he tears the cloth from his face, then he quickly corrects himself as the king gives him a look of disapproval. Back at the carriage, Pask let's out a strange noise, his eyes bright as he watches on, and I grin and wink at him.

"If you're quite finished," the king hisses beside my ear, stepping up behind me. "Need I remind you of what happens when you don't behave? Take my hand, my beloved. We enter the water as a pair."

Ah, there was that word again. *Behave.* I pivot, smiling sweetly at him. "Oh, I remember," I reply, but I still ignore his hand and saunter toward the water alone. I hear him huff behind me, but I don't care. Shade's not in her cage anymore, and I highly doubt he's going to kill my mates because I'm not holding his hand. *Then again, he is rather sensitive,* I muse. *Oh well, too late now.*

The water is pleasantly warm as it licks over my toes, and I don't pause as I walk further in, moving until the water is up to my ribcage. King Celzar is quick to follow, only a pace behind me. When he makes it to my side, his hand grabs mine, and he leans in close, bringing with him the overwhelming scent of roses as he twists and peers at the crowd still watching from the riverbank.

"I'm not sure why you're making this so difficult," he murmurs in my ear. "You must realize by now that there is no escape for you. I don't know what you're trying to prove."

"The only thing I'm intent on proving is that by taking me, you made a poor choice for a bride," I hiss back. "And by the time you realize the full extent of your failure, it'll be too late."

His eyes flash with anger, and he grips my hand painfully as he drags me into the water.

~ Princess Blake ~

One moment I'm in the water, enveloped by warmth, and the next I'm standing in a dimly lit hexagonal room. A fire crackles in a hearth in the centre of the space, and King Celzar stands beside me still dressed in a silver shirt and trousers.

"What just happened?" I blurt, looking down to see I'm still dressed in the skimpy glittering outfit, though I appear to be completely dry. *Well, this isn't weird at all.*

The king is staring at a section of the wall in front of him, and when he doesn't answer, I turn to a table where there's an ornate candlestick. I go to grab it because wherever we are I have a bad feeling, and I plan to bash him over the head with it, but my hand passes right through the object, almost like I'm a lost spirit in the shadow realm. *What the fuck?*

I whip my head around, peering at the king who hasn't moved. "Where are we, Celzar?"

When he turns toward me, his eyes flash with amusement and a bittersweet smile lifts his lips. "She would have loved you, you know."

"She?" I take a step closer to him.

He faces the wall in front of him again, and I follow his gaze. There's a large frame there, and before my eyes tiny shards of crystal move together until I can make out the image of a young female dressed in long robes. Her hair is dead straight, reaching down past her hips, and her eyes are soft and kind.

Curiosity gets the better of me. "Is she your mother?"

He chuckles, and then his smile turns solemn. "Try my lover."

I'm about to crack a joke about that being impossible because he's clearly heartless, when I note the flash of genuine pain in his eyes. He blinks and the emotion is gone, but it's enough to shock me into silence.

When I don't speak, he goes on, "Her spirited nature was what drew me to her, and it wasn't long before I was lost and entranced with her. She made me forget all I had lost, and for a time, it was enough."

I frown in confusion, staring at the flickering flames of the fire, and scanning the small room. On each flat section of wall there's another frame, though the others are all blank. "We're still in the water, aren't we?" I say, somehow still feeling the warmth of the water sliding over my skin, even though my mind isn't in the lake anymore.

"Your body is," King Celzar confirms. "And while we're here it will be as if no time has passed though eons could go by."

I grimace at the idea of spending eons in this room with him, and he smirks. "You flatter yourself, demon. I have no wish to keep you here for eternity."

"Then why *am* I here?"

His gaze softens, and when he walks to one of the empty frames, I follow him. Again, tiny shards of crystal appear in the frame, this time forming an image of the same female. Her arms are in the air, and her robes are twisted to one side as she spins in a circle.

"I never bothered to tell my other brides about her. They were too broken by the time I found them, so lost from the absence of their power, that they were more than happy to surrender to me. All for the chance to feel their power again, even if it was only for a moment before I took it all away." He turns to me, and there's a vulnerability in his eyes that makes me uneasy.

"Look, I don't need your life's story—" I say, because I still fully intend to kill him when I get the chance, and I don't want to feel any sympathy for him.

Before I can finish, he cuts me off. "But you...you're

an outsider. And behind that," he swirls a finger in the air, "*harsh* demeanor, I get the feeling you understand the struggles of responsibility."

I want to argue that while that's true, it's obvious *he* doesn't, but I don't. It's painfully clear he's in a talkative mood, so I figure I'd better let him. If he wants to use me as his therapist, I'll play along, and maybe I'll learn something useful.

"Okay, so you had a lover," I say. "And then what? She died? It's a sad story, but it doesn't justify what you're doing to your kind. Let me guess, the witches stole her from you? Or was it—"

"Me," he replies abruptly.

"What?"

"She died because she loved me."

I stare at him blankly, not liking where this is going.

"I never was good enough for them, my mother and my siblings. The royals of Perstalia. While my siblings thrived under mother's gaze, I was the black sheep, the outcast. No matter what I did I was never good enough," he says bitterly, and he walks to another frame where the image changes to show a younger Celzar crying with his head in his hands. "And then the day came when my mother named my sister as her successor rather than me, her eldest son. And I, despite all that I had done and given, was banished from the kingdom..."

I listen, not daring to interrupt.

"But I didn't leave empty-handed. One of my

mother's most powerful advisors had just created an enchanted object. He became fanatical and swore that it would lead to new lands, and new opportunities for allies. But mother wouldn't have it. She banned the object and forbade it from being used. Of course, I knew that was a mistake."

A new object? My gut churned. "So, you used it? And you found her?" I say, referring to the female he'd been talking about.

"Yes," he replies with a small smile. "Yenna was the one who found me wandering around that foreign forest. She called herself a witch, though at the time I didn't know what that meant."

My stomach plummets. *A witch?* One-hundred questions pop into my head.

"She lived in the forest, you see," he goes on. "She helped heal me on the inside, and for the first time in a long while, I was happy. Those were the best months of my life. But then came the day when she told me she had to return home. I was desperate to keep her with me. *Marry me.* I asked her. And when she agreed I could have sworn the stars themselves danced overhead."

The image before us changes, showing the two of them dancing. Yenna is now wearing a flowing dress covered in flowers, and their smiles are so big and joyful it makes me grin as well. I stare at the side of King Celzar's face, and for once there isn't cruelty in his expression. Now, there's something soft tinged with sadness.

"But it doesn't last," I say slowly.

His smile falls, his expression becoming hard again, and I almost regret saying it. "That night as she surrendered herself to me, as she took her vows to become my wife, I didn't understand what was happening. Her power leeched into me as I held her, and she grew limp and cold in my arms. I was desperate to give it back. I thought I'd do anything to keep her with me, but then I felt the rush of it. The power swelled inside me, and I knew I could do great things with her magic at my fingertips. I realized then that while my wife was gone, her love was a gift, and I would not waste it." A manic gleam enters his eyes, and if I wasn't in this weird ethereal state, bile would have crept up my throat.

"You're talking like you're glad she died. I thought you loved her?" I question.

His eyes sparkle, the same cruel king I'd come to know, returning in an instant. "How could I be sad? With her power, I could do so much good. I could do... anything!"

"Good?" I ask incredulously. "What good have you done? Perstalia is destroyed and your kind are underground!"

"I saved them!" he snarls back. "I had no idea that my Yenna was one of the witch anchors."

"Anchors?"

He nods. "It turns out she was one of three witches with the power of their ancients. It was through their rituals that the power filtered to their people. And when the witches came to find their sister dead in my arms, they didn't understand it had been an accident. They didn't give me a chance to explain my own power, one which I had not known about. No, they attacked, and I was forced to flee or waste my Yenna's sacrifice."

Wait, what? I can barely speak. Can barely utter the words. "And the witches followed you back to Perstalia," I say, almost in a whisper. "All because you'd taken the power of their ancients, and they wanted it back. You *stole* their power." The room spins, and I can hardly breathe, even in this prison of my own mind. "Y-you're the reason for all of it. You didn't save the Perstalians, you doomed them!" *And you doomed the demons.*

King Celzar doesn't look the least bit remorseful. "Mother didn't have the power to stop the witches when they descended on the city, and they couldn't be reasoned with. Even my brother, the so-called 'Defender of the Realm' as he was called by our kind, couldn't stop them. While Mason led our warriors into battle and was overwhelmed on the battlefield, it was I who had to take control and save those who were left. With the power I had, I was able to create an underground haven for us. A new world where we could escape the witches. I couldn't match the power of the two anchors they had left, but I could give us a chance."

I try to place my hand on the wall to ground myself, but I end up touching a frame and the image flickers, this time showing an intense battle scene littered with bodies. A centaur male stands with a sword in his grasp, surrounded by witches on all sides. His large wings are spread wide, arrows embedded between the feathers, and there's such sorrow in his defeated expression that it makes my heart hurt. The shape of his chin and coloring of his hair are the only features marking him as a relative of King Celzar.

"So, you stole what was theirs and you hid," my words are quiet, like I'm afraid to say them, because I can't believe this is true. I think of the graverobbing back in Seral. Of the great war and how the witches had fought to steal our power. How many demons had died? I tried to imagine what life was like for the witches without the power of one of their anchors. I hated them. My entire life I had been told to detest everything about their kind. I'd assumed they were power-hungry monsters, intent on dominating the realms. They tortured demons to figure out how to harvest our power, and no matter what King Celzar is telling me, I can't ever excuse that, but for the first time in my life, I realize there's more to their story. So much more.

"You should have told the truth," I tell him, sickened by what he's telling me. Sickened by the idea that he would let his kind suffer for his mistake. I think of Pask and every other trapped being in The Haven. "Why didn't you return the magic?"

"Return it?" His gaze darkens. "Now, why would I do that?"

I stare at him like he's an imbecile. "Oh, I don't know. Maybe to prevent a war? To prevent genocide?"

"Everything happens for a reason," he replies, his voice devoid of emotion. "Yenna gifted me her power, and I wasn't about to squander it."

"Gifted?" I scoff. "You *stole* it, and you murdered the female you supposedly loved!"

He juts out his chest. "War was merely an opportunity to elevate my kind."

Elevate? It seems a strange word to use when he quite literally brought them underground, but it's clear this guy isn't going to see sense no matter what I say. "If you were so keen on helping everyone, then why cuff them? You say you're stronger. Why not let everyone have their abilities in The Haven?"

He tilts his head, observing me. "Not everyone who's given power has the ability to wield it properly," he replies coldly. "Just like yourself. You let those males all fight over you, when going by the power I felt radiating off you when we were on the surface, I'm guessing you could have done something to put them in their place. No, I'm not going to let anyone ruin my utopia. This way, there is guaranteed peace."

"Peace?" I snort at the ridiculousness of the statement.

One moment he's standing before the frame, and the next he's in my face, towering over me. "I'm not sure why I thought you'd be different to my other brides. I expected you might be one of the few to understand. With your power, I thought you must be able to view the true world. That you would understand the weight of responsibility when it came to ruling a kingdom." His eyes soften, resignation seeping in. "But I guess, in the end it doesn't matter. You'll fade like the others did. Just like her..."

Unfortunately for him, I really struggle to feel sympathy for kings who are this deluded. "Why do you need me? You said yourself, you're powerful and juiced with witch magic. Why keep stealing from others? And why bother with marriage?"

He grows thoughtful then. "I might be powerful, but my power is not infinite. While my lovely Yenna, was able to draw on the power of the ancients, once I took it from her, that connection was cut off."

"So the more power you used, the more of it you depleted," I supply for him, keenly interested in this part of the conversation. "And while her power was great, you've now started taking power from your new brides." I hesitate, thinking through my next move carefully. A moment passes before I force myself to relax and smile. "But...what if you could have your bride *and* more power?"

He frowns at me, clearly suspicious of my dramatic change in attitude. "You've made it abundantly clear you want nothing to do with me, demon."

"Well, that's true," I tell him bluntly, "But that was because I hate being imprisoned, and it was before I realized just how powerful you are. What if we come to a mutual agreement? I don't want to die, and you said yourself, you were the happiest when you were with

Yenna. I'm not her, but I can be more than a fleeting sacrifice." I rest a hand on one hip, subtly jutting out my breasts, and a hint of interest touches King Celzar's eyes.

"It can't be an accident what happened with Yenna, and it's not an accident that I'm here now," I say. "Lady Fate has plans for us, and maybe this time, your bride can live."

Saying the words 'your bride' makes me want to gag, but I keep my posture relaxed. I think of his past lover. He hasn't explained why he always tries to make his new victims his brides, but I wonder if it's because in a way he's subconsciously trying to replay the past. Even though, he knows it'll always end the same way.

"How so?" he asks cautiously.

"What if, instead of dying, I become your queen?" I say, giving him a coy smile. "A *real* queen. Not a prisoner in your palace, but a partner."

He still stares at me suspiciously. "Now why would I want that?"

I shrug. "Oh, I don't know, maybe because it can be damn lonely being the only powerful being in a kingdom. And maybe, because I'm way more powerful than you realize." I lick my lips tentatively. "You weren't wrong. It was near insufferable having those males fighting over me, and I was close to wanting to end the lot of them, but it wasn't just a competition for fun. For my kind, we have predestined mates. And when we bond with those mates, our power increases exponentially." I pause for emphasis. "*My* power will grow far beyond what you felt before this cuff was placed on me."

His eyes get so light they almost glow.

"So they are your fated mates," he mutters.

"Yes," I nod. "But I don't think you understand the real reason I want them alive. You see, I need them to seal the bond so I can unlock my power. Once I have that power, you could imprison them for eternity, and I wouldn't care. But when I'm that powerful, you can take most of it, making you strong again, and instead of killing me, leave me a little and let me rule by your side. As long as you let me keep enough to be comfortable, and you don't keep me locked away, I'm happy to be yours."

His gaze drops then, and instead of staring at me with the same scrutiny he has used since the first time I'd met him, this time I see longing and desperation. His chest rises and falls as he considers what I've said, and when I see that longing, I almost feel bad for him. *Almost.* Until I remember the horrible things he's done, including to his first wife, let alone all the ones after that.

"I can't guarantee that I can stop when the power transfer begins," he says.

I smile reassuringly. "Sure you can. What happened with Yenna was a long time ago, and I'm sure you've perfected the art of using your magic by now."

He crosses his arms, his expression becoming

thoughtful. "And bonding with these mates of yours. What does that entail?"

I give him a saucy smile and bite my lip. "Well, yes, you will have to learn to share just this once. But on the bright side, let's just say you should enjoy the show."

His pupils dilate. "A mating ritual? It's been so long since my kind have encountered fated mates. I'd forgotten this was part of it."

"It is in a way," I reply. "Let's call it a basic ritual to unlock my power."

His gaze shines with hunger, and I have to force myself not to cringe. Truthfully, I'm not sure if he's lusting over the idea of more power or the idea of me with my mates, but either way, my proposition seems to be getting the job done.

"So," I say, still making a point to tease my bottom lip. "Will you marry me, my king?"

His eyes sparkle in the light. "I suppose there would be no harm in letting myself have a true queen for as long as you remain useful. But you must know if you cross me, I'll make you and your mates suffer fates worse than death."

"Like I said, the only reason I care about them, is because I need them to unlock my power. After that, I have no loyalty to them."

King Celzar's smile stretches wide. "Well then, let's see about this bonding ritual, shall we?"

CHAPTER

ELEVEN

~ Alaric ~

I drive my pickaxe down with such force that the cave wall shudders. The rock cracks to reveal a cluster of golden crystals that sparkle like diamonds, and for a moment, all I can think about is my demon enchantress. My *mate*, though I'm still reluctant to believe it. The golden color reminds me of her eyes, and a new rush of anger has me gripping the handle of my pickaxe so tightly my knuckles turn white.

In the past, when I was given a target by the Order of the Drozac, I always had this calm certainty that I'd get the job done. There had been times when I'd had to track my target for weeks before being able to terminate them, and throughout, I'd remained patient, never losing sight of the end goal. But now, my patience is wearing thin, and I'll be fucking lucky if I can stop myself from killing the three males mining next to me. For every minute that I'm away from the she-demon with the smart mouth, I lose a shred more of my control and more of my sanity. *I always knew the demon princess would be the death of me.*

My thoughts spiral, and soon I'm imagining the one-hundred different ways I'll torture and kill her captors. *As soon as I'm out of here.* I hold out hope for the princess's little bird companion, but if the rebels don't come soon, I'm going to have to make my own exit.

"Axes down!" Javier, our guard, orders. He's been wary since Dante jabbed his hand into the male's throat, but no less cruel. We all drop our pickaxes, letting them thud to the ground, and we turn to the guard.

"Don't know about you guys, but I'm ready for another round," Nate jokes with a grin, though his left eye is still bruised from the last beating we were all given.

Javier doesn't look impressed.

"It's a little sad that you enjoy our company this much," Dante drawls, his tail poised in the air behind him like a snake ready to strike. "We're starting to wonder whether you have any friends."

The guard's lip curls. "Just move it," he snaps. "The king has given us orders."

The king? I glower at him.

Three more guards join Javier.

"Try anything, and the king's orders be damned, this time we'll leave you so bloody it'll take your bodies a long while to heal with that cuff on," Javier bites out, and he gestures for us to walk in front of him.

I imagine my fist connecting with the surly guard's face, blood spraying from the blow, but there's something about the male that's giving off a strange energy. It's like he's nervous...or excited.

Nate is the first to step forward, following the order, and I step in line, knowing that with the cuff around my ankle, I won't be able to match the guards. We pass where our new prisoner friend, Mason, as he calls himself, is mining with a group further in the cavern, and he subtly watches us as we leave the mines, walking past the cells until we enter another tunnel and come to a narrow door. One of the guards opens the door, and we're ushered inside. I observe the white tiled walls surrounding us on all sides, and the circular drain in the middle of the room.

"What is this?" I growl, my muscles tensing as I prepare to fight.

Two hoses are connected to the walls on either side of us, and a couple of the guards pick them up.

Javier smirks, his face contorting as a sadistic gleam enters his eyes. "Strip," he commands. "The king has requested that you be cleaned."

Nate folds his thick arms in front of his chest. "Fuck that. Usually, when someone asks me to take my clothes off, at least I know I'm gonna have a good time."

The guard on the right points his hose at the shifter and presses on the handle. Before the jet of water hits him, Nate dodges out of the way, and the stream connects with Prince Callan's face instead. The prince scowls, lifting one arm to block the water as droplets trail down his reddening cheeks.

A wide grin stretches across Nate's face. "Ooh, yeah that one was my fault," the shifter admits.

The guard turns off the hose again as Prince Callan glares at the shifter.

"Why does your king want us cleaned?" I ask.

"How the fuck are we supposed to know?" Javier snaps. "If the king wants you in a dress and prancing around like concubines, you do it. So, drop your drawers before we decide to strip you ourselves. Either way, you aren't leaving here until your asscrack is clean."

Dante smirks, looking intrigued. "Well, that's rather specific. Does your king have certain kinks by any chance?"

The other guard points the hose at the demon's face, and Dante lifts his hands in a placating gesture. "If you're that desperate to get me naked, you won't get complaints from me." At that, the demon starts stripping off, and begrudgingly, the rest of us do the same.

"What are you doing, Nine Lives?" Prince Callan asks harshly, and I turn to see Nate staring at each of us. The stupid fuck is making an already odd situation even weirder.

"Just checkin' that I'm the biggest," the shifter replies with a shit-eating grin. "You get to see mine all the time, it only seems fair. Besides, I wanna know that I'm gonna be Blake's favorite."

Prince Callan lets out an insufferable sigh, and I shake my head. Despite the shifter's idiocy, the archangel drops his gaze, scrutinizing everyone.

"See, knew you wanted to know," Nate teases. "Hate to break it to you, though. Looks like I'm bigger."

My brows slam down. The room is as frigid as the ice mountains in my realm, and this isn't my true size, but I'm not about to argue with the male about the size of his cock. Going by the way he talks, I'll be surprised if he knows how to use it anyway.

Dante stretches his arms above his head and cracks his neck. "You don't need to come up with excuses to admire me, shifter. We're going to be bonded brothers after all."

I repent internally for whatever transgression led Lady Fate to hate me and place me in this situation. "You're all fucking stupid," I growl.

"If you're quite done," Javier shouts, and both guards turn on their hoses.

I curse, cupping my front as a powerful jet of ice water pounds onto my chest, knocking my broken rib. They pelt us for long enough that I start to wonder whether they aim to strip the skin from us, when

Javier commands, "That'll do." The hoses are turned off, and I peer at my bloody clothes that are still covered in grime.

"You're not to redress," Javier says with a stern expression. "Let's go." He jerks his head to the door, and the rest of us follow, escorted by the guards.

I determine we're not about to be executed, or they wouldn't have bothered bathing us, but I stay alert as we're led down another tunnel. This time when we reach a wider door, two guards in pristine royal armor are waiting outside. I take note of the weapons they're carrying and the image of a fierce bird etched into their breastplates.

"Keep alert," Prince Callan mutters under his breath, not that I needed the warning.

The guards open the door, and we stride into the room without hesitation. None of the guards follow us, and as soon as we're inside, Javier pokes his head through the doorway. "Make it a good show for us, won't ya?" he says with a smirk, and he slams the door.

Nate peers around and whistles. "Well, fuck me, is this a—"

"Conjugal visit room?" Dante finishes with amusement. "Going by the furnishings, I'd say this resembles many of the pleasure houses I've seen."

I scan the area, taking in the large bed that's situated at the far end of the room, complete with crimson sheets and multiple embroidered cushions. The room is dimly lit with crystal lanterns attached to the walls, and multiple plush couches line the area. The red carpet is soft beneath my toes, and a floral-patterned wallpaper covers the walls, stretching everywhere except on the right side of the room where there's a long wall-length mirror.

"As nice as it is to be out of the mines, somethin' tells me we're in for a surprise," Nate comments, staring at his reflection in the mirror.

I crack my knuckles and move to one side of the door.

TWELVE

~ Princess Blake ~

"I'll see you the entire time, my beloved," King Celzar tells me as he leaves me standing outside a wide steel door. "Retrieve your power. Then tomorrow, we shall be wed."

I smile tightly, hiding the fact that my heart is galloping in my chest. "Can't wait."

Before he leaves, King Celzar waves his hand, and my wings reappear, bursting from my back and tearing through the thin robe I'm wearing. A giddy grin erupts on my face, and I flap my wings twice before folding them behind my back.

"Better that they see you like this," King Celzar says dispassionately, like he doesn't care how happy he's just made me. "There'll be less questions that way." I only have time to mumble a quick 'thank you' before he disappears into a neighboring room.

Facing the door, I let out a long breath through my nose. *What if they're not here?* The nasty thought slithers through my mind, and I push it back. King Celzar might be cruel, but he hasn't played mind games like Dad would have. No, they're in there. My males. My *mates.*

I step inside and a guard closes the door, sealing me in. I don't have time to react before a body crashes into me. Large fingers curl painfully around my throat and push me against the door, and I don't try to fight. My mate's scent slams into me, and the relief is near crippling, leaving me speechless. If anything, I'm glad for his hand on my neck, because in that instant my legs feel weak. For days, I'd tried to tell myself that it didn't matter if we were apart. That my mates didn't want me anyway. But now, as the warm and bitter scents of dark chocolate and mint fill the air around me, all I want to do is climb onto the assassin and remind him why the fuck he should never leave my side again. Because he's mine, whether he believes it yet or not.

Furious gray eyes bore into me, but then Alaric blinks, his gaze softening with surprise and recognition. "Enchantress?" he rasps, his grip loosening. Slowly, his gaze lowers and as he realizes just what I'm wearing, or more so, what I'm *not* wearing, his eyes heat, his expression becoming feral. My lips part, my body responding to him—to his smell, his touch—and the magic binding us together. He leans down, his lips closing in on mine, and my heart races as I think of how good he'll taste. As I think of how badly I need this. But just when our lips are about to touch, he's ripped away from me.

And then my three other mates are closing in. Dante. Nate. Prince Callan.

They stalk closer like wolves surrounding their prey, and I grin as my body tightens, a potent mix of excitement, joy, and lust flooding me. *Yes.* I want them. More than I've wanted anything, but just as I get the overwhelming urge to jump on one of them, I remind myself of the king. *Because he's watching.* I try to quell my rising desire and focus on calming my frantic heartbeat. I force myself to suck in a few more deep breaths in an effort to gain some control. Because I can't let the king know what these males mean to me. I need him to think that they're dispensable.

I work on shutting down my emotions, and a cold mask comes over my face, even as Dante cups my cheeks with his hands. The smile that forms on his face makes my heart squeeze. "Princess? Thank Lady Fate." His midnight blue eyes bore into me, and the look of relief on his face almost has my mask cracking. *Fuck.* Before Dante can say another word, I glance at the long two-sided mirror that lines the right side of the room, hoping my warning is obvious.

Nate raises a brow, clearly not understanding my message. "And here I thought she'd be happy to see us," the shifter complains. "Well, happy to see me, anyway," he amends with a lop-sided grin.

I roll my eyes.

"Pay attention, Nine Lives," Prince Callan says coldly, subtly glancing at the mirror, and it takes a moment before understanding shows on Nate's face.

I stare at Prince Callan. If it's possible, he looks grumpier than usual, but I guess that's not surprising given his stay in the mines and the bruises marring his body. In fact, all of my mates are sporting injuries, even Dante. I keep my face passive, careful not to give away how much this bothers me. We were all blindsided, but at least we're alive.

My mates move even closer, creating a wall so they're blocking my view of the mirror, and I struggle to keep a clear head as their intoxicating scents surround me. *Keep it together, Blake.*

I wobble a little on my feet, and Dante steadies me by placing a hand on my shoulder. "You all right there, princess?" he asks, his devilish lips twitching up.

I'm tempted to knee him in the crotch, simply because I love it when I get to wipe that smug smile from his face, but instead I subconsciously lick my lips. I am definitely *not* all right.

"You're naked," I squeeze out. I really should have expected it given my own lack of clothing, but I hadn't thought the king would be this practical.

"Seems we have something in common," Dante drawls, blatantly admiring me and not at all helping me keep my control.

"Actually, I have a robe on," I point out, indicating to the white gown that's covering my naked body, though my arms are exposed, along with a fair amount of cleavage.

"That's not a robe," Alaric growls, his expression looking pained.

"King Celzar thought this would make the situation more efficient," I say carefully, not sure whether the king can simply see into the room or if he has ears in here as well. When I'd mentioned the bonding ritual to the king, all I was thinking about was the fact that it would allow me to see my mates again, but now that I'm here, I wonder if I've made a mistake.

"What are you talking about?" Prince Callan asks.

"Efficient," I repeat. "For us to complete the bonding ritual."

Shock flashes on Prince Callan's face before his expression hardens. *Perfect.* Of all of them, I'm counting on Prince Callan and Alaric to really sell this.

Alaric's nostrils flare. "What have you gotten us into, demon?"

I'm aware the king is probably growing impatient, so I speak up loudly. "Me? We all know this is Lady Fate's doing. Luckily for you, all we need to do is seal the bond, and I'll be on my way. I won't need anything else from you."

"Seal the bond?" Alaric growls, looking like he wants to wrap his hand around my throat again.

"Yes," I say with a tight smile. "That way *I* can

have my power, and you'll never have to see me again. I think you've made it obvious you don't want me, and as long as I have my power, I'll have no use for you."

"*Your* power?" Nate repeats, his lips twitching.

"Yup," I say with a nod.

Everyone knows that when fated mates bond, the female gains the most, unlocking the power within her, but the males also gain increased abilities. Everyone knows it, that is, except the Perstalians and King Celzar. At least, I don't think he does. As far as King Celzar knows, the whole bonding thing is merely a way for me to level up. I failed to mention that my mates and I would also solidify a bond that would tie us for eternity.

"So..." Dante says slowly, "you want us to bond so you can have *your* power, and then you want nothing more from us? We can leave the prison?"

I honestly have no idea about that last part. When I was convincing the king, my focus was on getting the five of us together. After that, my plan got a little hazy.

Noise blares from a little speaker in the left corner of the room, the king's voice ringing out. "Bond with my betrothed, and I'll free you from the mines. You can return to the surface where you can unite with your people."

It's obviously a blatant lie, and I'm sure my guys can sense it, too. There's no way King Celzar is going to allow the others to go back to the surface and blab the location of The Haven.

"Betrothed?" Alaric growls low, his gray eyes shooting to me. "So it's true?"

I give him a sheepish smile remembering how Shade had said they'd made a mysterious friend in the prison who was divulging information to them. Clearly, he must have told them about the wedding. "Yep. Looks like I'm going to become queen of this place," I explain casually like I'm not basically telling my mates I'm rejecting them and getting hitched with someone else.

Alaric and Prince Callan scowl, while Dante and Nate give me questioning looks.

"Like I said," I say loudly. "None of you want me, so I may as well unlock my power, and you can be free to do whatever you want back on the surface."

My mates are still blocking the view of the mirror, and Dante smirks as he steps forward, loosening the knot that's holding my gown together at the front. His hand slides between the opening of my robe, and he grips my bare waist, leaning in close. "You're lucky I didn't try to fuck you the moment you came through that door, princess. He's not going to believe we don't want you," he whispers. "I know you, Blake, and you won't so easily give up on the demons. So, what's the real plan?" He moves his hand down, and I shiver as his fingers glide between my legs. He slides a single finger along my center, and I press my lips tightly together to stop my gasp. My mates press in closer, and the room starts to spin again.

"I don't know," I admit quietly, even as Dante pulls

my robe back enough to press a kiss to my shoulder. "The king is power-hungry, and this is the only way I could think of to get him to bring me to you," I whisper, hoping King Celzar can't hear me. "The way I see it, our best option is to fake the bonding ritual, and when the king enters the room, we act quickly to try and take him out, knowing that we might completely fail and doom ourselves in the process."

Dante's expression grows thoughtful, and he swipes his finger along my center again, undoubtedly simply because he enjoys torturing me. I curse, but I don't ask him to stop, because it feels too damn good. "That sounds like a terrible plan, princess," my demon drawls.

"We can't bond. It might give the king the power he wants. And this plan has got to be better than you sending Shade blindly into the tunnels," I whisper. "Which, by the way, if anything bad happens to her, I'll make you all personally suffer."

Nate winces. "You know about that, huh?"

I nod. "Now, are we faking it or not?" I ask quietly, and my heart thunders.

"We put on a show for the king," Prince Callan agrees slowly, though his voice is hard and clinical.

"And we hope your little bird friend pulls through for us in time," Alaric growls low.

"But do you really think you can fake it, princess?" Dante whispers with a seductive smile. "What does the king think bonding involves? Going by our lack of clothing, I'd say it's not far from the truth."

It's becoming hard to breathe, and I reach down, forcing Dante's hand to stop moving. "Only that it involves physical intimacy with my mates," I squeeze out.

Nate grins. "Shouldn't be too hard to make him think it's real."

Prince Callan and Alaric look less enthusiastic about this, but neither of them complain.

"I'll take one for the team," Dante says with a sensual smile that makes my insides melt. "The rest can make a show of busying themselves." He runs his other hand over the silky collar of the robe I'm wearing. "With this, we can make it look like more than it is."

"Or I could actually make Blake feel somethin'" Nate suggests hopefully, moving even closer. "Without all four of us gettin' involved, the bond won't be sealed."

Holy Lady Fate. I seriously overestimated my willpower.

"She's more comfortable with me," Dante argues. "Besides, I'm a demon. If she's only going to fuck one of us, it makes sense that the main bonding partner would be one of her own kind."

Nate grumbles something under his breath.

"*Pretend* to fuck," I clarify, but I don't know if Dante is listening. As much as I want my mates, I haven't forgotten about what happened to Kai, the last lover I'd been with, and now isn't the right time to test out whether my vagina will accidentally kill any one of my mates.

There's a buzzing from somewhere overhead, and King Celzar's voice rings out. "I have places to be, my beloved. Seal the bond or I shall assume this was simply a ploy for you to see your friends. You do not want to disappoint me."

Honestly, I'm not sure if the king is going to believe our act, but we have to do something. "Okay, if we're doing this, we have to do it now," I whisper.

"The robe stays on," Alaric growls, and I have to stop myself from rolling my eyes. I'm not scared of having an audience. I'm sure it's not just the king behind the two-way mirror that lines the wall. For all I know, there could be a dozen guards eagerly watching on, but none of that matters. Demons don't really care about nudity or public shows of affection as long as it's not putting us in a vulnerable situation.

"It stays on," I agree to appease the assassin.

"All right then. Ready, princess?" Dante asks me quietly.

I force a smile. "It's not like any of us have a choice."

His grin turns wolfish. "I don't care who it's for, as long as I get to do this," he murmurs into my ear, and then his lips are on mine. *Merciful. Lady. Fate.* The male tastes like the best damn spiced apricots I've ever eaten, tangy and sweet with a hint of spice, and I can't get enough. His tongue sweeps into my mouth, and sparks of pleasure shoot through my body. A moan slips out of me, and while I'm quick to cut off the noise, it's like a siren call drawing my other mates even closer to me. Dante claims me like a demon possessed, and his hand slides behind my head, tangling in my hair as he utterly consumes me.

I hadn't planned for this. Hadn't planned for the way I'd feel when I had them with me. Around me. I'd intended to make this appear forced. I try to stop myself from showing just how badly I need my mates, but a rumbling starts in Nate's chest, and I lose myself.

"More," I gasp when Dante finally breaks the kiss, his eyes completely black as he pulls me toward the bed, licking and sucking on my neck the entire way. His legs hit the end of the mattress, and I press on the demon's chest, pushing him onto the bed. He falls onto his back, and his lips curl as I climb on, straddling his hips. Holding myself up, I rock above him, hoping that my robe is hiding enough for the king to think this is believable. My thighs tremble as I fight against my desire, but I don't let myself drop down onto Dante's cock.

Nate comes up behind me, his teeth grazing my shoulder as he plays with my breasts, and I fight to keep control. Because none of this is about me, or about us. *It's all a show,* I tell myself. *Just make it convincing for the king.* But my body doesn't believe it's a show. She wants her mates, and my muscles strain from the effort of holding myself back. *Think of Kai,* I tell myself. *You don't want that to happen to them, do you? Besides, Prince Callan and Alaric don't want to bond anyway.* At the thought of my reluctant mates, I turn my head to where the giant and my archangel stand beside the bed, both with their backs to the mirror like they're hoping to block the king's view of me.

Did they not get the message about making this look real?

"Bond with me," I call out to them. "Give me the power that was predestined to become mine and obtain your freedom in return." My words sound stilted and wrong to my own ears, but I hope the king finds it convincing. There's a war raging in Prince Callan and Alaric's eyes as they battle their own desires, but they move closer to the edge of the bed. Prince Callan's eyes are hooded as he kneels on the mattress, and I don't think when I reach out, grabbing his massive length in my hand. To my surprise, he doesn't pull away. He only stares at me, half with uncertainty and half with desire as I stroke him in time to my rocking, imagining he isn't just in my hand. I don't stop to think about the fact that the last time I saw him, the archangel looked like he wanted nothing to do with me. All I can focus on is my mates, and the demon between my thighs.

I can't stop myself. Desperate for more friction, I drop down, my core clenching as Dante's cock slides against my center. Nate pinches and teases my nipples with his fingers as his lips press against my neck, and sensations fire through my body. *More. I need more.*

"Fuck, Blake," Dante curses, his voice tortured as I slide against his cock, enjoying every bump and ridge.

I know I should lift up again, but I only rock my hips harder, enjoying the feel of him beneath me. I don't care that the king is watching. Really, I wouldn't care if the whole damn kingdom was watching, these are *my* mates, and everything in me tells me that this is right. I need their skin on mine as badly as I need...

"Princess," Dante says the word as a breathy warning. "Stop."

But I can't. They had been taken from me, and I need this.

Dante curses again, and I moan as I stroke Prince Callan's hard cock. When I look up, the archangel is staring at me with an intense gaze, like he wants to pluck me from Dante and steal me away, but he doesn't. I'm distracted by the archangel, and I don't notice Dante reaching his hand down between my legs. He aims himself, and the next time I rock my hips, his cock slides in, pushing in deep. I gasp at the sensation of him filling me, stretching me so much that a whimper falls from my mouth. The sting of pain is chased away as pleasure makes my entire body come alive. *Fuck.* We should stop. The memory of Kai clings to the edges of my mind, a warning I promised myself I wouldn't forget, but the pleasure chases it away.

Alaric is still standing, but his chest heaves, and his temple pulses as his gaze drops, watching as Dante slides in and out of me, the robe pulled back enough to give him a nice view. His hand lowers to his cock, and then he's stroking himself in time to the rest of our movements. The assassin growls a curse, and the rumbling sound in Nate's chest grows louder, almost frantic. *Shit. Stop, Blake. You need to—* This isn't part of the plan. I try to remind myself of Kai, of the risk involved, but as Dante's hands move to either side of my hips, I can't stop myself from enjoying the way he makes my body feel. Tingles rush through me as the pleasure builds.

Nate's teeth clamp onto my shoulder, and I throw my head back, my nails clawing down Dante's chest.

"Have your power," Alaric growls, his voice hoarse, though he's obviously the only one of us still level-headed enough to keep this ruse going. I rock my hips faster, needing more as the pleasure blooms inside me, delicious and all-consuming. But just as I think I'm about to tip over the edge, I gasp as fear makes my body lock up. I can't do this. Not now. Not when I could lose one of my mates forever. Dante's hands still on my sides like he knows what's going through my head. His cock is still deep inside me, and I pant, trying to control my emotions. Seconds pass, and I force myself to remember why we're in this mess. *To convince the king.* Pushing my worries from my mind, I stretch my arms out dramatically, and make a show of staring at my palms like they now contain the secrets of all the realms. "Finally!" I exclaim, my voice maniacal. "I feel it. The power."

Dante breathes heavily beneath me, his eyes hooded, but a small smirk graces his lips. I take that to assume that my act was believable, but it's hard to tell.

It takes all of my willpower to lift off my demon and move away from my mates, and I stand facing the mirror. A smile creeps across my face. "I'm ready my king. The power we both desire is now mine."

The king doesn't speak, but my mates move behind me, lifting to their feet. I start toward the door, but I stop when I hear shouting. There's a brief moment of silence, and then another scream comes to us from the tunnel.

"Fuck it, I don't even care if he sees," Nate says as he moves in front of me, blocking my path to the door and taking up a defensive stance. My other mates do the same, all four of them forming a wall between me and the door.

Clenching my jaw, I scan the room, looking for a weapon. *Why are there so many damn cushions?* Aside from smothering someone to death, they're pretty useless. I'm still searching when the door flies open. I drop into a crouch, ready to attack, but a familiar prickling sensation touches my mind. *"Hold on girl! We're here!"* Shade's voice fills my head, and my mouth pops open.

"Shade?" Relief crashes into me. *"What are you doing out there?"*

"Saving your ass, of course," she tells me. *"Now get out here already."*

I peer at the tall, muscular male standing in the doorway. He's covered in dirt and blood, his torn clothes hanging off him and his dark hair is a mess of matted knots, but he has the most vibrant glittering blue eyes I've ever seen. He looks a little different now, but I still recognize him as the male I saw when I was in the water, the male who'd been on the battlefield surrounded by witches. *Celzar's brother.* But unlike in the picture, the sorrow is gone from his eyes, replaced with a fierce determination.

"Looks like your bird friend came through for us," the stranger says to my mates, and the deep timbre of his voice has goosebumps rising on my skin.

"Coming through!" Shade shouts in my head, and my attention is pulled from the male as a black blur flies past him, diving straight for me.

Before she reaches me, Shade extends her wings wider, slowing her descent until she lands on my shoulder. She tilts her head to the side, observing my naked mates. *"Looks like I missed out on one hell of a party,"* she teases, and I grin, reaching up to stroke her feathers.

"I missed you," I tell her with a smile.

"I'm serious, Blake," she replies. *"I fully expect you to explain this."*

I chuckle, but I find myself staring again at the stranger in the doorway again. "This way," he orders, indicating with his head to the tunnel beyond, and as my mates start to move, I go with them.

THIRTEEN

~ Princess Blake ~

There's a large group of rebels and prisoners already in the tunnel, and it's chaos as we step over the bodies of fallen guards. My mates and I grab the guard's discarded weapons, and my males stay close to me as we make our way through the prison, and past empty cells that reek of urine and mold.

"*Looks like you've been busy,*" I say to Shade as we pass a guard that's lying in a pool of blood, his head severed from his body. "*Why didn't you warn me you were almost here?*"

"*I thought you were still with the king in The Haven,*" Shade replies. "*I didn't want you to risk using magic around him.*"

I nod. *"Well, you obviously found the rebels."*

At the front of our group the rebels lead the way, charging at any guards who cross our path. It takes a group of around ten cuffed rebels to take on a single centaur guard, but somehow, we keep moving, making our way through the tunnels.

A few paces in front of us, one of the female prisoners falls, crying out as her knees buckle, but the male with the blue eyes scoops her up, barely missing a step. She wraps her thin arms around his neck, and I note the scars visible on the male's back through the tears in his ripped clothing. I'm still struggling to believe this male is Celzar's brother, and the image of him on that battlefield haunts me.

He walks faster, picking up his pace. "We need to move quicker!" he shouts to the group. "The other rebels won't be able to distract the remaining guards for long. Reinforcements will arrive soon."

No one argues, and everyone matches his speed, surging onward through the prison.

"Blake, look out!" Shade squawks as two guards come from a tunnel on my left, shouting obscenities as they gallop toward us. I brace, ready to fight, but then my mates are there. I'm guessing it's due to their pent-up rage from being imprisoned, but I've never seen them so angry. They work together, cutting down one guard in a matter of minutes, and quite literally leaving him in pieces, while a group of prisoners and rebels take down the other one.

There's more shouting from the prison mines, but

we avoid the guards, navigating to an exit the rebels have opened up and slipping into the tunnels adjoining the prison. It takes a while for all of us to make it out of the gap, but then we're scurrying down a series of winding tunnels that grow darker. The light dims as we turn down one tunnel then another, and soon we're walking in complete darkness. My vision adjusts, allowing me to see the edges of the tunnel walls and the path ahead, and everything is silent except for the shuffling of feet, and the sounds of panicked breathing.

"*Soooo, are you going to explain why you're all naked yet?*" Shade asks, sitting relaxed as she remains perched on my shoulder.

"*I'm not naked, I have a robe,*" I protest.

"*Yeah, a robe and hooker hair,*" she teases. "*Did you have to play out King Celzar's weird fetishes as punishment?*"

"*What? No. Faking the bonding ritual was my idea.*"

"*Faking the bonding ritual?*" Shade squawks.

"*It was the only way to get King Celzar to bring me to Dante and the others,*" I explain. "*I knew if I told him about the power increase that comes with bonding, he wouldn't be able to resist letting me bond with them.*"

"*Hold up. So, you just turned up to the prison looking all bangable, and the king watched you get freaky? I'm guessing you didn't actually...*" she trails off.

I grin in the darkness. "*No, we didn't bond. I still have the cuff on, remember? I couldn't risk the king getting control of that kind of power.*" I go on to tell her about

King Celzar's confessions and of what happened with the witches.

She whistles in my head. *"Well that is..."*

"I know," I reply. *"So fucked up."*

"You can say that again," she says. *"Well, in any case, I guess it's lucky we turned up when we did."*

My lips curl upward. *"Never doubted you."*

"Oh, puhleeze, even I doubted me!" she retorts.

"That's because you forget about all the awesome things you do."

She's thoughtful for a moment. *"Hmmm, yeah I guess I am pretty amazing."*

"And seeing as you're amazing," I tell her. *"Do you know what his story is? Celzar's brother?"*

Shade adjusts her grip on my shoulder. *"From what I've heard, after King Celzar created The Haven and started cuffing everyone, Prince Mason and his sister Princess Nerelia started speaking against the king, trying to convince centaurs not to agree to the cuffs."*

"Nerelia?"

"The princess in the palace," Shade tells me. *"The one in the crystal garden."*

I'm not sure how she's figured this all out, but I'm grateful she's helping me piece this all together. *"And so what, King Celzar imprisoned them?"*

"Yep. And anyone who was loyal to them."

I blow out a breath.

"Our new princely friend here is second in line to the throne after Nerelia," Shade explains. *"I'm pretty sure he's been in prison for a long, long time."*

My expression softens, and I stare ahead at where the male, Prince Mason, is still carrying the female prisoner. I think about how lonely I'd been as an only child. *"And to think I always wanted a sibling,"* I muse. *"Maybe I was better off alone."*

"It's times like this when it's good to remember that you can choose your friends, but you can't choose your family," Shade replies.

"Unless they're friends who turn into family," I amend, and she practically preens on my shoulder.

Nate brushes against my right side as Dante keeps close on my left, and I suppress the urge to reach out and grab them. *And you also don't get to choose your mates,* I muse internally as I clench my fists to stop myself from touching my shifter and my demon. Even now while we're escaping, I can't help but think about the way it felt to have my mates around me, to have Dante *inside* me, and I bite my lip, glad for the darkness. Dante is the only one who has happily accepted that we're mates, and his hand curls around my waist, pulling me tighter against him. I lean closer to the demon, trying not to make it obvious how badly I want him, because I hate that he has power over me. That all of my mates do. Everything in me wants to be around them, but now that I am, I'm reminded of how out of control they make me feel.

I try not to think about it as the minutes blur by, and eventually we reach what appears to be a dead end. There's chatter up ahead, and then the massive wall of rock that's blocking our path starts to move, revealing a wide opening. Light floods the tunnel, and we pass through quickly before the passageway is sealed again behind us.

"I hope we're doing the right thing by following these guys," I mutter, blinking as my eyes adjust to the light.

Dante's hand squeezes my waist. "We're together and out of the prison. I'd say it's a good start."

We continue to follow the rebels and prisoners ahead of us until the tunnel starts to widen even more and then opens out into a large cavern. I stop walking. *"Okay, when I heard we were going to a rebel camp, this is not what I pictured,"* I say to Shade.

"What had you expected? A tiny group of refugees huddled in a cave?"

"Uh, yes. Something like that."

"Yeah, well, me too," she laughs in my head. *"It's amazing, right?"*

I peer at the small city still some distance away. The narrow streets are packed with rebels who are chatting and rushing to and fro, weaving between buildings made from stones. Bird creatures, just like Prax, the creature I met in The Haven, pull carts amongst the crowd, and crystal lanterns line the streets, emitting a warm glow. Around the cavern walls, large holes dot the space, separated by thick, rocky walls, and I stare in fascination as I see even more rebels milling about inside these spaces.

"Are those...houses?" I ask out loud in disbelief.

Shade follows my line of sight. *"Yup. But with an*

open area that overlooks the city. From what I've learned, they started building those homes as the city grew larger."

"Looks like it," Nate replies, unaware that Shade has already answered my question. "Reminds me of the bunny burrows back in the beast realm."

I raise a brow at him. "Bunny burrows?"

"Yeah, you know. The burrows the bunny shifters make. What? You didn't think all shifters were sexy jaguars like me, did you, gorgeous?"

I stare at him. "I know there are different types of shifters. I guess I'm just wondering what you were doing in a bunny burrow."

He grins and winks at me. "Let's just say, sometimes I go there when I'm feelin' hungry."

My cheeks heat as he holds my gaze, and I purse my lips.

"Yeah, I'm pretty sure he's not talking about eating food," Shade points out unhelpfully.

"You think?"

"Hey, don't take it out on me," Shade squawks. *"He's the one talking about banging bunnies. Remember that place, No Bunny Blues? You don't think that's where he's talking about, do you?"*

I think of the club we'd once had to visit in the beast realm. Dad had tasked us to collect information from an informant there, but the shifter had come out to meet us on the street, so we never had to enter the club.

"I'm still salty about how we never got to see any

bunnies," Shade says, and it's only then that I realize she's still been rambling this whole time.

"Maybe Nate can take you there one day," I reply bitterly, not annoyed at her, but at my shifter mate. I know I shouldn't care that Nate's been with other shifters. Just like I shouldn't care that Dante has probably bedded half the demons in Seral, but the thought of my mates being with other females has irritation spiking up my spine.

Like he can sense it, Nate leans close, his lips brushing along my warm cheeks. "Somethin' bothering you, gorgeous?" he asks wickedly.

I force a breath out through my nose, and I turn my head so my lips are almost touching his. "Just thinking about those innocent bunnies," I lie.

He chuckles, and the rumbling sound in his chest makes my insides twist. "Oh, I can promise you, love, they're not innocent." His gaze turns predatory. "How 'bout I tell you all about it?"

"Uh, yes please," Shade says excitedly in my head.

My heart pounds as Nate waits like he's actually expecting me to answer. *"Does he really think I'd want to hear about all the depraved shit he's gotten up to with other females? Hard pass."* I force my lips to curve as I press even closer to him. He responds, his nostrils flaring as he breathes in my scent. I part my lips like I'm going to kiss him, but instead, I say, "And to think I was almost considering fucking you," I murmur, then I pull back, continuing to walk through the tunnel and leaving Nate standing there.

Dante smirks, clearly amused by the situation, and even Prince Callan's lips lift slightly. It takes Nate a few seconds to wipe the look of shock from his face, and then he's striding through the mob of prisoners and rebels, finding his way back to us.

When we near the edges of the rebel city, a guard shouts, "They're here!" That's all it takes for the message to spread, and soon dozens of rebels are streaming out of the city, swarming our group and fussing over the freed prisoners who collapse with relief.

"Your highness," one of the newcomers says as the group rushes forward. They each stop before Prince Mason and bow their heads in a gesture of respect.

I watch the prince, noting the way his body becomes rigid, and a look of unease crosses his face as they await his command. "Rise," he tells them. He passes over the female he's holding to the one of the rebels. "See to it that she gets the care she needs. The rest of you assist the other wounded."

The rebels are quick to follow his orders, separating and joining our ranks. Quite a few of the rebels openly gape at me and Prince Callan, and it takes me a moment to realize they're staring at our wings.

"We've worn these cuffs for so long, there are many who can hardly remember what it feels like to have our own," a feminine voice says, and I turn to see one of the female rebels close to us.

My brow creases. "What?"

"Your wings," she goes on. "There are many who will be envious of you, and many more who will be wary because you're outsiders."

"That's Eliza," Shade quickly explains. *"She's one of the main rebel leaders."*

"We're not interested in causing trouble," I reply.

She nods as she assesses me, and I get the sense that she hasn't yet decided whether she believes me.

"How long have the rebels been here?" I ask, indicating to the city.

"Many have resided here since the first uprising three decades ago," a masculine voice answers before Eliza can speak, and I turn as Prince Mason strides toward us accompanied by a male rebel.

"And we've been building on it ever since," Eliza adds. "With so many residents in such a confined space in The Haven, it took a while before the king noticed some of the residents and his resources were missing."

The male on Prince Mason's other side smiles at us, and I recognize him as one of the rebels who came to the prison. "Name's Waylen. Good to have you here."

Nate grins. "Glad to be here. Thanks for breakin' us out."

Dante squeezes his hand around my waist, and Nate, Alaric, and Prince Callan stand nearby, all of them so close that I'd barely have to reach out to touch them. Prince Mason, Eliza, and Waylen stare at us curiously, and considering my mates are still butt naked, it's a credit to them that they're able to keep a straight face.

"Thank the bird," Eliza says, tipping her head to where Shade is still perched on my shoulder. "You're only here because of the message she carried."

"Finally, someone appreciates me," Shade preens.

"I appreciate you all the time!"

"Yeah, but you're biased because you like me," she replies. *"It's nice to be appreciated by others."*

"Hmmm note to self: show Shade less gratitude so it doesn't go to her head," I muse, and she shoots daggers at me with her beady black eyes.

"You have my thanks as well," Prince Mason says, his glittering blue gaze lingering on me before moving to Shade and my mates. "I've waited for this chance for some time."

"Is it just me..." Shade chirps in my head, *"or are his eyes dreamy? It's hard to tell with all the hair and dirt, but I'm already starting to see why King Celzar hated his brother so much. Clearly, this guy got all the good genes."*

"Do you have to perve on everyone?" I ask her.

"I'm just saying," she hisses, *"that for a prince who's been beaten, tortured, and forced to carry out manual labor for decades, if not centuries, he's looking pretty good."*

I'm not sure why, but my stomach cramps at the thought of the prince being tortured for such a long time. I decide it's because I can still picture him on the battlefield, the witches closing in around him. Scars cover the prince's body, and I wonder just what he's been through. When I lift my gaze again, I realize he's watching me.

"So, you're royalty, huh?" I blurt, not sure why I feel like I'm caught out.

Shade cackles in my head. *"Guess, I wasn't the only one who was perving."*

"Shut up," I send back, and she laughs again.

"I was," he replies, his expression hardening. "Now, it's just Mason."

Waylen and Eliza shift uncomfortably at his response, but they don't comment.

"Eliza will see to it that you're given clothes, supplies, and a room where you can rest," Mason says.

"And the cuffs?" Prince Callan asks, speaking for the first time in a long while. "How do we remove them?"

Eliza lifts up one of her pant legs revealing a cuff around her ankle. "If there was a way, we would have found it by now. Only King Celzar can take them off. We do, however, have a barrier around the camp so it's harder for the king to detect us. That's as good as it gets."

Dante frowns. "So, we still won't be able to access our power?"

Eliza purses her lips. "No." Someone shouts something behind us then, and she takes that opportunity to turn and start leading us away. "Now, let's get you to a room."

CHAPTER

FOURTEEN

~ Princess Blake ~

"It's not much, but it'll have to do. With our sudden increase in numbers, housing is limited," Eliza says to us as she opens a door and leads us into a small room. It's one of the spaces we'd seen along the cavern wall, and at the other end of the room, there's a gaping hole that provides a view of the city. "I'll give you time to rest and collect yourselves, and I'll be back when Mason wants to discuss with you further." At that, she disappears from the room, and I glimpse Waylen taking up a guarding position outside before the door closes.

"Well, this is pretty nice," Shade says, flying around the space. *"It's, uh..."*

"Cozy?" I suggest.

Shade perches on the back of a wooden chair. *"Yeah, that."*

I take in the couch and two armchairs, small table with four more wooden chairs, and two large beds that sit the closest to the gaping hole. Lines of knotted rope stretch across the bottom of the hole, the only barrier to prevent someone from falling to the rebel camp below. *Well, that seems like a poor design choice.*

A pile of clothes is neatly folded on the table, accompanied by two jugs of water, some loaves of buttered bread, and a bowl of fruit. Prince Callan and the others stride further into the room, not hesitating to grab a pair of clothes and slide them on.

"Not bad," Nate says, admiring his new shirt and pants, then he flops down onto the closest armchair.

Alaric scrutinizes every part of the room like he's searching for hidden traps, and Prince Callan plucks an apple from the fruit bowl and sinks his teeth into it. Dante smooths back his hair and doesn't move from my side.

I remove my robe and start dressing into the smaller shirt and pants that has been left for me, not caring that I'm naked. I'm still wound up tight after our encounter in the prison, and I feel like adding some layers might help. The moment the robe is off, four pairs of eyes find me, and their heated gazes make my temperature rise a few more degrees. Even Prince Callan and Alaric don't hide their attention.

Shade ruffles her feathers. *"Well, is it just me or did*

it get hotter in here? I'd offer to wait outside, but that just seems a little unfair. For me, that is."

"You are such a perv," I tell her.

"I'm kidding," she defends. *"...Maybe. I mean, look at these guys."*

She doesn't need to tell me to look at them. I'm all too aware of how ridiculously attractive my mates are.

Nate grins mischievously. "So, now that we're back together and not stuck in prison, I vote we make the most of our situation." He pats his muscular thigh in invitation for me to sit down, and I struggle to focus as I pull on my clothes. Thankfully, the shirt I've been given has slits for my wings, and it's surprisingly comfortable. The others all watch like they're waiting to see how I'll respond to Nate, and I can't tell if they're hoping I'll climb onto the shifter's lap or not.

"I think we need to discuss a few things," I say slowly, trying not to think about Nate's predatory gaze.

No one speaks for a long moment, and then Prince Callan swallows his mouthful. "I agree, we need a plan to remove these cuffs and find a way back to the surface." But even as he says it, his eyes linger on me, like he's afraid that if he looks away I'll disappear.

"Oh, I thought she was referrin' to the bed situation. I'm thinkin' Blake and I can have that one, and the rest of you can take the other bed." Nate winks at me, and I have to force myself not to grin because his damn attitude is infectious.

Prince Callan glares at him, and Dante moves

closer, sliding his arms around me. "If anyone's sharing a bed, it'll be me and Blake."

I step away from my demon, because if I don't get some space, I'm going to go right back to trying to bone all of them, and as good as that sounds, we have bigger problems right now. "Where we sleep doesn't matter," I say. "Being kidnapped by the Perstalians wasn't exactly part of our plans. We need to discuss—"

"Fine," Nate muses thoughtfully, cutting me off. "Dante, Blake, and I can share that bed, while Alaric and Callan can have the other one."

Alaric and Prince Callan scowl, looking annoyed, though I'm not sure why they care.

"*Why not just push them together!*" Shade chirps sounding strangely eager. "*Then there's only one bed! Gosh, I love the one bed trope!*"

"*The what?*" I ask, because I have no idea what she's talking about.

"*You know, where the boy and girl are reluctant but there's only one bed, and they have to share, and the tension...*"

"Can we please focus," I say aloud, mostly to Shade because she's starting to sound way too enthusiastic, and I don't have the energy to work out her rambling. There are moments when I wonder just what happened to her in the human realm, and right now is one of those times.

"We should start by discussing what we've each learned about King Celzar," I say to the others.

"Agreed," says Prince Callan, and I gape at him because I'm not sure when the two of us started seeing eye to eye.

Prince Callan smirks and goes on to explain everything Mason told them while they were in the prison. I do the same with the information I've learned, and when I get to the part about the witches, they all curse, and Alaric starts pacing the room.

"So, it was King Celzar's fault the witches attacked Perstalia?" Dante repeats for the second time like he can't wrap his head around this bit of news.

"Apparently," I say, still hardly believing it myself.

"Then we force the king to give the power back to the witches," Nate suggests. "If they're startin' to resurface, it might stop any future conflict."

"Too much blood has been spilled," Alaric growls, his eyes darkening. "They're just as likely to use that power against all of the united realms."

"King Celzar can't simply return the power anyway," I say. "From what I gather, over time the king's power has depleted. It's not self-sustaining for him. It's like a weapon he's stolen, and without the witches' connection to the ancients, that power is being used up. It's why he's started taking power from his brides."

"Yeah, what's with that?" Nate says, lifting a finger. "He could just take what he needs from all of his citizens. He has everyone under his control, no one is going to say anythin'."

My lips thin as I go on to explain how the king murdered his lover.

Nate frowns. "So, he's playin' out the memory, as a form of what? Punishment?"

I shrug. "Maybe it's his therapy? I don't know. But part of the reason he let me try to bond with you guys is because I promised him he'd finally get a different ending with me." I wince. "That I could be strong enough to be his...queen." I don't know why I care what my mates think. It's not like they're all on board with being my mates anyway, but I still feel a little guilty when all four of my guys don't look happy with this bit of news.

"Wowee, Blake. Way to turn the mood in the room," Shade comments.

"There's no point in sugarcoating it," I reply.

I sit on one of the wooden chairs at the table, and we spend the next while theorizing how we can get out of this place. When my stomach growls for the third time, I reach over to grab a strange pink fruit, but Alaric immediately snatches it before I can. He sniffs the fruit before taking a small bite, his face scrunched with concentration as he chews and then finally swallows.

"Hey!" I protest. "If you wanted one, you could have just grabbed your own."

The assassin gives me a funny look, then he holds the fruit out to me. "Here."

I stare at his bite mark on the pink flesh. "You're kidding, right?"

Shade hops onto her other leg. *"Whoa, did he just check that for poison?"*

I blink in surprise. It hadn't even occurred to me that's what he was doing. He's still holding out the fruit, but suddenly, the assassin looks as shocked as I feel. Like he can't believe what he's doing, either. *Great, so this is weird for both of us.*

"So, does this mean you're not trying to kill me anymore?" I ask, utterly confused.

His face twists into a deep scowl, and when he doesn't reply, I grin. Taking the fruit, I sink my teeth into it, almost moaning when the tangy juice slides down my throat. It's so good that I devour the entire thing in no time and it's not until I'm licking my fingers that I realize all four of my mates are staring at me intensely.

"What?" I ask. "They're amazing."

A smile teases Dante's lips and Nate looks just as amused, but Alaric stares at me with irritation. "Like I said earlier, if you want one, you can just grab your own," I tell him, and this makes Nate outright snort with laughter.

Dante cracks his knuckles. "All right, I think it's about time we get some rest. None of us know when Mason will call on us, and I don't know about the rest of you, but I could use some down time."

I sigh, knowing he's right. I haven't slept since we arrived in this place, and I get the feeling they haven't either. Standing, I walk over to the beds, and my mates follow me. I stop a few feet away from the closest mattress, hesitating.

"Now, this is why I tried to get us to sort this out earlier," Nate comments, indicating to the two beds.

"We could push them together," Dante suggests, and Shade squawks in my head. *"That's what I said!"*

I'm considering it when Prince Callan strides past the rest of us and moves to the farthest bed. Without a word, he drops down fully clothed, and he closes his eyes as he rests his head on his hands.

"Or not," Shade says, disappointed. *"It seems our grumpy angel still isn't keen on the whole having a mate thing."*

I don't reply, and I try not to think about the sinking feeling in my chest.

"I'll keep watch," Alaric growls, going over and positioning himself in the armchair that's closest to the door.

I want to argue, but something tells me he won't listen anyway, so I don't bother.

Dante gives me a seductive smile. "I don't mind sharing with the shifter."

I'm sure he means he doesn't mind sharing *me* with Nate, but his comment reminds me of all the other females he's bedded in Seral, and I jab him hard in the side and move to the bed where Prince Callan is. "Guess it's settled then," I say, and Dante and Nate groan. As tempted as I am to squeeze between the shifter and demon, now that I'm level-headed again, I keep reminding myself about Kai and the risk I take every time I'm with them. I'd rather not accidentally kill them when I've only just gotten them back.

Prince Callan tenses when I move onto the mattress beside him, but he doesn't open his eyes.

"Well, that's fucked," Nate grumbles, and I swear I see the hint of a smile form on Prince Callan's face.

Dante's eyes are bright as he moves to the other bed with Nate, and I close my eyes.

I can't sleep. *No surprise there.* Prince Callan's scent of crisp green apples and bergamot is so good that twice I doze off, only to jolt awake shortly after and find myself drooling. Yep, that's right, actual spit is soaked into my pillow. I wipe my mouth with my hand and peer over at where Dante, Nate, and Prince Callan appear to be having no trouble sleeping. They lie still, their breathing steady, and I finally give up on the idea of rest.

Standing, I slide from the bed and move to where Alaric is still sitting in the armchair with his back to us. His gaze is fixed on the door with an intense focus like he believes we might be attacked at any moment. Which is possible, but if the rebels wanted to kill us, surely they would have tried to pick us off during the escape.

"Your turn," I say, stopping beside the armchair. "I'm not sleeping anyway."

When he doesn't immediately respond, I lean

down, wondering whether the male is sleeping with his eyes open. *Well, that's super creepy.* I go to wave my hand in front of his face, and the next thing I know, he has grabbed me and I'm on his lap with his large arms around me. His gray gaze fixes on my face, and he looks as shocked as I feel. I fully expect the giant to throw me off now that he realizes what he's done, but then his lips crash to mine and his massive hands roam over my body. The kiss is hard and frantic, and it swallows me, sending warmth burning between my thighs. The tension that has built up since the encounter in the prison pours out of me, and I can't get enough of my assassin mate.

His hands press into the curve of my back, pulling me harder against him, and my knees slide further in, tucking into the sides of the chair. Reaching forward, my hands dive into his long hair, his silky strands sliding past my fingers as my nails run down his scalp. He lets out a tortured sound and breaks the kiss.

"What's the matter, assassin?" I tease, breathless. "Surprised that you don't want to kill me anymore?"

Like my words have broken whatever spell was over him, he growls and stands, intending to make me slide off, but I instinctively wrap my legs around his waist. My lips find his neck, and he groans, the rumbling sound vibrating between my legs. Stepping to the side, he pivots, one hand sliding under my ass as he slams my back against the nearby wall and presses up against me, showing me just how badly he wants me. My lips part, and I look over to see Shade and the others are still sleeping.

"Enchantress," Alaric hisses through gritted teeth, and my heart races at the mixture of hate and affection in his tone. "Why is it that when you're around, you are the only thing I can think about." His nostrils flare. "But when you're not around…" He trails off, and his expression darkens as his whole body starts to shake with anger. His words are so deathly calm, I stop breathing for a second.

"When I'm not around?" I squeeze out, not sure why my throat is so tight.

"When you're not around," he rumbles, "it makes me want to destroy everyone and everything until you are."

The lump that forms in my throat is so sore I can't speak, and then his lips are on mine again, hot and sweet with the taste of chocolate and mint. His tongue sweeps over mine, and I moan, grinding against him, desperate for more. More from my mate. My giant.

"Birds are snacks that can fly into your mouth!"

Birds? I jolt, my head jerking to the side in a panic. It's only when I see Shade is still sleeping soundly perched on the back of a chair that my chest eases.

"Bony, but fuckin' delicious," Nate mumbles in his sleep, and rolls over, draping his arm over Dante in the process. I gape at him and make a mental note not to freak Shade out by telling her what I've heard. *Also, I'm going to have to keep an eye on Nate when she's around.* I'm still feeling a little unsettled when I turn my attention back to Alaric. His eyes are hooded, his cheeks flushed, but the moment is broken and before I can protest, he sets me back on my feet.

"Wake me if anyone enters," he mutters, and he's rigid as he walks away, settling next to Prince Callan on the bed.

What. The. Fuck? I fume as I stare after him, and it takes a good moment before I can breathe evenly again. Even if he can feel me staring, the asshole doesn't say anything more, and soon his breathing grows steady like the others. *Either he's asleep or he's a pro at pretending.* I curse internally. *Great, so it's only me with a current bout of insomnia.*

Settling in the armchair, I glare at the door feeling even more agitated than when I rose from the bed. Rationally, I know I would have stopped things with Alaric anyway, but I'm still annoyed. I sit like that for what feels like an hour before I decide I can't stay there any longer. Standing, I peer at my sleeping mates before creeping toward the door.

"Where are you going?" Shade's drowsy voice fills my head, and I turn back to see her staring at me with beady eyes.

"I need to get out of here for a little while. Just to clear my head." I know it's probably a bad idea to venture out on my own, but right now I can't seem to care.

"What you need is sleeping on those beds over there. Just squeeze in there and take what's yours," Shade counters.

I shake my head. *"It's not that easy."*

"Isn't it? You didn't see how stressed they were when they were in the prison without you. Even if you don't bond, you could have some fun. They're your mates, Blake, no matter how reluctant some of them are."

"I can't. Not until I know they're not going to end up like Kai," I tell her. "It's too risky. Besides, they seem fine now."

She sighs heavily in my mind. *"At some point, you're just going to have to trust Lady Fate."* She spreads her wings as if she's about to fly over to me, but I hold up a hand to stop her. *"You stay here and let me know if they wake up. The last thing I need is my mates making enemies with the rebels because they think I've been taken."*

"You can't be serious."

"You know I am," I reply, opening the door.

"You'd better not get into trouble."

"I'll be back before you know it," I reassure her, and walk through, closing the door behind me.

Waylen and another guard are waiting outside the room, and they stand straighter when I step between them.

"So, who's coming exploring with me?" I ask before either of them can speak.

Waylen's brow scrunches with confusion. "Exploring?"

I smile. "Yes. I'm either going with one of you or I'll be going on my own. So, what'll it be?"

The guards share a look.

"You're meant to remain here," Waylen starts, but I

don't wait for him to finish the rest. Striding forward, I start down the tunnel.

The guard quickly falls into step beside me. "We're under strict orders to keep you under watch."

"Then keep watching," I reply dryly. "I'm not hiding. I'm *exploring*. And your guard friend is still back at the room to report on the others." I'm not sure if it's because of my no-fucks-given expression, but after that he walks with me in blissful silence as we traverse the tunnels and make our way to the main cavern.

When we reach the rebel city, I don't stop but walk straight into the crowd. Cursing, Waylen charges after me, determined not to lose me in the throng of rebels.

CHAPTER
FIFTEEN

~ Mason ~

My shoulders feel heavy as I cut through the streets, the hood of my cloak pulled down, shadowing my face. You'd think I'd be used to it by now. The crushing weight of expectation. For years, the other warriors in the prison had looked up to me. When they were on their knees at the point of breaking, they'd look to me for the strength to continue on. But now, as the rebels cry out to me, hope once more shining in their eyes, I withdraw further inside myself.

Defender of the realm. Whenever the name leaves their lips, something inside me cracks a little more. Most of these rebels weren't on the battlefield during the war. They didn't witness as our kind was

182

slaughtered, bodies littering the ground as the witches laid waste to the strongest of us. Only a few of the warriors who were imprisoned alongside me heard the cries as our light was snuffed out, our once mighty kingdom falling into darkness.

I had thought it was over. As my most loyal warriors and friends were cut down before me, I'd surrendered to defeat. But then he had come. *Celzar.* With a power he was not born with, he had struck back, saving my life and countless others. He drove the witches from our land for long enough that we could escape to the safe haven he created. Well, that was what he called it anyway. *The Haven.*

But it was merely a prison. I couldn't save us from the witches or from my brother. My parents and our other relatives never received an invitation to the new city. Whether they were slaughtered by the witches or by Celzar it did not matter. Perstalia as we knew it had been destroyed, and we were all that was left to wallow in the ashes.

And now, the rebels look to me once again, just like they had when the witches first came to our land. Just as they did before I failed them. Even now that I'm washed and dressed in clean clothes, looking less like a prisoner and more like the prince again, I feel like merely a shadow of the male I had once been.

I think of the bed waiting for me high up on the cavern wall. Eliza had been trying to acquire me a house in the city, but I'd made it clear that no one was to relocate because of me. A small room would be more than sufficient, and even as I tell myself I must go and rest, the bone-weary exhaustion so deep it's an effort to stand, I shudder at the thought of spending a single night on the plush bed they're offering. After countless years of sharing a cell with multiple others, I know only nightmares await me there. Or should I call them memories?

I slip down another street with the intent to head into the tunnels on my left, when I spot Waylen standing sentry beside a water trough. His posture is awkward, and he fidgets with the hilt of his sword nervously as he scans the area. *Now, what are you up to? You're supposed to be guarding the newcomers.*

I pause, ducking behind a merchant's stall, and that's when I see her. The female with the long dark waves stands a short distance from the guard, her golden eyes alight with wonder as she observes the city around her. Blake. That's what my new friends from the prison had called her. She's a marvel with high cheekbones and sensuous lips, but it's the lethal grace to which she moves that always captures my attention. Most wouldn't notice it, but even without a weapon in her hands, I see the strength in her movements and the confidence in her gaze.

My new male friends had called her their mate, and while I can't be certain the claim is true, it hadn't escaped my notice how all four of them arranged themselves around her during our escape. Whether they're doing it intentionally or subconsciously, I can't tell, because half the time two of the males look like they hate her as much as they want to be close to her. Not that I can blame them for the latter part. I, myself, find her alluring, even from a distance. And up close, I can taste hints of her suppressed power. It's no wonder she caught Celzar's attention.

All Perstalian royals can sense the power of others, but Celzar is the only one who can take that power for himself. Our parents had always thought he was powerless—the only Perstalian royal without magic—and because of this, their relationship had been strained. When they'd announced our sister, Nerelia, would rule rather than Celzar, my brother was inconsolable. In the days that followed, it was discovered that he poisoned one of our cousins, and though no one truly understood the motivation behind the murder, my brother was banished from our kingdom. No one knew, that in a way, the reaches of his power far surpassed our own, and that his return would result in our ruin.

I wonder how mad Celzar must be now that he's lost his latest betrothed, Blake, and then I think of her mates again. All *four* of them. It is an uncommon number for Perstalians. My kind have fated mates just as hers do, though the connection is extremely rare, and some don't believe in it at all. Most pair up simply for convenience, or to follow a mutual affection or attraction not determined by fate. But if I had a fated mate, I suspect I wouldn't want to let her out of my sight. Certainly, not so soon after having been separated from her. *So why is she out here alone?*

I watch in surprise as Blake approaches a large Pecos bird without fear. The creature is strapped to a metal cart and is busy pecking at seeds scattered about its feet while its owner chats to a merchant. It's clear the owner notices Blake, but he continues his conversation while watching her from the corner of his eye, uncertain on how to handle the unusual intrusion. Little has been said about the newcomers who arrived with the rest of us prisoners. Some have already deemed them our new saviors, convinced that they are new foreign warriors who will fight by my side. Others are wary.

In either case, their presence has made the idea of battle against my brother a little more complicated.

Letting out a long exhale, I force myself to stop thinking about the needs of my kind for a moment, and simply observe the female instead. I'm surprised when the Pecos bird doesn't startle when she approaches. Instead, it lifts its large head and stares at her inquisitively, then it stretches out its neck in invitation. Smiling, she reaches forward, stroking its smooth rainbow scales.

I move from the shadows, striding into view. "They're not usually the friendliest of birds," I tell her, and she doesn't look the least bit startled when she peers over at me. Her hands glide down the creature's scales, stroking with confidence, even as the bird stares warily at me.

"It's well known they often only let their owners

touch them," I go on to explain, stopping a short distance away from the creature.

Waylen's face blanches at the sight of me, like he thinks he's about to be reprimanded for letting our new friend wander the streets, but he doesn't need to worry.

Blake grins. "Is that why you're standing all the way over there?"

"I give respect where it is due," I reply simply.

She thinks on that, lines creasing between her brows.

The bird's owner bows his head to me. "Defender," he whispers with reverence, and I have to stop myself from reacting to his comment, the wound inside me growing a little bigger. The moment the name leaves his mouth, others around us turn toward me, peering at the face beneath the hood and whispering the same thing.

Blake studies me, concern flashing on her face before her lips stretch into another grin. "And here I thought your name was Mason," she says, speaking louder than before, and when the voices around us hush to hear her speak, I wonder if she did it for my benefit.

The hint of a smile teases my lips. "It is," I confirm. "Can I not have many names?"

"I guess it depends if all of the names are true," she replies, and her attention goes back to the bird again. Before I can warn her against it, she reaches down and takes a handful of the bird's seeds. I tense, ready to intervene if the bird reacts aggressively to the intrusion, but the creature merely continues eating as she shoves the seeds into her pocket. *Well, that was highly unexpected.*

I'm not the only one who notices the unusual encounter, because gasps come from the rebels milling around us.

"What?" Blake asks, confused. "Haven't you guys heard that sharing is caring? We all have mouths to feed, and mine just happens to belong to a feisty crow who gets mean when she's hungry." She peers down at the large pile of birdseed that remains on the ground. "I mean, it's not like I took much."

I smile. "That you managed to take any without losing a hand is a wonder. No one would dare take food from a Pecos, not even me. Many of the birds were warriors once. Now they help us in other ways, but they're still to be respected."

"It's not like I stole its food," she defends. "I asked politely. Maybe if more did the same, it wouldn't be such a big deal."

I'm not sure what she means, but she turns and walks down the street and away from me before I can question her. Waylen goes to follow, but I wave him away and move quickly to catch up with her.

Blake walks until she finds a stall laden with different colored crystals cut into intricate shapes, and she stops to browse. "What is with all the crystals?" she asks without looking at me. "Is it simply a resources thing, and because you have tons of them you figure you may as well utilize them, or are you all genuinely obsessed with crystals?"

She picks up a green crystal that's shaped into a winged centaur and appreciates the small sculpture. The merchant watches kindly, stepping back to give us privacy, even though his eyes are practically bulging out of his head as he stares at us.

"It's a long story," I reply.

"And let me guess," she says. "One that you're not willing to tell me right now?"

I don't answer, and she places down the crystal. "I get it. You've only just met me, and I'll bet after what happened with the witches, any outsider must make you nervous."

My brows slam down. "What do you know of the witches?"

She frowns, and even now, even as talk of the witches has painful memories flashing in my head, those golden eyes draw me in.

"I guess I can't be sure of anything now. Not after what your brother told me," she replies. "My kind, the demons, have been at war with the witches for as long as I can remember, but for the first time..." She trails off, shaking her head before continuing. "Well, I'm second-guessing everything I thought I knew about them."

"So he told you, then?" I mutter.

She studies my face. "It's true, isn't it?" When I don't immediately reply, her expression hardens, and she turns to another crystal. This one is shaped into a star with six points. "Countless lives could have been saved if the witches knew the truth."

The pain I've worked hard to bury rises to the surface. Because she's right. And it's that truth that I can never seem to escape. "I only found out what he'd stolen from the witches when it was too late," I admit, regret tugging at my chest.

I'm not sure why I do it, but as she turns toward me again, as the memories of the past threaten to overwhelm me, I step closer to her.

Her rich scent of honey and cinnamon rushes at me, and it instantly dulls the pain building in my chest, and replaces it with an intense hunger unlike anything I've felt. It's not the hollowing pain I had grown accustomed to, from the periods of starvation in the prison, but a hunger that comes from the deepest parts within myself. A hunger that could only mean one thing...

I don't think, I only act as I pull the dark-haired female to me. When my lips press against hers, her warmth chases away the darkness inside of me, and for a moment, I'm not drowning in my mistakes. In my failures. For a moment, all there is, is *her*.

A moan slips from her lips as her arms slide around my neck, and I realize that every rumor about having a fated mate is true. Because she is *mine*.

She's panting when she breaks the kiss, and she blows away a stray strand of dark hair that has fallen in front of her eyes.

"Lady Fate can't seriously be doing this to me right now," she says, her breathing labored.

I can't stop staring at her. At the way her lips move when she speaks. At the way her golden eyes glow brighter as she stares back at me. And at the obvious flush in her cheeks betraying her own desire.

"How?" It's all I can manage to say as I keep holding her.

"That's a great question," she replies. "I tend to go with asking 'why' instead."

"A fated mate pairing hasn't happened for any of our kind since our arrival in The Haven," I tell her gravely. "And it was uncommon even before that."

"What can I say, Lady Fate likes to make the weirdest matches," she replies, then looks at me oddly. "Now when you say 'pairing,' you do realize that Dante and the others are also my mates, right?"

I breathe in deeply again, and my cock throbs, my body responding to her scent. *My mate.* It's so strange saying the words in my head. Like something from a fable I had once read as a child. An impossible dream, just like the notion that my kind might one day again be above the surface, able to soar through the clouds.

"It's already weird with the four of them, and adding you is going to be...strange," she goes on when I don't respond.

"The only thing that matters is that I have you," I reply, not bothered by the idea of having to share her. "To be bonded by fate to another is a privilege I never thought I'd experience." My fingers skim gently over the side of her face, and I press a kiss to her forehead. "Provided your other mates treat you with the respect and adoration you deserve, I am sure we will all get along."

"Respect and adoration?" She grins. "Okay, maybe you're just what we need."

And then my lips are on hers again, and I relish the warmth that sings through my body. A warmth I never thought I'd feel after that night on the battlefield. It doesn't fill the hole inside me, and it could never make me forget the brothers I've lost, but for once, I don't feel dead inside. The numbness that had spread through me, taking root over the long years, starts to fade, and suddenly, I don't feel all alone.

~ Princess Blake ~

Five mates. I have five freaking mates. I keep repeating it in my head, not sure whether I should be happy or horrified. In demon history, there are no records of a female ever having five mates, but the moment Mason's lips connected with mine and I smelt his amber and leather scent, I knew.

He is our missing piece. Our missing mate, and the last one we need to complete our bond. My heart races, and I'm a tangled mess of tension as Mason walks me back to my room. Scars still cover the prince's body, betraying the years he spent in the prison, but he's cleaned up, the layers of dirt washed away to reveal beautiful brown skin, and he has groomed, so it's easier to make out the lines of his chiseled face. The male is sexy as sin, so I guess I can't complain about Lady Fate's taste there, but honestly, I was hardly handling the four mates I already have.

We stop outside the door, and the way Mason looks at me sends a rush of heat through my body, drawing my awareness to the spot between my legs. "If you do not wish to return so soon, we could escape to my room for a while," he offers, and there's a hopeful gleam in his glittering blue eyes.

I smile, feeling oh, so tempted, but I shake my head. "I need to tell them about you. We've been through a lot lately, and the last thing we need is more secrets."

With a nod, he pulls me into a kiss that leaves my lips swollen before he releases me. Waylen and the other guard standing watch shift uncomfortably, but neither of them comment.

Closing his eyes, Mason rests his forehead on mine. "You do realize that now that I know I'm yours, I'll do anything to keep you safe." He exhales loudly. "I will do...anything." His voice cracks with emotion, and I know there's so much he's not telling me. I swallow hard. With the others, it had been so different. Even with Dante, given our history, I'd been resistant to accept that he's my mate, but with Mason it's different. I hardly know him, and yet, it's so easy to let myself enjoy being with him.

"I know," I reply, surprising myself with how much I believe it. This is what I thought it would be like when I found my fated mates. That there would be this instant connection, an instant certainty that we were bound by fate, even before performing the actual bonding ritual that unlocked our powers. While I felt it with my other mates, it all got so complicated so fast. And though, logically, I know it should be complicated with the fallen prince, his instant acceptance of the connection makes it feel so simple.

"Are you a good teacher?" I ask.

Opening his eyes, he pulls back. "I have trained soldiers in the past, on matters related to combat and the use of different weaponry. If you wish for me to give you lessons—"

"Oh no," I say casually. "I was just thinking my other mates could use some lessons on how to treat their female."

Mason's lips curve upward. "Whatever you need, *my mate.*" When he says the last two words bumps prickle on my skin. *My mate. My fifth mate.*

"Uh, thanks." I hadn't actually thought he'd agree to that, but if I get the chance, I'll definitely have to take him up on it. Smiling, I turn toward the door. "You know, you don't have to be here for this. I have no idea how they'll react, and I kind of slipped out without telling them."

Mason reaches over, resting the palm of his hand on the doorknob. "I'm sure they will be eagerly awaiting your return, my mate."

I grin because I'm pretty sure he's about to get the

shock of his life when he sees what my other mates are like.

~

"You could have warned me they woke up!" I tell Shade, feeling ambushed when I walk into the room to find four very pissed-looking males glaring at me. Okay, to be fair, Dante and Nate look more relieved than angry, but Prince Callan's glare could make any beast cower, and Alaric looks like he's contemplating tying me up and strangling me. Which, now that I think of it, actually sounds pretty hot.

"I could have, but then this wouldn't be nearly as funny," Shade replies.

I shoot her a glare, and her laughter rings in my head. *"Kidding! They only woke a couple minutes ago, and I've been a little preoccupied trying to stop them from charging from the room. You're welcome, by the way."*

I feel a little guilty for the position I put her in then, and I reach into my pocket, pulling out the handful of seeds the Pecos bird, Shanda, let me have. I place them on the table.

"Annnnd all is forgiven," she says as she pecks at the seeds hungrily.

Dusting my hands, I give the others a chipper smile. "I trust you all slept well."

Prince Callan gives me an incredulous look, and I'm about to point out that it sure looked like they were having no trouble sleeping when I left, but then I notice his fatigued expression.

"Where did you go?" Alaric growls, folding his arms across his broad chest.

Dante comes over and presses a kiss to my neck. "He means to say, we were worried about you," he drawls.

"Thought you were taken for a minute there," Nate adds. "Lucky your crow friend made a fuss, or we would have made a mess tryin' to find you."

I give Shade a grateful smile. "I wasn't far," I tell them. "I just explored some of the city. "I couldn't sleep, and I—"

"Alone?" Alaric questions gruffly, and for the first time since I entered the room, all four of them seem to finally notice Mason standing there.

The Perstalian prince steps forward, his shoulders pulling back as he peers at my mates. "No, not alone," he says. "I was with her."

"I bumped into him," I add quickly, "and, well, things got a little interesting from there."

"Interesting how?" Dante asks, but there's a twinkle in his eyes like he knows exactly what I'm about to say.

I lick my lips, and all four of my mates track the movement. Actually, make that five. All *five* of my mates watch me carefully. "Well, you know how I thought I'd found all of my mates in Perstalia?" I say slowly.

"Yes," Alaric growls, and from the way he's staring

at Mason now, I'm guessing he's also pieced together what I'm about to say.

"No," Shade squawks in my head. *"You're not trying to tell us that—"*

"Mason is also my mate," I blurt.

Silence. The room is completely quiet as everyone processes what I've just told them, and Mason moves closer to my side.

"So, I guess Lady Fate wasn't done with me after all," I say with a tight smile.

Prince Callan curses, Dante shakes his head smirking, and Nate laughs.

"This can't be Lady Fate's doing," Alaric mutters.

"Well, it sure isn't mine," I grumble, giving them all a pointed stare, because let's face it, if I had my way, a Drozac assassin, shifter thief, moody archangel, playboy demon, and now, a fallen prince, wouldn't have exactly been my picks.

"Whoa, Blake, five mates? Even having four is unusual for demons," Shade reminds me.

"Yep, Dad's going to be so proud," I reply sarcastically, and then I wish I'd never thought about him, because I'm reminded that Dad is in Seral alone.

"As long as I get my time with you, princess, I don't care if you have dozens of mates," Dante says with a smirk, and I get the feeling he's remembering how I judged him for the number of females he's been with. I want to argue that it's still not the same thing, but I don't.

The others look at me like they're expecting me to

rattle off the names of more mates I've discovered, so I say instead, "Thankfully, there won't be dozens. Just you five."

"You sure?" Nate asks with a shit-eating grin.

"Yes," I reply, jutting out my hip. I don't tell them how I know. But, somehow, I can feel it in my core.

"And how do you feel 'bout all this?" Nate asks Mason curiously.

The prince doesn't hesitate in saying, "I feel like I've been given a second chance. Having a fated mate is an honor, and I intend to never leave my mate wanting."

Nate makes a face. "Great. He's a romantic."

I grin, already liking having Mason as part of our group. *Now if only I knew I wasn't going to kill my mates when I bed them, then this would be a whole lot more fun.* As the sobering thought of Kai enters my mind, I step forward, intending to grab the jug of water on the table, but I stumble before I can reach it. Mason and Dante are quick to each grab one of my arms to steady me. "Whoa there, I can grab myself a drink," I tell them.

Knowing that Dante is holding me, Mason pours a glass of water, and hands it to me. "When is the last time you rested, my mate?"

Considering the lines around his eyes, I don't think he's one to judge, but I take the drink and down the whole thing before saying, "Probably not since before we were kidnapped."

Alaric's brows lower.

"Even a demon princess has limits," Prince Callan tells me. "We need to be strong when we face King Celzar."

"Strong? With these cuffs on, that's not likely to happen," I point out.

"We should bond," Dante says. "Now that you're certain we're all your mates, maybe your increased power could break the magic of the cuffs."

"It doesn't work like that," Mason says. "Once the cuffs are on, they'll block whatever magic the prisoner holds."

There's a knock at the door, and we all turn as Waylen pokes his head into the room. "Mason, Eliza wants to see you. She says it's urgent."

The prince's body goes rigid, and there's reluctance in his eyes. "I'll be right there," he replies, and when Waylen disappears from the room, Mason turns to me. "I need to tend to this. Will you join me, my mate?"

Instinctively, I want to say 'yes,' but it wouldn't make sense. "It would look strange if we all turned up to your private meeting. Go and do what you need to do. We'll still be here."

When he continues to hesitate, I add, "Don't worry, I'm not going to be doing any more exploring on my own."

At that, he finally relaxes. "Even if you did, I trust you would be fine, but times are uncertain and sometimes individuals do unexpected things."

"It's fine," I reply. "I probably should try to rest more, anyway."

He nods, seemingly satisfied with that, and he kisses me stupid before exiting the room, leaving me a grinning, near panting mess.

"So she'll listen to him," Alaric grumbles as the door closes.

Ignoring the assassin, I start toward the bed, and Dante moves with me, dropping onto the mattress before I can.

"What are you doing?" I ask.

"You didn't think you were sleeping on your own, did you?" he drawls. Before I can protest, he pulls me down, and tucking me against him, he wraps an arm around my body. *Sweet Lady Fate my demon smells good.* Unlike earlier when I had laid there alone and unable to shut down, now sleep claims me easily. Despite the desire that has me wanting to climb my demon, my eyes flutter closed, and as warmth rushes through me, the tension in my muscles finally eases, and my body calms. Before I drift off, I hear Dante whisper, "I've got you, princess."

SEVENTEEN

~ Dante ~

"Remind me why you keep doing this?" Luna asks as she focuses her power, morphing my features until I'm unrecognizable. She's hazy in my memory, her features a little blurred, but she's still unmistakable with her fire red horns. "This is the third night," she points out. "I'm pretty sure you'd know by now if she's your mate."

I stare at my reflection in the antique mirror across from us, and Kai's face stares back at me. Not Dante's. "I'm not paying you to ask questions," I drawl.

"You're not paying me at all," she quips back, and my lips quirk into a smile.

"Yeah, the smile doesn't work the same when you don't have your face anymore," she teases. "Maybe I should leave *you like this permanently. Then, at least, the females in this city would be safe from you."*

"And deny them the joys of Dante?" Noah chips in from where he lounges across the room. "Where would be the fun in that?"

"There would be less broken hearts for one," Luna points out, waving her hands again as she fixes my lopsided eyebrow.

"Their hearts will heal when they find their fated mates," I point out. "Then I'll be easily forgotten."

Luna shrugs. "Maybe, but anyway, stop skirting the question. Are you going to tell us why you keep doing this?"

I stare back at her quizzical umber eyes. Luna's a pretty demon with thick auburn hair and red horns, but we grew up together, and she's always been immune to my charms. It's probably why we get along.

"He's still afraid to show his face after the princess kicked his ass during the tournament," Noah answers for me through a mouthful of cheese.

"Says the demon who was out within the first five minutes," I counter, pinning Noah with a stare. "I would have made it to the end if Zoran hadn't caught me by surprise and knocked me out."

"Mhmm... See I told you, being invisible isn't all that," Noah says, stuffing his mouth full again.

I turn my attention back to Luna, and the shapeshifter watches me carefully. "You're playing a dangerous game, you know. If you're not the princess's mate, you shouldn't keep visiting her. If she finds out that I've used my shaping abilities on you, it's not just you who'll be in trouble. I get the feeling she won't be happy to hear she's been deceived."

"She'll never know," I reply seriously, because Luna's not wrong about this being dangerous. "And this will be the last night, I promise." I don't point out to Luna that the magic she's been using on me has made it harder to detect whether Princess Blake is my mate. Luna's shaping abilities not only disguise my appearance and scent, but it's made my senses duller. Knowing the princess would be well aware of my reputation, the first night I visited her, it seemed an interesting experiment to go in disguise. I'd thought it would be an uneventful dinner, but enough to satisfy my curiosity about the formidable female I'd witnessed breaking demons during the tournament. To my surprise, even with my dulled senses I found her company to be refreshing. There was more to the princess than I'd previously thought, and I was driven by the need to find out everything about her. A difficult task considering for most of the dinner, she seemed to prefer comfortable silence. But tonight, will be the last night. Luna is right, and if the princess isn't fated to me, I'd be an idiot to continue.

Luna stares at me for a moment longer, but when I still don't explain myself, she throws her hands up in the air and joins Noah on the lounge. "I hope you know what you're doing, Dante," she says. "For once, I think you're going to have to accept that there's at least one more female in this city who's out of your reach."

Standing, I stride closer to the mirror and fix my tie. "We shall see."

I breathe in Blake's alluring scent as she finally relaxes, giving in to sleep. *So perfect.* It had never felt like this with the others. When I'd bedded demons in Seral, the moment of bliss was fleeting and the emptiness I always felt after the act left me wanting to chase the high again. I wanted to find those brief moments when I could truly feel alive.

But with Blake, just to have her sleeping in my arms fills me with a vast pool of warmth that is deeper than anything I've felt. I know she still doesn't think she can have us. Not in the way she wants. The rumors that circulated after her last lover's departure have been more damaging than I expected. I breathe in again, thinking about how her scent haunted me for so long. It's been so long since I first tasted her. Since Blake walked into that dining room and demanded that Kai take her. That *I* take her, and even the magic Luna had placed on me couldn't stop me from seeing who the princess was. My fated mate. My princess. Mine to bond with. Mine to protect.

But as she was coming apart in my arms an unknown force attacked me. A cold vice clamped around my throat suffocating me, the dark power squeezing my life force, and it wasn't until I'd turned invisible that I'd managed to slip free of its hold.

Fuck, watching the princess, *my* princess, search for the demon she knew as Kai had me wanting to show myself again, but I'd had to break through

Luna's shapeshifting magic to use my own power, and if I revealed my true form I didn't know how she'd react. I was also certain that someone or something had tried to kill me, and that the source of the magic was close to the princess. So I remained quiet, waiting until the princess left the room before returning to my clan house, and I've spent the time since trying to discover where the unknown power had come from.

It was only my lack of restraint that had me violating the rules and bringing humans to my house, and in turn, luring the princess to my home. Each time, I'd hoped she might realize who I was. That somewhere deep down she'd see I was her fated mate, but Kai's death had made her even more wary, and I still hadn't discovered where the threat in the palace was originating, so I'd waited.

I think about that night over and over as Blake sleeps, finally getting the rest she needs. Eventually, Alaric, Nate, and Prince Callan slip out with Shade, leaving me to watch her. I know they're going to distract themselves while she sleeps, because though Blake doesn't seem to believe it, she's all we think about. My cock has been hard since the moment she entered the room again, and my balls ache just thinking about everything I want to do with her. But she needs her rest, so I don't move as she sleeps soundly beside me, and the others left. Shade was reluctant, but all I had to do was comment about how upset Blake would be if her mates got themselves into trouble, and the bird was following after them.

I stay beside Blake for hours until she slowly starts to rouse. Yawning, she blinks blearily up at me and stretches.

Smiling, I tuck her hair behind her ear. "Feel better?"

"You're still here," she replies, and I frown. I think about all the females and males from my past. I'd always left straight after being with them, and it never occurred to me that I should stay. But with Blake, I never want to leave her side.

"Of course," I say, admiring her tousled dark hair and puffy cheeks. "Where else would I be?"

She shrugs. "How long was I out?"

"It's hard to say. Hours, probably."

"Hours?" Her eyes snap wide, and she peers around the room. "Where are the others?"

"Exploring. You needed sleep, and they needed a distraction," I drawl.

Her expression flattens. "Exploring? This is because I went out without them, isn't it?"

I chuckle. "Actually, I'd say it's because they didn't know what to do with themselves while you were resting."

She grows thoughtful, and her gaze goes to the open space that overlooks the rebel city below.

"It's beautiful down there, you know," she tells me, and there's a faraway look in her eyes.

"As beautiful as our depraved city back home?"

"In its own way," she replies, and then the smile falls from her face. "You know, if the witches attack while we're gone, Seral might not look the same when we return."

I think of my clan and my friends. Of Noah and Luna, and the other demons. "King Dalton has stopped the witches before," I tell her, thinking back to the great war.

Sadness enters her eyes, and her words are soft when she speaks. "He won't be able to do that this time."

Her comment surprises me, and I want to ask if this has something to do with the announcement of the king's unexpected retirement, but now isn't the time. "Let's just work on getting out of this place and back to Seral, shall we? If we get out of these cuffs, we can bond, and with the five, uh six, of us having heightened abilities, surely we'll be able to take on this King Celzar."

She sighs heavily, rolling onto her back. "I don't think Prince Callan and Alaric have changed their minds about bonding."

"Oh, I don't know about that. There's a difference between words and actions, princess."

"Well, right now Alaric and Prince Callan's actions say they're not sure what they want," she counters.

My lips twitch, and I comb my fingers through her hair. "The Drozac assassins are taught to live on a diet of hatred and pain, but it's obvious Alaric's already coming around. As for the archangel...there's more to him than he's letting on. He was just as upset at the idea of being away from you in that prison as the rest of us."

She raises a brow, clearly not believing a word I'm saying.

"Perhaps if you let us act more like your fated mates," I drawl, my fingers trailing lower and brushing against the side of her right breast. "I'm more than happy to lead by example."

Her lips part at my touch, her skin warming in response, and desire ripples through me.

"You've heard the rumors," she whispers. "If I accidentally kill my mates, we won't be able to seal the bond. And, I'll have to live with that loss."

"We're your mates. None of us will die because of you," I assure her.

"You don't know that."

"I do."

"Trust me, you don't," she insists. "There's something wrong with—"

My lips find hers, because I can't let those words keep tumbling out of her mouth. That lie. She tenses, but I devour her mouth, my tongue tangling with hers, and slowly she softens. I pull her closer to me, and my tail wraps around her thigh, squeezing tightly, and reminding her that she's mine. By the time our lips part, she's breathless and panting, and her golden eyes are bright with desire. *So incredibly beautiful.*

"It's you who doesn't understand, princess," I tell her, my heart pounding faster. Because this is the moment I've dreaded. I made a mistake, but keeping this from her was never the answer. "And it's my fault you don't."

She pulls her head back to stare at me. "What are you talking about?"

I steel myself and finally let myself admit the secret I've held on to for so long. "You didn't kill me that day."

"Kill you? Do you mean in the tournament?" she asks, puzzled.

I think of the deadly tournament the king made us fight in, and how I'd been knocked unconscious that day. "Not then," I say carefully, my finger trailing up and down her side. "In the palace."

I can see her mind working as she tries to understand what I'm telling her, and I stare into her golden eyes, guilt squeezing my chest. "I've got you, *princess*," I repeat the phrase Kai uttered, wondering if this time it'll trigger the memory. Seconds pass, and I can tell familiarity is tickling at the edges of her mind.

I go on, "It wasn't your fault I almost died. There's a power in the castle. Something reached out when you were coming apart in my arms. A dark magic that's unlike anything I've experienced, and it wasn't until I'd turned invisible that I'd managed to slip free of its hold."

Her face drains of color.

I run my hand over my horns. "I wanted to tell you the truth sooner. When I saw you searching for the demon you knew as Kai, fuck I wanted to tell you, but

I'd realized you were mine, and I couldn't risk it. Not until I knew where that dark power was coming from."

Her mouth opens, closes, and then opens again. "So, I never killed Kai?"

"No."

"But you can't shapeshift," she rasps, and before I can explain she connects the dots. "Luna," she croaks. I'm not sure if she's angry or relieved.

"I wanted to discover who you were without my reputation ruining things," I explain, though it sounds so stupid now. "Be honest, if I'd gone as myself, would you have agreed to a meeting?"

She purses her lips, proving my point.

"I promised myself I'd stay away from you until I discovered the threat," I say. "But I knew you were mine, and it was driving me mad. So, I came up with excuses for you to visit me."

"Wait. You violated the rules, bringing humans to your home so you could lure me there?"

I smirk, not in the slightest regretting that part. "I only have so much control, princess."

"Unbelievable," she mutters.

"The thing is, it can be hard to function when your mind is constantly filled with thoughts of the only female you're destined to spend your life protecting and pleasuring." My fingers brush against the side of her breast again, and she shudders.

"You should have told me," she says. "Did you find out where the power is coming from?"

I frown, hating my answer. "No."

She nods like it's the response she was expecting, and she peers up, scrutinizing my face. I know she's imagining his features. Kai's, that is. "His horns were longer," she says, a wicked grin slowly tugging at her lips.

"Were they now?" The corners of my mouth tease up, because we both know that isn't true.

Her gaze trails downward, and she bites her bottom lip. "Also, I'm pretty sure his cock—"

I silence her words with my lips again, and for the first time since that night when I had a different face, she doesn't hold back. *I've got you, princess,* the words vibrate through me as true today as they were that night in the palace.

My hands slide to her ass, and she breaks the kiss, lifting to straddle me. She doesn't say it, but as her golden eyes look down at me, I know what she's thinking. In a way, I just set her free.

CHAPTER

EIGHTEEN

~ Princess Blake ~

I didn't kill Kai. I can hardly breathe. Can hardly wrap my head around everything that Dante's just told me.

I'm torn between feeling annoyed that the asshole lied to me, and relieved that it wasn't my vagina that killed the demon. *It wasn't me.* I mean, sure, there is some evil magic that tried to kill Kai, erm I mean, Dante, and I can only guess it has something to do with whatever is behind the forbidden door in the vault, but that's a problem for another time.

Right now...well, right now, one of my mates is between my thighs, and for the first time I don't feel like I have to stop. At this thought, my desire burns brighter, and my body heats like lava is traveling along my veins. Leaning down, I kiss Dante, sliding my tongue against his, and he groans into my mouth, his hands moving behind my back and pressing me closer to him. It's not long before I'm grinding against him, our breathing shallow, and it takes a lot of effort for me to lift up and pull my shirt over my head. Dante's midnight eyes remain fixed on me, his eyes hooded as he watches me peel off the layers. *My demon mate. Mine.* And I can have him.

His hands skim along my body, and I reach down, unfastening his pants. I help pull them off his thick thighs before removing my own, and he continues to watch me. His eyes are so dark they're almost black, and I smirk at the burning desire in his gaze. But he doesn't move. It's like he knows I need control, at least for now, and he's happy to let me take my time. Climbing back up, I admire the dark tattoos inked over his body, and I run my hands up the hard lines of his abs.

"Mmm, how did I get so lucky?" he mutters, his muscles hardening at my touch.

As I straddle him, I start moving my hips, neither of us wearing clothing now, and he groans as I slide against him, teasing the length of his very impressive cock. "I'm not sure lucky is the word I'd use," I say, teasing myself as much as I'm teasing him. "Have you seen the mess we're in?"

I let the tip of his cock enter me, moaning before I let it slide out again.

"Fuck Blake," he curses, gripping my hips tighter.

His eyes flick to mine, and his face is dead serious. "All I see is you, princess. And you're fucking stunning." Bursts of blue spark in his eyes as he speaks, like his magic is pushing against the power of his cuff, straining to be free, and for a moment, I stop moving, unable to speak.

"Let me in, princess," he rasps, his eyes wild and desperate. Desperate for me. For *us*.

And this time I don't have to say, 'no.' Because he's my mate, and merciful Lady Fate I need more. "Yes," I whisper, and it's all Dante was waiting to hear. His expression turns completely feral, his fingers digging in as he flips me onto my back and moves between my legs, pushing his cock inside my body with one smooth thrust. I gasp at the sensation of him filling me, his cock burying so deep it makes me cry out. Pleasure tears through me, and I grab hold of his horns, my thumbs rubbing over the ridges, and making him shudder.

"Stop," he warns me, his deep voice a throaty rasp. "I've waited too long for this, princess."

I chuckle darkly, continuing to rub his horns because I enjoy the way it makes him groan, his lips parting. He curses, and pulls his cock out, and then he's lifting my legs and resting them on his shoulders, practically folding me in half. I'm barely in position when he thrusts in, pushing in even deeper than before, and his name is a moan on my lips. He gives me a sensual smile, picking up speed as he moves his cock in and out of me. "One taste of you, Blake," he says hoarsely between labored breaths. "And I knew I could never get enough."

My heart squeezes as the pleasure builds inside me, tingles racing over my body as I near my release. "Dante," I whimper, and his tail reaches around, the tip sliding between my legs and teasing my clit as he slams inside me again, his cock forcing in as deep as it can go. My inner muscles clench around him as I'm left practically screaming, but he only chuckles, fucking me harder, his tail practically vibrating as it moves against my clit.

It's too damn much. I open my mouth, and I'm intending to say that I can't breathe, because as he drives into me in this position the air is knocked from my lungs, but the next time he slams into me, I swear I see stars, and I cry out instead, my nails tearing through the fabric as I fist the sheets.

"Never," he says, thrusting into me again. "I could never have enough of you."

Tears spring to my eyes. "Good," I tell him, "because you're mine, Dante."

My words shatter him, and he fucks me like this is our last time together, though if I have my way, this is only the first of many, many times we'll be like this. A surge of power rises in me, despite the fact I need all five of my mates to seal the bond, but then the magic of the cuff comes alive, sending a wave of agony up my leg. The pain is chased away by pleasure as Dante pulls his cock all the way out and thrusts it in again. His tail continues flicking my clit at the same time, and my orgasm rips through me. Dante keeps pumping into me, the wooden bed protesting at the strain as he tries to drag out the orgasm for as long as possible, and I let go of the sheets, reaching up to grab and stroke his horns. Groaning, he comes not long after, his dark eyes sparking with blue as he spills into me, filling me with warmth.

My demon. Because he is fucking mine, and there's nothing stopping me from having him now. It feels so damn *right,* and I shudder beneath my demon.

Dante hangs his head down, pressing a passionate kiss to my lips. "You all right, princess?" he asks as he moves back and lowers my legs, propping himself beside me.

I'm not sure if he's asking because he endured the pain of the cuff as well, but I smile, because not even a reminder of our cuffs could ruin this moment. "Never better," I tell him, and he grins, his sensuous lips curving upward.

"Told you I wasn't going anywhere," he says, reminding me that he didn't die while we were together. He kisses my hair, pulling me close, and I trail my fingers down the hard panes of his sweaty chest, need already building in me again.

"And I finally believe you," I tell him simply. "But if you'd told me you were Kai sooner..."

"I know," he replies, blowing out a breath. "Any chance you can forgive me, princess?"

I grin, making a show of tapping my head

thoughtfully. "Hmmm, I'm sure there's more you can do to earn my forgiveness."

He gives me a wicked smile. "Then I'll gladly spend eternity making it up to you."

He wiggles down, sucking my nipple into his mouth, and my laugh turns into a moan as I breathe in his scent. *Fuck I love apricots.* I sink my fingers into his hair, but my eyes snap open when the door opens.

"Whoa, you go girl! Get it!" Shade's comment sounds in my head as the others all filter through the doorway and stop abruptly, staring at where we're on the bed. Dante still has my nipple in his mouth, and for a moment I think he's just going to ignore them and keep going, but then he pulls back, turning to the others with a smug grin.

Ah, crap.

Nate's eyes heat, and he looks like he's contemplating shoving Dante out of the way and taking his place, but Alaric and Prince Callan both tense like they're preparing for battle.

"Get dressed," Alaric growls, and I bristle at the order.

Dante chuckles. "Jealousy doesn't look so good on you, assassin."

Alaric's jaw ticks, but before the giant can retaliate, I slip out from beneath the covers. I stand there completely naked for a few seconds before slowly starting to dress. "And here I thought my mate would enjoy seeing me unclothed," I tease, giving Alaric a saccharine sweet smile. I know I'm pushing the assassin's buttons, but now that I realize there's no risk that bedding my mates will kill them, I'm enjoying teasing the asshole.

"*Oh, he does,*" Shade comments. "*Look at those tight lips pressed together. I bet he even has his ass cheeks clenched going by how tense he is.*"

"*Thanks for the visual, Shade,*" I reply dryly.

"*You're welcome!*" she sings.

Nate's smile is predatory as he watches me. "I know I do. Now that you're finished playin' with the demon, how 'bout you let me show you what a shifter mate can do?"

I grin, biting my bottom lip, and Alaric glares at him. "Stop encouraging her," he growls.

"Now, why the fuck would I do that?" Nate replies. "We're not all made of stone like you." My shifter takes a step toward me, and my pulse skitters, but we all turn when the door opens again, and Mason walks into the room.

CHAPTER
NINETEEN

~ Prince Callan ~

Blake's honey and cinnamon scent is stronger than usual, and I know I have Dante to blame for that. For whatever reason, the demon princess has finally decided to start enjoying her mates, and I wasn't prepared when we'd returned to the room. Her heightened scent had hit me the moment I'd walked through the doorway, and it had taken everything in me not to march over to her and worship her body like an archangel mate normally would. *Like I want to.*

I'm still breathing in her scent when Mason strides into the room. The fallen prince looks different now. His long beard has been trimmed, and the dirt and

220

grime has been washed away, though his many scars remain, inside as well as out, I'm sure.

According to Blake, the male is another one of her mates, and going from the way his steps falter and he inhales, his eyes pinpointing Blake like a hunter who's found his prey, I don't doubt it. A smile creeps over Blake's face at the sight of him, and a twinge of jealousy goes through me. Because I want her to look at me like that. Not that I fucking deserve it.

"Mason?" Blake says with surprise.

The male walks to her in a few strides, and he captures her mouth with his, and slides one hand behind her head while the other presses into her back. The small noise she makes has my cock hardening even more, and I glower as she melts into him, seemingly completely comfortable with the fallen prince.

Nate's temple pulses. "Get in line, brother," he complains, and then the shifter is there, pulling Mason away and taking the prince's place. Mason only smiles at the intrusion, and Blake kisses the shifter like she's enjoying every moment of this. I side eye Alaric. The giant is scowling, his hands balled into fists, but he doesn't move forward. Dante watches from his position on the bed, and I cross my arms, hating every fucking moment of this.

When Blake pulls away from Nate, her golden eyes are glowing, and her lips twist into a smirk. She winks at Mason. "See, I told you you'd be good for us."

I narrow my eyes, wondering what else the little demon has told our new bond brother.

"That you did, my mate," Mason replies as he lifts Blake's hand and kisses it gently.

Nate glares at the prince. "Would you stop? You're makin' the rest of us look bad."

Mason's eyes sparkle. "If that's true, then you haven't done a sufficient job at taking care of our mate."

"We were doin' just fine," Nate replies, but Mason doesn't look convinced. I don't blame him.

I think of my words to the demon princess when we first discovered we were mates, and now all I feel is regret. Angels are known to shower their mates with gifts, pampering them beyond their wildest dreams, and giving them as much as they desire. It has taken all my willpower to go against that, and now I realize I made a mistake. There is no denying your fated mate, and I'm going to have to find a way to repair the damage with Blake, and still keep my promise to my sister.

Dante stretches and smiles smugly as the sheet falls off him. "Welcome to the group, brother," he tells Mason.

The fallen prince dips his head in acknowledgement.

"Don't get me wrong, I'm happy to see you, but why are you here, Mason?" Blake asks, and I know she's picked up on the same thing that I have. The prince is giving off a strange energy that's making me feel on edge.

Mason's expression hardens, and once again, he looks more like the male we met in the prison. He hesitates before explaining, "A scout has returned from The Haven. Preparations are almost complete for King Celzar's royal wedding, which is being held in the palace tonight. Invitations have been sent out across the city."

Blake takes a step back. "What? But that doesn't make any sense. Why would Celzar send out invitations when I'm no longer his captive?"

Mason's face is grave. "Because he knows me too well. He's been searching for this rebel camp for years, and he knows he may never find it. So he's decided on a different approach to reclaim his bride. Blake, if you aren't there in time to complete the marriage ceremony, my sister, Princess Nerelia's life will be forfeit."

Rage flows through me, and I try to access my power, dipping my head slightly as pain shoots up my body. "Blake can't marry him," I say simply.

Alaric's eyes darken with the promise of violence. "She's not going anywhere near him."

"There's nothing Celzar hates more than looking like a fool," Mason replies. "He promised The Haven a royal wedding, and he intends to give them one. He also knows that using Nerelia is his strongest move. She's the rightful ruler, and the only other family I have left. But..." His gaze goes to Blake. "I agree that our mate shouldn't go anywhere near him. I only came here to tell you to keep her safe."

"Wait, what?" Blake's jaw slackens. "You're joking right? You just said Nerelia is your sister, and the rightful queen. Of course, I'm going."

Shade squawks and flies over, settling on Blake's shoulder.

Mason straightens, a severe expression on his face. "My warriors are readying themselves as we speak. I'll confront my brother alone. When he's defeated, I'll come for you."

"When he's defeated?" Annoyance flickers in Blake's eyes. "You mean when you're all dead? You and your warriors are all cuffed just as we are. What makes you think you can win against him? There's a reason Celzar rules your kind."

"I won't let my sister die," Mason replies.

"Then let me go," Blake retorts. "Because you turn up without me and she's as good as dead."

Mason pulls Blake into his arms, and she doesn't fight him. "This isn't just about you," she says, her tongue darting out to wet her lips as she stares up at him. "We all need this. I'm your best shot at defeating King Celzar and you know it."

"You're also my mate, something that I never dreamed was possible," he says softly. "I won't let him take you from me as well."

Before Blake can protest, Alaric growls, "Listen to him. This isn't our fight."

She frowns, not looking the least bit impressed by

his comment. "Celzar is the reason the witches came to Seral. It *is* our fight. Besides, this might be the only way to ensure we can remove these cuffs and get back to the surface."

"The king wants to steal your power, gorgeous," Nate reminds her, but it's obvious Blake has already made up her mind.

"You can either stay here or come with me, but I'm going," she says as she pulls on her boots. "Now, where the fuck can we get some weapons?"

"There's no point arguing with her," Dante drawls, rising from the bed. "There's a reason she's lasted against the cutthroat demons of our realm."

Mason exhales, nodding. "Fine. Then we do this together."

Blake braids her hair quickly, and gulps down a glass of water. "I'll attend the wedding," she says, placing the glass back on the table. "The rest of you can figure out how to get us out of these cuffs. A servant in the palace revealed that after the wedding vows are complete, there's a brief moment when Celzar will unlock my cuff so he can feed on my power. I just have to be faster than he is."

"And if you're not?" Alaric asks.

"Then I guess you'd better be good little mates and kill him before he kills me," Blake says with a wink, though from her stubborn expression it's obvious she has no intention of letting the king take anything from her.

"Well, then," Nate mutters, and cracks his neck. "Let's go spill some blood."

TWENTY

~ Princess Blake ~

Thirty rebels march with us as we make our way through the tunnels and away from the rebel city. Mason walks beside me with Dante and the others at the head of the group, and the prince's eyes are steely and focused, his brows furrowed in a determined frown. There was no way I was staying behind at the camp while my mate went to face King Celzar alone, but now I wonder whether we can pull this off.

None of the rebels complained when we joined them in the armory, and Mason advised them that we'd be joining the party. Truthfully, a few of them looked relieved that I was there, probably because they knew it was suicide to attend the wedding without me. But then Mason had pulled me to him, pressing his lips to mine and declaring that he was my mate. It's funny how quickly the mood changed then. At first, the centaurs had stared in disbelief, but as the realization had set in, they'd dipped their heads to me in respect. Like the simple fact I was mated to their prince meant I was someone to be honored. Which was weird, but kind of sweet.

"I don't know about this, Blake," Shade's worried voice fills my head, breaking me out of my thoughts. *"We've made it through some things, but this seems like a bad idea."*

"You're not doubting me now, are you?"

My friend paces on my shoulder and flutters her feathers. *"I'm being real. I don't want to see you get hurt."*

Reaching up, I stroke her feathers. *"You know me better than to think I was ever going to stay behind. Who knows what the situation is back in Seral, and this is our best chance of getting out of here."*

"I just..." she trails off. *"I hope you know what you're doing."*

Honestly, I don't. I'm taking a risk. A big one, but it's not like I could let Mason go without me. King Celzar would likely kill Princess Nerelia if I didn't turn up, and then he'd turn his sights to Mason and the other rebel warriors. I think about Sassia in the palace, and the rest of the Perstalians, including the bird, Pask. They're all cuffed, stuck in this state of imprisonment, and as much as I tell myself I'm not going for them, as much as I remind myself that this is all simply to get back to Seral, my heart squeezes at the thought of what might happen if I don't turn up for the wedding.

I think of Celzar's initial lover and the witches. *"Celzar caused this mess,"* I tell Shade. *"He's the reason the witches attacked Seral. The reason Perstalia was destroyed."*

"I know. But if he takes your power, it won't help anyone," Shade points out, more serious than I've heard her in a long while.

"Then I'll have to make sure he doesn't."

We're silent the rest of the way as we move through a series of secret tunnels, and then we're skirting the edges of the city in The Haven.

"It's quiet," Nate mutters, scanning the buildings near us.

"Many will already be at the ceremony," Mason replies, resting his hand on the hilt of his sword. "I don't think attendance is optional."

"Meaning there will be more collateral if we attack during the ceremony," Eliza points out bitterly, the female striding behind me.

We don't encounter another soul for the remainder of the journey to the palace, but when we near the massive crystal structure, we stop, sheltered by a row of smaller buildings.

Mason rests his large hands on my shoulders and warmth goes through me. "It's not too late to turn back, my mate."

I swallow and smile, though my heart rate has

picked up. It's different this time. I wouldn't say it was easy facing the challenges the demon king had thrown at me in the past, but the stakes had never been this high. If I fail, King Celzar will take my power, and the Perstalians will never be free. If I fail, things are about to go very badly for me and my mates. *My confusing, addictive, and annoyingly handsome mates.* "And let you have all the fun?" I reply to Mason. "I don't think so."

The prince's gaze remains serious. "Remember, Blake. Once your cuff is off, you can't let his magic take hold of you. If you do—"

"I know," I say, waving a hand in the air. "I won't get another chance."

He nods, but his expression is strained. His hands grip tighter onto my shoulders, like he's afraid to let me go. Reaching up, I place one of my hands over his, and I think of the rules Dad has drilled into me since I was a child. "Rule number one for a demon royal," I tell Mason. "Never show weakness." I pause, grinning at the prince. "And Rule number two...*Never show mercy.*"

"No mercy," he agrees with a nod, and I step back from him. Taking a deep breath, I smooth my hands down my silky black dress. "Think the king will be happy with it?" White crystals are embedded into the black lace pattern stitched on one side, and the sweetheart neckline shows a generous amount of cleavage. It's the best dress Eliza could find on short notice. Well, one of them anyway. There was a white one that would have been much more suitable for a wedding, but this seemed more fitting.

Mason smiles but worry still shines in his eyes. "Celzar is never happy."

Dante comes from behind and wraps his hands around me. "I look forward to tearing this off you, princess," he murmurs into my ear, and I grin.

I tilt my head back at him. "Does that mean you're going to try not to die?"

"Oh, I'm not going anywhere, sweetheart," he replies.

I turn my attention forward again as Mason leans in close and presses a kiss to my lips, and for a moment, I'm deliciously sandwiched between my demon and the fallen prince.

"*Have I mentioned that it's not fair?*" Shade comments, still on my shoulder. "*Where are my irritating, but sexy mates?*"

My laughter sounds in her head. "*I'm sure they're out there, Shade. Just waiting to make bird babies with you.*"

"*Bird babies?*" I can't tell if she's delighted or horrified by the sound of it, but I'm distracted when Eliza steps up behind Mason and clears her throat. "It's time, Mason. If we're doing this, she can't be late."

Mason pulls back, and I straighten, trying to ignore how hot I feel right now.

"*You should stay out here,*" I tell Shade. "*Away from the ceremony.*" *...And the danger.*

"And miss your big day?" she teases. *"I don't think so."*

I want to argue, but Shade can be stubborn at the best of times, so I don't bother.

"All right, let's go get our powers back," I say cheerfully to the others.

Alaric, Nate, and Prince Callan look like they want to argue, but they don't stop me when I move away and start walking the rest of the way to the palace on my own.

"It's settled, Mason and Dante are both winning at this whole being a mate thing," Shade tells me as I cross the street, striding from the cover of the buildings and approaching the front of the palace. Four centaur guards are stationed at the top of a flight of stone steps, guarding the crystal entrance doors.

"The others are all drool-worthy to look at," Shade goes on, *"but Dante's been there for you before you even realized it, and Mason has the whole tortured warrior thing going on, and he treats you nicely. Like, was that so much to ask?"* I'd explained to Shade that Kai was really Dante in disguise, and my friend had literally hopped up and down with excitement.

My lips still tingle from Mason's kiss, and I grin, but I force myself to focus as we approach the guards. *"None of it will matter if I can't keep us all alive."*

The guards don't address me, but they open the doors when I reach the top of the stairs, and I move into the entranceway of the palace. A group of four soldiers in pristine, royal armor are stationed there, and the moment I draw close, they surround me and start escorting me further into the building where I assume the ceremony is being held.

"Looks like Celzar expected you to turn up," Shade mutters in my head as she eyes the guards in front of us.

No one speaks as we make our way along a series of hallways, but when we near the ballroom, idle chatter and lyrical music drifts out from the open doors. The guards in front of me move to the side, and then I'm standing there, just inside the doorway. Thousands of faces all turn to me and the chatter tapers away, the music abruptly stopping. *Ah, crap.*

"Gee, this is beautiful," Shade comments, peering at the wide pieces of glittering white cloth that are suspended from the massive crystal chandelier above, the fabric streaming to all sides of the room.

"Yeah, for a funeral," I counter. The room is filled with countless bouquets of white scalloped roses tied together with gossamer white ribbon. They're deposited around the space, set in glass vases atop white pedestals, and attached to the walls in an even pattern that makes the arrangement look too artificial. Too...unnatural. *Too forced like this whole damn ceremony.* White roses are the standard flower used when having a burial back in Seral, and I have the distinct feeling of being the one in the box about to be covered with a pile of dirt. ...Except I'm not about to let King Celzar bury me.

A plush white carpet stretches down the center of

the ballroom to the dais at the other side, and I finally let myself look at where King Celzar stands with a confident smirk on his face. His pressed white suit is completely covered in crystals, the tiny stones catching the light, and his oily dark hair is slicked back from his face. He doesn't look the least bit surprised that I turned up, but even from my position, I can see the hint of irritation in his eyes as his gaze roams over my black dress. *Perfect.*

With a wave of his hand, the band starts up again, playing a tender, melodic tune that sings through the room, and I stand there, feeling like I must have dozed off and slipped into a bad dream, because I swear this is some kind of nightmare. The Perstalians watch me, enraptured, like they're waiting to see me do something fascinating, yet I know they're just waiting for me to walk to my death. Most of those standing in view are high born individuals, dressed in rich garments of a variety of colors, but behind them stands rows of commoners dressed in simpler clothing in shades of cream and brown.

"Look at her wings!" a female whispers, her cheeks flush with excitement.

"How is that possible?" questions another.

"She must be from above," whispers a third, her eyes glued to my black feathers.

"So much for not wanting his kind to ask questions," I say to Shade. *"The Perstalians aren't going to believe I'm a low born from The Haven now."*

"Yeah, something tells me he doesn't care," she replies.

Lifting my chin higher, I turn my attention back to the king and try to ignore my racing heartbeat. From his look of impatience, he's about ready to order the guards to march me up the carpet, so I start walking, ignoring the whispers and gasps of the Perstalians as I pass them. No doubt this ceremony will be the talk of the city for some time.

It feels like an eternity passes as I stroll along, the music matching my steps, but then I'm standing beside the king, feeling completely exposed. A few paces away, Princess Nerelia stands between two large centaur guards, and her expression is somber as she watches us.

King Celzar continues to examine me, and a look of distaste crosses his face when he peers at Shade on my shoulder. "Why you insist on having that rat close to you is beyond me," he mutters, his voice thick with disgust.

Shade bristles, her feathers puffing up. *"Girl, what the hell did he just say? That's it, he's clearly not using his eyes anyway, so he won't mind when I peck them bloody."*

Anger heats my blood, but I stroke Shade's feathers to calm her down, and somehow, I manage to keep my own cool. "What can I say, it's called having a friend, King Celzar. You should try it sometime." *Maybe then you wouldn't always look like you have something stuck up your ass.* Thankfully, I'm smart enough to keep that last part to myself. I wouldn't want the king simply deciding to kill me and get it over with. Or worse, have him kill Shade.

King Celzar's back goes ramrod straight, his eyes narrowing to slits, but a humorless smile curves his lips. "Perhaps when I have your power, I can entertain such a notion. And speaking of friends, I presume your other male companions are here as well. Not to mention my brother..." His shrewd gaze scans the ballroom, but I don't give anything away.

When his gaze cuts back to me, frustration makes his temple pulse, and I smile. "Looks like it's just you and me, buddy. If you can't count on your own family to attend your wedding, you must be doing something wrong."

His hand twitches, and for a moment I think he's going to strike me, but he only reaches up and straightens the collar of his suit jacket. "Not to worry," he says calmly. "I'm sure he'll show his face in due time. Mason is nothing if not predictable. But now that you're here, let's not waste the precious time of our guests." He turns to a male who's dressed in white silk robes and standing close by. "Proceed with the ceremony," he commands, clicking his fingers, and the elder dips his head and steps to one side of us. The robed male addresses the crowd, and he launches into a long talk welcoming everyone and discussing the topic of commitment and devotion, and the importance of marriage. The male must think it's his time to shine, because I'm pretty sure he's gone on a tangent, and he's busy talking about the fundamentals of a good relationship when King Celzar barks, "Get to it! I think we've all waited long enough."

"Geez, he really is a ray of sunshine," Shade comments dryly. *"Now, I'm glad I didn't get him a wedding gift."*

I have to work hard to suppress my laughter. *"And the fact he's about to kill me has nothing to do with it?"*

"No, because he's only going to try to kill you. Obviously, you're not going to let that happen. And when he's the one who's dead, that means all the wedding gifts will be yours." She pauses. *"Wow, okay, I am an asshole for not getting a gift then."*

I grin as I listen to her rambling, glad to have her in my head to take the edge off the situation. But I quickly tune her chatter out when the robed male becomes flustered, rushing to the last part of the ceremony. He lifts my hand, placing it onto King Celzar's, and he drapes a strip of silky white cloth over our hands.

Sweat beads on my brow and makes my hands clammy. I know this isn't real. Not in the sense that I'm really intending to commit myself to the Perstalian king, but as the citizens of The Haven watch on intently, and even the guards standing stationary along the walls appear to lean forward to hear the next part, my heart thunders in my chest. I can't see my mates, but I can sense they're out there. Undoubtedly, the other rebels have slipped inside, too. If all goes to plan, they shouldn't have to reveal themselves until the dagger strapped to my thigh is through King Celzar's neck, but a slither of doubt slides through me. Because what if I'm not fast enough?

"D-do you, Blake, daughter of …" the robed male trails off awkwardly, a flash of panic entering his gaze as he stares at me, and I supply, "demons." The male's face blanches. I'm pretty sure he was wanting me to list off my family names, but I don't. Irritation ticks along Kings Celzar's jaw.

"Uh, do you Blake, daughter of demons," the male says quickly, "take King Celzar, first of his name, ruler of The Haven and savior of our kind to be your wedded husband?"

"Savior? Well, that's rich," Shade scoffs in my head.

I lick my lips nervously. In Seral, if a demon husband or wife dies before a single night has passed since they voiced their vows, the marriage is considered voided. I remind myself of the rule, and it helps to ease the tightening of my stomach. I hesitate only for a second, before blurting, "I do." The moment I say it, King Celzar's face changes. The corners of his mouth twist into a cruel smile, and his eyes are icy and unfeeling, devoid of the slightest hint of warmth. My blood chills, and the malice in his eyes has me wanting to grab my dagger.

The robed male stutters as he asks King Celzar the same question that he asked me, and the king is quick to say, "I do."

"Then, it is so," the robed male says, pulling the cloth away from our hands and turning to address the crowd. "Let us celebrate King Celzar's new bride, and our new queen!"

The crowd erupts into applause, and though I

know they've likely been ordered to respond like this, for a moment, I panic. It feels too real. Like I've just sealed my fate and sworn myself to the Perstalian throne and their king. But then I hear the faintest growl from somewhere further in the ballroom, and it's enough to ground me. Saying that vow is the least of my worries. Now I have to try and stay alive.

My heart races even faster. *All right, Blake. The moment the cuff is off, you need to seize your power and kick his ass.* From what I've been told, this is the point in the ceremony when King Celzar would remove the cuff from his bride, so I'm surprised when he leans down, his scent of roses invading my senses. Before I can react, his ice-cold lips are on my cheek, and my skin prickles as his power seizes me. I feel the curve of his lips as he smiles, but I can't seem to pull away. His power holds me in place, my body paralysed, and my energy slowly starts draining into him as his magic takes what's mine.

"No, no, no! He was supposed to remove the cuff first," Shade squawks in a panic. She flaps her wings, lifting into the air, and she outstretches her claws like she intends to scratch his face. Before she can get to him, one of the guards comes for her. She dodges the guard's hand, moving to the side, but another guard clamps his large hands over her.

King Celzar's lips remain on me, and repulsion rolls through my body, chased by a bout of nausea. It feels like eons pass, though in reality it's likely only seconds, and then the king is stepping back. The moment he's no longer touching me, my knees buckle, and two guards step forward, grabbing me roughly under my arms and holding me up.

None of the Perstalian's are cheering now. The ballroom is eerily silent as they all watch me with pity...and relief. Pity because the king is about to take my soul, and relief that it's not them. I don't blame them. It's hard for me to imagine myself in their shoes when they've lost their home on the surface and lived for years without their magic and power.

For a moment, I think I see Sassia amongst the crowd, her eyes wide with hope and determination, even when it's obvious I'm doing a crap job at saving her kind. Steeling myself, I try to stand...and fail.

"Let her go," I rasp at King Celzar, my frantic gaze going to where Shade is still trapped in the guard's hands. Shade screeches, struggling in his grasp, but he only clamps onto her tighter.

King Celzar's cruel gaze is sharp and unkind. "The fact that you care for that little wretch is proof enough that you could never be a true queen."

I'm not sure why he has such a hatred for birds when he has a half animal form himself, but I croak back, "And the fact you have a stone for a heart is why you'll never be a decent king." Holy Lady Fate my body feels so heavy. I struggle to keep my eyes open, fighting against the darkness that's at the edges of my vision.

There are shocked whispers from the crowd, and King Celzar's lips form an ugly sneer. "*I* keep my subjects alive," he spits. "They understand your sacrifice will benefit us all. Without me, they would have been dead on the surface long ago."

My nostrils flare as I glare at him, my hatred so strong it sends a small surge of energy through me. "If it weren't for you, then the witches—" My words die off as King Celzar grips my throat, his fingers tightening and cutting off my air supply. My mouth opens and closes as I struggle for air that doesn't come, and energy starts draining from me again.

He leans in close, his lips a hairsbreadth away. "Usually, I remove the cuff from my bride and make a spectacle before they die, but I suspect you can't be trusted. I can smell it on you—the power that races through your veins, just waiting to be released." He chuckles, and it's a dry, humorless sound. "Oh no, I'm going to take what energy you have now and wait until you're close to death before I free you." He inhales and exhales deeply, the tip of his nose brushing against the curve of my ear. "It is a shame. You know, you almost had me when you said you wanted to change the ending of my story."

Black spots start to dance across my vision, but I'm powerless to stop him, my limbs hanging uselessly by my sides. I was so stupid to think I could best this male. So fucking stupid. Pain blooms in my chest, a searing, aching agony, and just as I think he's not going to stop, just as I'm certain he's going to simply kill me now, a bellow rings out across the ballroom. "Ceeeelzaaaar!" The cry is long and low, and full of an anger that resonates in the depths of my being. "Release her!"

"Mason!" Princess Nerelia gasps, struggling against the guards that hold her back and staring at where my mate must be standing further in the ballroom.

A sinister smile crawls onto King Celzar's lips, and he releases me, taking a small step back. I sag in the guards' arms, my knees slamming to the stone dais as air returns to my lungs, and pain races along my bones. When the king twists his head to the side, I try to move my head as well, but my body is too heavy, like these limbs don't even belong to me anymore. I can't feel my connection to Shade. I can't feel any remnants of my magic at all. Had I really thought I'd be fast enough to best King Celzar if he removed the cuff? It looked like I wasn't going to get to find out.

"The defender!" Awed whispers ring out amongst the crowd of Perstalians, and while I can no longer see King Celzar's face, I note the way his hands curl into fists at his sides.

"How nice of you to attend my wedding, little brother," the king says, an undertone of amusement in his voice.

Though I can't see them, I hear the shuffling of the crowd, and I sense all of my mates as they move a little closer to the dais and stop.

"Well, I appreciate that," Dante drawls like the king had been addressing him. "I do enjoy a good party."

"Especially ones with such entertainment," Prince Callan adds, and I've never heard his voice so cold. It makes all the times he spoke to me seem like casual banter in comparison, and a chill slides down my spine even though the ice in his words isn't directed at me.

King Celzar's body goes rigid, and the guards holding me tense as well.

"Release Blake," Mason commands. "We both know I'm the reason you demanded her return."

"To the contrary," King Celzar replies. "I have plans for my new bride, and I was bereft when she was taken from me. You're simply a nice bonus. I knew you would do the honorable thing and try to save her and our darling sister. It's your predictability that always was your weakness."

There's the clack of hooves on stone, and the clanging of steel as more guards march into the ballroom. My heart skips a beat. *Fuck.* It's bad enough that the king has me. I can't let him have my mates as well. A tiny shred of energy has returned to me, likely due to my dulled demon healing ability, and I try to struggle against the guards restraining me, but I'm still so damn weak. They merely grip me tighter, their fingers digging painfully into my arms.

"She's a fighter, this one," King Celzar says, turning to me again, and lifting my chin with a single manicured finger. I grit my teeth, seething at him because it's all I can do. "She has such fire," the king goes on. "It's such a shame that for her power to become mine, I'll have to snuff out that bold spirit of hers."

He moves so fast that I don't realize what's happened at first. Not until the searing hot pain spreads from my chest, and my gaze drops to where he's buried my own dagger into the flesh close to my heart.

There are roars, and screeching, and the clang of steel, and barked orders, but the noise fades as I stare at that blade. Ordinarily, if I had my power, such a wound wouldn't bother me much. I'd heal from it quickly. But now, I know it's the final straw that will lead to my true death. Blood leaks down my chest, and with it, my remaining energy pours from me.

King Celzar's distinct floral scent is overpowering as he leans in close once again. "Say hello to Yenna for me," he whispers by my ear, and I feel the exact moment he removes the cuff.

Power floods my system, crashing through me in a rush so great it further cripples my already weakened body. I scream, feeling as though I've been set on fire, but my natural demon healing ability kicks in a second later, working hard to repair the damage that's been done. Still, I know it won't be fast enough for me to escape death.

King Celzar clamps his hand onto my arm, and he throws his head back and laughs. It's an abrasive, harsh sound that fills my ears, and my power starts funneling into him instead.

CHAPTER
TWENTY-ONE

~ Prince Callan ~

I want to flay the Perstalian king for daring to put his hands on my mate. I want to sever his head and gift it to my demon princess as a trophy, while pissing on the remainder of his ashes.

It had been agony watching from the crowd. An agony watching, and waiting, and letting Blake have the time she needed and a chance to defeat the king. But this Celzar has proven himself to be even more wicked and cunning than we had anticipated, and rage and fear makes my body tremble as I watch in horror as he slides his hand between my mate's legs and steals her dagger, burying it into her chest.

Before I can fight my way to her, more guards filter in through the doors to one side of the dais, adding to the guards who are already assaulting us from behind. The rebels have all joined us now, striding from the crowd to take up arms, but with our powers limited, the fight is uneven, and it's not long before the rebels start to fall.

Using one hand, I tear off my cloak, tossing it to one side before drawing another blade. I fight side by side with Mason, Dante, and even Nate, snarling as one of my blades sinks into a centaur guard's eye. The guard cries out, swinging his sword wildly in my direction, but I easily avoid his attack, my own sword slicing along his neck deep enough that blood pours from the wound. The guard stumbles backward into the path of two rebels, and they take pleasure in finishing him off.

The crowd screams, some of the citizens trying to get away while others take up arms as well, fighting back with whatever they have on them. Soon, there are eight guards bleeding on the ground, which is a valiant effort, but I try not to think about the much larger number of rebels and innocent civilians who have fallen in the chaos.

Dante spins, his tail flicking as he slices at the guards near him, and Nate growls, jumping into the air before driving his sword into a centaur's back, just above its wings. I peer over at Blake, my jaw set as I keep fighting to get to her, my blade always moving, always cutting a path to her. But just as a clear space opens up before me, more guards stream in, shouting as they charge at us, four guards abreast. I brace with

Dante on one side and Mason on the other. *Kill them all.*

~

~ Princess Blake ~

I'm so cold that my fingers and toes ache as my body begins to shut down. I've died multiple times before, but it's never been like this. Seemingly agonizingly slow. I can feel the depths of my power being pulled from me, stolen, like my very soul is being torn from my body.

I know I won't come back from this. This isn't just my body dying. For an immortal demon, this is a true death. Eternal.

The air is as cold as ice as it passes between my lips, and there's this strange sensation like I'm being carried away, the claws of shadow monsters already sinking deep into my essence. King Celzar's hand remains on me, and I know it won't be long now. He's taking everything from me. I feel his magic syphoning away my power, consuming it.

Truthfully, at this point I'm not sure if I care. I struggle to remember what I'd even been fighting for as my body grows lighter, the pain starting to ease. My eyelids fall shut, and the cold spreads up my limbs, bringing with it a numbness, like I'm turning into... nothing.

"Fight!" The angry growl comes from somewhere close by, and the command vibrates through my body, familiarity tickling my senses.

My lips part a fraction more as I suck icy air into my lungs. I hadn't even realized I'd stopped breathing.

"Fight *Enchantress*." This time the words aren't simply a command. They're a choked, guttural plea from one of my mates—*Alaric.*

My assassin mate cries out in pain, and I struggle to open my eyes, fighting against the edge of death. As some of the pain returns, so do my senses, and I fight harder as the sounds of the battle rush at me—the clang of steel, the cries of the fallen, and King Celzar's manic laughter as my power fills his body.

No, not his power.

Mine.

Fury surges through me, obliterating the numbness that I'd embraced not long ago. The day would come when I'd happily sink into the abyss of death. But not today. Not like this. Not when Shade and my mates are battling for their lives, and an entire kingdom is in shackles. King Celzar doesn't deserve my power.

I focus on where King Celzar's hand is on me, his fingers digging into my shoulder. His magic is still reaching into me and stealing what's mine like some kind of parasite. I focus on that transfer of energy, and for the first time since he started taking from me, I feel a little tug. Before I can investigate further, the scent of chocolate and mint fills my senses, and I gasp as King Celzar is thrown backward. With the loss of contact, the connection is severed, his magic no longer inside me.

"You're stronger than this," Alaric growls as he scoops me into his arms, blood trailing down the side of his head from a shallow gash on his temple. My chest heaves as I struggle to regulate my breathing, and I try to pull away from him. He's too hot, his body like an inferno against my ice-cold skin, but he doesn't let me go. "Where's the feisty demon who fought me in the ruins?" he demands, sounding appalled, though worry shines in his eyes.

"She's out of action right now," I reply, and the hint of a smile lifts my lips. "Knew you didn't want to kill me anymore," I mutter, somehow still able to tease him despite our messed-up situation.

"I mean it, demon," Alaric growls angrily, lightly shaking me. "Fight this."

I try to swallow but my throat is so dry I end up coughing instead. "I can't," I admit, my limbs still completely useless and refusing to work. King Celzar might no longer be stealing from me, but he's already taken almost everything I had. *Fuck, I miss my crows.*

Alaric's furious gray gaze bores into me like he's not willing to accept my bullshit response. "I said *fight*, Blake!" the assassin snaps.

A spark of annoyance flares inside me, because he's clearly not hearing a word I'm saying, but before I can hurl abuse back at him, a trickle of energy starts flowing into me from… somewhere. I try to reach out and connect mentally with Shade, but I can't feel her, and panic makes my chest tighten.

I'm jerked back as a guard lunges for me. Alaric holds me tightly with one hand while fighting with the other. His sword blocks the blow of the guard, and when they break apart, he twists, driving his blade into the centaur's throat.

"Princess." Dante appears beside me, and his voice is soothing as Alaric passes me into the demon's arms. "I've got you." If I had my power and, you know, working limbs, I probably would complain at being manhandled so much, but his words are tender, and it makes my heart hurt. I try to lift my arms, but they still won't budge, even with the small flow of energy that's slowly warming me. My physical body is mostly healed now, but it's the lack of energy that's keeping me immobile. Dante presses me against his hard chest, and even though he's even hotter than Alaric, I relish the heat now. Glad that it's helping to chase away the remaining ice in my veins.

"Thank fuck," I hear Nate mutter from somewhere close, and even Prince Callan looks furious as he peers at me, twin swords in his hands, the blades coated in blood.

My mates circle where Dante holds me, forming a barrier between me and the surrounding guards. They're disheveled and covered in blood, but my mates are *alive*, and they continue to fight. The power slowly building in me is fragile at best, but a spark of hope shoots through me when I realize I can move my fingers. *Yes, come on.* I grit my teeth.

Before I can get too excited, laughter booms in my ears, and as if the sound is a command, the fighting ceases. The guards stop their assault, standing at attention, and we all turn our gazes to where King Celzar stands near Princess Nerelia.

Angry tears spill down the princess's cheeks. "Don't do this, Celzar!" she pleads, struggling against the guards restraining her.

Mason stands at the head of our group, covered in sweat and blood as he faces his brother.

King Celzar ignores the princess, his laughter turning maniacal as he lifts his hands into the air, staring at them like he can see the power radiating from his fingertips. "Oh, I knew our new winged friend was powerful, but this—" He sucks in a breath through his nose, letting his chest expand before breathing out. "Now this will sustain me for some time. I feel…incredible."

I peer at the king. At my mates. At where I spot Shade unconscious on the ground, her beak bloody, but her chest moving as she breathes. Rage tears through me, and the warmth inside me continues to build, that trickle of power flowing a tiny bit faster.

King Celzar grins, completely self-absorbed. "I'll admit this isn't how I planned my latest wedding to go, but I guess the end result will be the same." He cracks his neck as a menacing smile stretches across his face, and then he's in front of Mason, moving so fast I hardly register the motion. He lifts my mate into the air by his throat, clearly using my strength power. "I kept you as a warning to the others in the prison." King Celzar sneers. "But oh, how I've wanted to do this. Defender of the realm?" He scoffs. "I don't know how they still believe it after all these years. Even after you *failed*."

Mason struggles against King Celzar's grasp, slamming his fist into the male's arm, but he can't break free. The centaur king might have diminished his own power, but now he has mine. The cuff shines bright around Mason's ankle, and from the expression of agony on my mate's reddening face, it's clear he's trying to access his own magic.

"Mason," I croak, struggling to get out of Dante's arms, but my demon mate holds me tight. Nate and the others go to help Mason, but the guards block them, layering up and countering their attacks.

"They still believe in me because I've never lied to them," Mason squeezes out. "I've only tried to protect our kingdom."

"Noble as always," King Celzar replies with disgust, and my heart races as Mason struggles to breathe.

"Please, brother," Prince Nerelia begs, fighting even harder against her guards. Her face scrunches in agony like she's trying to access her own power as well.

"That's *King Celzar* to you," he snaps back, but he doesn't turn his attention from Mason.

"Oh, if only you'd chosen differently," King Celzar says as Mason's movements weaken. "Mother, Father, and the rest of the forsaken royal family deserved to die for how they treated me, but you brother. You could have chosen to stand by my side." His expression hardens, a mixture of hatred and pain. "But instead, you ignored my offer, my warning, and you went onto that battlefield like a fool, trying to save those who were already lost. If it weren't for me, you would have been dead that day."

"You kept me alive because you thought you could sway me," Mason rasps, his voice weak as he clings to the edge of consciousness. "But how could I side with a brother who is the one responsible for destroying our kingdom, killing our family, and imprisoning anyone who's left. No one's been living under your rule since we came to The Haven. Everyone's been merely surviving."

I fight to move my body. My limbs are still heavy, but I have feeling all the way up to my wrists now, and I clench my jaw, fighting harder to regain movement.

"You never understood me," King Celzar replies bitterly. "No one did. But I'll give you this last courtesy, brother. I'll let you die by the sword. A warrior's death. It's more than you deserve." He releases Mason's neck, and my mate falls to the floor, coughing as he lands in a crouch.

A nearby guard hands King Celzar his sword, and

my heart thrashes wildly. *No. Fuck no!* Crying out, I clench my teeth, hissing through the pain of my battered soul as I draw upon the small pool of energy that's welled inside me, and struggle from Dante's arms. My demon reluctantly lets me go, but he walks with me as King Celzar watches in amusement. "Now this is precious," he laughs. "Tell you what, I'll even let your new...*ally* die at your side."

"Blake, no," Dante snarls as the guards step forward, separating us and depositing me next to Mason. I tumble to the stone floor, my bones feeling brittle, and Mason grabs hold of me, his strong arms wrapping around my body. His voice is filled with hatred when he says to his brother, "She's not simply my ally, brother. She's my *mate.*"

"Mate?" King Celzar's gaze ignites with interest, and he laughs again. "Now that is the rarest of connections, and a cruel twist seeing as she's my bride."

I fight against the nausea that's gripped me. I used most of my energy to stumble toward Mason, and now all I can do is pray to Lady Fate that this will work. "Mason couldn't join you because you're right, he didn't understand you," I say, surprising everyone with the clarity of my words. "He only blamed you. He didn't understand that you loved Yenna, and that taking her power was an accident."

Regret and the reemergence of old emotional wounds twists King Celzar's expression.

"He never understood your pain," I say even

louder, and I steel myself, hoping the king connects the rest of the pieces himself.

King Celzar's expression grows contemplative, his mind working. "You're right, he never did," he finally says slowly, and he peers back at Mason. "But, perhaps, if you watch your mate die before you, you might just understand something before you join her."

I don't see the king move, and then his hand is on me again. Mason bellows, his face filled with fury as he moves to attack him, but King Celzar slams his free hand onto Mason's chest, throwing my mate backward. I hiss as the talons of King Celzar's magic sinks into me again, and the connection snaps back into place. "Now, I'll finish what I started," he says, his top lip curled, and I gasp as the energy that had started to replenish inside me starts to drain away. My mates' cries sound in my ears, the sounds of battle starting up again, but I focus on the king.

I struggle to breathe, my chest feeling like it's capsizing as that cold seizes me again, but this time I'm ready for him. I focus on the flow of power, and I grab hold of the thread tying us together. I grab hold, and I pull, sinking my own claws into the magic. Because like fuck if he's taking everything from me.

I strain, mentally fighting against him, and I'm rewarded when the flow of magic slowly changes, the power no longer draining into King Celzar but back into *me*. Like a damn has burst, power races through my body, filling my veins, sparks of energy exploding inside me like tiny fireworks. Magic twirls and dances as it fills every part of me, and the golden tattoos light up on my skin, the color so bright it's like my entire body is lit up from the inside. I feel the moment all of my power has returned to me, and a comfortable warmth spreads through my body, but I don't stop there.

King Celzar lets out a garbled sound as he struggles against my hold, but I don't release him. Reaching forward, my nails dig into his arm, the scent of his blood in my nose as I keep him there. Different types of magic I've never felt before flow into me, and I know it must be remnants of the power he's stolen from his other brides, and the witch, Yenna. And then, through our connection, I feel them. King Celzar's connection to the thousands of cuffs he has created and used to magically bind the power of the Perstalian citizens. I realize now that the reason Sassia could alter the cuff slightly and let me access a slither of my power, wasn't because she'd found a way around the king's magic. It was because as the king's magic depleted, so did the magic of the cuffs. They were all connected. And now I was, too.

Crying out, I send out a burst of power across The Haven. The magic pulses and ripples in the air, and I'm rewarded with the steady 'click' as simultaneously, every magical cuff unlocks, dropping to the ground. King Celzar lets out a stream of abuse, still struggling against me, and I finally let him break free, knowing his power is almost depleted. He staggers back, glaring at me, and a roar shatters the air followed by screams. Moments later, Nate lands on the dais beside me, no longer on two legs but in his powerful jaguar form. The cat's massive claws scratch deep grooves into the floor, and his maw drips with blood, a trail of fallen guards behind him. He bares his fangs at the king, his slitted eyes not moving from the male.

Mason's body changes, growing in size as he turns into a majestic, winged centaur with a glistening brown coat and large brown wings, and Alaric, Dante, and Prince Callan step up as well, their bodies pulsing with power. Prince Callan sends out a burst of wind that sends all of the remaining guards flying backward. They slam against the walls of the ballroom, their bones cracking before they fall to the floor.

"She did it," a feminine voice cries, and I turn to see Sassia and a handful of the servants watching from the doorway. Instead of standing on two legs, they stand as winged centaurs with glittering, glistening coats. I smile, and she grins at me as if to say she never doubted me.

"This can't happen," King Celzar spits, shaking his head furiously as the windows at the back of the dais shatter, glass raining down. I watch as Pask, and three other Pecos birds fly through the windows, their rainbow scales glittering in the light.

"No!" King Celzar shouts, staggering back.

I step forward, smiling grimly as they swoop down. "Oh, did I not mention? I passed on a message to some of your friends. I don't think they're too happy with how you've been treating them."

Pask screeches as he lands, his large taloned feet pushing King Celzar to the ground and pinning him there while the other birds circle their prey.

"Brother!" the king calls out fearfully, his frantic gaze going to Mason who stands beside me. "You know The Haven will not survive without me."

My centaur mate stays by my side, his gaze devoid of emotion. "This is your doing, Celzar. The Pecos have suffered just as the rest of us have."

Realizing Mason won't help, King Celzar turns his gaze to Princess Nerelia, his throat bobbing as he speaks. "Sister, have I not kept you alive and well all these years?"

The princess strides forward, no longer restrained, and when she lifts her arms, white crystals form on the ground, surrounding the groaning guards around the room, and half encasing them, so they're frozen in place. I think of all the white crystal around Perstalia, including the palace itself. *It was all her power. The king hadn't just been feeding on the energy of his brides. He'd been stealing the power of his sister.*

"You have kept me," Prince Nerelia says softly, and there's a sad but resigned look in her eyes. "And that is your mistake. I never wanted to take the throne, but you have shown why our parents selected me. Without you, we have a chance to heal."

"N-no!" King Celzar splutters, and when Pask and the other birds cock their heads, asking for my permission, I give it to them. The king's screams carry throughout the palace, but then it's silent as his blood seeps onto the floor.

Pask's talons release the king, and he picks up the king's crown in his bloodied beak, and he walks over, offering it to me. I take it from him and turn, holding it out to Mason.

"I was never meant to rule," Mason says with a shake of his head, peering over at his sister.

I walk to Princess Nerelia instead, noting the way her body shines, tiny crystals now glistening over her whole body.

"You're the rightful queen by marriage," she tells me with a soft smile. "And you freed us. You've earned this."

I smile. "Would you believe me if I told you I have enough to deal with at home? I have the demon throne to worry about."

"If the other demons are as powerful and strong-willed as you, I do believe you," she replies with a grin.

I hold the crown out to her, and she takes it gingerly. "Be the ruler your kind need," I say. "After what they've been through, they deserve it."

Nodding, she takes a deep breath, standing a little taller as she places the crown on her head. It's not until the applause starts that I realize citizens of The Haven have poured into the ballroom again, streaming through the doorway. Except instead of cuffed subordinates, hundreds of winged centaurs walk in, their heads held high, and their faces glowing with relief and awe as they stare at their new queen. And as they stare at me.

My mates crowd around me, and Alaric opens his hands, revealing Shade's battered body. I realize he must have scooped her off the floor. *...Because he knows how much she means to me.*

I swallow hard, terrified that in the time since I last saw her, she might no longer be breathing, but then she lifts her head, peering at me with those beady eyes I love. *"What happened?"* she asks groggily, and her gaze finds King Celzar's torn body. *"Oh crap, I missed seeing him get his ass kicked?!"*

Laughter bursts out of me, tears springing to my eyes, and my mates press in closer. Nate nudges me with his large nose, and I stroke his soft head, letting his fur slide through my fingers. A loud, possessive rumble starts in his chest, and I grin as the vibration works its way up my arm.

"So, princess," Dante drawls. "Can we go home now?"

CHAPTER
TWENTY-TWO

"I'm just saying it's not fair that I missed seeing the massive birds in action," Shade complains for the second time as she swallows down her beakful of fruit.

I shake my head at her and spear another piece of cured meat with my fork. Sweet Lady it's delicious. In fact, all of the food on the table in front of me is mouthwatering. There's even a dish with apricots, and I'm about ready to worship the pie like it's a new deity.

After Princess Nerelia was officially crowned as queen, a grand banquet was called in our honor, but my mates and I requested a more private affair. The new queen sits at the head of the dining table with only Mason between us, both of the Perstalian royals in their non-centaur forms. Dante is on my other side, and Alaric, Prince Callan, and Nate sit opposite us.

"Is something wrong, my mate?" Mason asks, resting his large, callused hand on my thigh beneath the table. It takes me a moment to realize he must have noticed me shaking my head.

"Not at all," I tell him with a smile, watching as Shade sticks her beak back into the flesh of a peach.

"So, what now?" Queen Nerelia asks softly, drawing my attention to her as she swirls her goblet of wine. "You've done us a great service. Will you stay and let us show our gratitude? You must be exhausted from all you have endured, and the celebrations will carry on for days."

"*Yesss, time for a vacay,*" Shade comments eagerly, her face covered in peach.

"*Vacay?*" My friend always comes out with the weirdest language.

"*Vacation,*" she replies, exasperated. "*We need to find out more about this Perstalian hospitality.*"

I grin. "*What we need, is to get home,*" I remind her.

She sighs in my head. "*How did I know you were going to say that?*"

"*Because it's true.*"

"Unfortunately, we need to get back home to Seral," I say aloud to Queen Nerelia, though I'm speaking to Shade as well. "Who knows what the situation is like back there?"

Dante spears an olive with his fork. "Yes, I can't

imagine King Dalton is happy about his daughter's disappearance."

"I understand," Queen Nerelia replies, not hiding her disappointment. Placing her goblet down, she turns to Mason. "And you, my brother. I presume you're going with her?"

My heart stutters, and I nearly choke on my latest mouthful. My new mate and I haven't had a chance to discuss what he plans to do now that King Celzar is out of the picture, and the Perstalians and rebels are free once again.

Like he can sense my stress, Mason's hand tightens reassuringly on my thigh. "I must go with my mate. She helped save us, and now I must help her and demonkind."

Queen Nerelia nods, and while there's sadness in her eyes, she smiles, and it's obvious she's happy for her brother.

"But I will return," he assures her. "While we are free from Celzar's rule, the Perstalians are still confined below ground, in a world we didn't choose. I will search for a way for us to return to the sun."

Guilt twists inside me. I want to offer for the Perstalians to come to Seral. To say they can live amongst the demons, but that's not a decision to be made lightly. There's no telling if the witches have further infiltrated Seral City, and until I'm queen of the demon realm, times are uncertain. "We'll figure something out," I tell Queen Nerelia, and I bump

Mason's shoulder with my own. "And don't worry, I'll take care of him."

Queen Nerelia's lips quirk up. "Of that, I have no doubt," she replies, her eyes sparkling. Still smiling, she lifts from her chair. "Well, if you'll excuse me, I'm going to get some rest. It's been an... exciting day, and I'm sure tomorrow will also be eventful."

She gives Mason one last look, and we all dip our heads respectfully as she leaves the room.

The moment she's gone, Nate blows out a breath and relaxes in his chair. "So, when are we plannin' to leave?" he asks, shoving three olives into his mouth at once, and then wrinkling his nose as he swallows them down.

Grinning, I say, "Tomorrow." But then I frown, turning to Mason. "Is that possible?"

My centaur mate nods. "Now that we're in possession of Celzar's ring, I can create a portal to the surface whenever I wish."

Relief trickles through me. "Good," I say, and I grab a large piece of the apricot pie that's sitting in front of me. It doesn't quite have the same flavor as the apricots from outside Dante's clan house, but it's still delicious, and I finish it within seconds. I'm busy licking my fingers when I notice my mates are all staring at me. Ignoring them, I eye the pie, wondering whether I can fit in another piece. After the whole ordeal with King Clezar, it was like I hadn't eaten in days, but the food I've already consumed tonight is starting to settle in my stomach.

"Apricots?" Dante questions, a slow sensual smile pulling across his face.

"What can I say? They're my favorite fruit." Grinning, I lick the jam off my bottom lip, and Dante's eyes heat as he watches me. "That is, they're my favorite, for now," I add.

Now that I know there's no chance of me accidentally killing my mates, I have no reason to hold back. No reason not to take what's mine, and I enjoy the attention as all of my mates fixate on me.

Mason's hand slides up my thigh, and Dante leans closer, reaching over to turn my head toward him. "For now, or for always?"

I hesitate, my breathing becoming shallow, and Shade makes a whistling sound in my head.

"Whoa, that must be one good apricot pie. I need to get me some of that," she comments.

"What?" I manage.

"Don't worry, girl, I get the hint. I'll meet you back in our room when you're done." Without waiting for me to respond, she launches into the air, swooping down to snatch up a small section of pie. Then she flies from the room, squeezing through the gap in the door.

I think about Dante's question as I watch her go. *For now, or for always?* Opening my mouth, I'm about to tell Dante that as my mate, he'll always be at least *one* of my favorites, but when I turn back to him, I find his chair is empty.

Right. Because he can turn invisible again. My gaze sweeps across the room, trying to find him though I know it's impossible, and I let out a surprised noise when my chair tips back, and I'm dragged a few paces away from Mason and the table. When all four chair legs are back on the ground, I feel Dante's warm breath by my ear as his tail wraps around my right leg, tying me to the chair.

"How long do you think it'll be before one of your other mates intervenes?" Dante whispers, his lips pressing to my neck. His invisible hand slides up my left thigh, and I guess that he must be kneeling beside my chair. Going by the way the other four are all staring at me, their food forgotten, I'm guessing they've heard what he said. My body heats as my demon moves his hand, my skin prickling with awareness as he slides his fingers up under my dress.

"What are you—" I start, but my words die off as he pulls my panties to the side, stroking a single finger along my center. I suck in a sharp breath, desire ripping through me as he slides his finger up and down my wetness slowly, teasing my clit and then moving down again.

"I think we should make up for lost time, don't you, princess?" Dante drawls against my neck as he touches me, his movements painfully slow, and I shudder as his breath puffs on my skin. "There's nothing to hold you back now."

His words aren't entirely true. Neither Alaric nor Prince Callan have said anything about changing their minds and being willing to bond, but when it comes to simply enjoying my mates without killing them...well, my demon is right. Nate's slitted gaze fixes on my flush face, his grip on his fork tightening to the point the steel utensil bends.

But it's Mason who comes over to kneel on my other side first. We'd all explained our powers earlier, including Dante's gift of invisibility, and the male doesn't seem the least bit bothered by it.

"I, for one, have no reason to wait, my mate," Mason murmurs, turning my head to him and claiming my mouth. His lips are soft and warm, and when his tongue explores into my mouth, I respond, enjoying the taste of him.

"That's two," Dante whispers, and like he's rewarding me, he pushes a single finger inside me before pulling it back out.

I whimper, wanting more, and across the table, Nate's fingers morph into claws as his expression turns predatory. "Like fuck if they're the only ones who get to have you," my shifter complains, his voice deepening like he's struggling to keep from changing into his jaguar form. Climbing over the table, he stalks toward me and drops to his knees in front of my chair. The moment Mason releases my lips, Nate turns my face to him, demanding his own kiss. I still have this feeling that Nate is hiding something from me, but that doesn't stop me now. Even if he's only after some fun, I'm more than willing.

"Three," Dante rasps, and this time he forces two fingers inside me, sliding them in deep. He pumps his fingers a few times before pulling them back out, teasing my entrance. I moan into Nate's mouth, and he growls, his chest rumbling.

My eyes are shut, so I don't see Prince Callan move. Not until a rush of air fans my body, the cool air pleasant against my hot skin. He pulls my chair back a little, and the prince's finger slides down the edge of my right wing. "F-fuck, what are you doing?" I gasp, pulling my lips from Nate's as I writhe at the sensation of him touching me like that. Because I had *no idea* my wings could feel that good. It's almost like there's a direct connection from my wings to between my legs, and merciful fates I can't tell if the sensation is torture or pure pleasure. Prince Callan chuckles darkly from behind me as his fingers slide through my feathers, pressing on the sensitive membrane of my wings, and my body coils at the rich sound of his laugh. There's no ice or reluctance, but only pleasure now as the archangel touches me.

"Four," Dante says, sounding almost as tortured as I feel, as he pushes three fingers inside me and slowly fucks me with them. Mason slides his hand under my dress, massaging my clit, and it's all too much. Too much sensation. Too much of *them,* and yet, I writhe, wanting more. Squirming, I pant in my chair, and all five of us stare at where Alaric is standing on the other side of the table. His face is tight, his brows pulled low, and the male almost looks like he's in pain. "I can't, Enchantress," he mutters, his voice barely louder than a whisper.

Dante doesn't stop, continuing to move his fingers

in and out of me. Nate kisses along my neck while Mason teases my clit, and Prince Callan continues to play with my wings, torturing me. But I don't tear my eyes from Alaric. My other mate.

"We should bond," I tell him through gasping breaths. "If we bond, we'll all be stronger."

Indecision flickers on the assassin's face, but his hands remain clenched at his sides. And when he doesn't come for me, the disappointment stings. I can still picture his face as he held me, telling me to fight and stay alive, and yet here we are. Still apart.

"There will be time to convince him when we're back in Seral," Dante murmurs reassuringly, his tail tightening around my leg.

"Fuck him," Nate says. Using his claws, he cuts down the front of my dress, and Dante and Mason move their hands away as the fabric falls from me, exposing me to the cool air. Nate tears his own clothes off next, and I'm distracted as my gaze slides over the perfect specimen before me, and the extremely *large* cock between his legs. *Holy Lady.* I'd forgotten how big it is, and I would be terrified if I wasn't already so sensitive, aching for more.

Mason squeezes my right breast, his mouth teasing my nipple as Prince Callan keeps playing with my wings, stroking and touching. Dante is the one playing with my clit now, and I moan as his fingers roll over the sensitive nub, teasing and torturing me. For a moment, Nate stays where he is, his eyes hooded as he drinks me in, enjoying the sight of me.

Reaching down, he fists the base of his cock and begins stroking himself as he watches me, and as Dante's fingers push inside me again, I shatter, gasping as I fall over the edge. My mates don't take their hands off me, and the orgasm is barely over when Nate prowls forward.

"Fuck me, shifter," I tell him, wanting more. I'm still so sensitive from all the teasing, and I'm relieved when he gives me a feral grin, desire swirling in his eyes. Dante's tail loosens on my leg as Nate slides my ass to the edge of the chair, and then my shifter leans back, sitting on his heels, and pulls me from the chair onto him.

Nate positions me, and I gasp as he pushes his cock in a few inches before pausing, giving me time to stretch for him. And then he slides his cock in the rest of the way. *Merciful Fates.* I reach forward, digging my nails deep into his shoulders, needing something to hold onto, and his chest rumbles with approval making my pussy vibrate. I feel so fucking full, and when his hands tighten on my ass and he slowly starts bouncing me on his cock, pleasure rolls through me.

Mason kneels on my right side, his hands finding my breasts again as he teases and pinches my sensitive nipples, and I whimper. My core clenches, and Nate curses, moving me faster as he peers down, watching his cock pump in and out of me.

"How can it feel this good?" he rasps, his voice ragged.

I claw at him, almost like I'm holding on for dear

life, and Nate removes one hand from my ass, sliding it down between my breasts toward my belly.

"That's because she's our mate," Dante drawls, and he says it with such certainty that my heart hurts. My demon crouches on my left, and his tail moves between my legs, teasing my clit as Nate fucks me. "Knew you would take it like a good little princess," he says, but his voice is strained. I turn my head, kissing the demon and clamping my teeth onto his lip, drawing blood before letting go. He chuckles, licking his lip and tasting his own blood. He's naked now, all bronze skin and defined muscles, and I reach down, grabbing hold of his hard cock. Wrapping my hand around the base, I start stroking him, and Dante groans.

"Fuck, Blake, I can't stop—" Nate rasps as he thrusts into me again.

I think he's trying to warn me that he's going to come, but then his cock fucking explodes. No, not explodes, but spines erupt on his cock, and a rush of pain shoots through me at the unexpected sensation. I cry out, and Nate curses as he stops moving immediately, panting as he holds me still.

"What the fuck just happened?" Dante asks, his voice suddenly serious.

"My barbs," Nate explains, his face strained as spotted fur sprouts on his shoulders. "I couldn't stop myself."

Mason frowns, concern filling his features. "Will it hurt our mate?"

Nate blows out a worried breath. "Hard to say. I've never been with a demon before."

Dante looks like he wants to pull me off Nate, but I shake my head, wiggling in Nate's hold. "It's okay," I say slowly, my breathing still labored. "I can take it." When I'd first met my mates, I was sure Lady Fate had made a mistake matching us. That I was somehow being punished. But now, I'm starting to think that just maybe, she wasn't wrong after all. And if that's true, then it makes sense that being with my mates shouldn't be an issue. *Not even if one of my mates has a massive, barbed penis.*

"Gorgeous, you don't have to—" Nate begins, looking unsure, but a smile forms on my face as I wiggle a little more, and the sensation of those spines turns from pain to pleasure.

"Fuck me, shifter," I tell him. "Don't hold back." Because I need this. Fuck, I need *him.* "And if all goes wrong, I have my power now, so at least I know I'll heal quickly," I reassure him.

Nate raises his brows, but he starts moving slowly, cautiously, as he tests me, all while watching my face. Now that the pain is gone, all I feel is an intense pleasure as those spines stretch me, and when I moan, throwing my head back, the uncertainty leaves his expression. A lopsided smile crawls onto his face, and when he thrusts into me, I feel like I'm unraveling in his arms. Realizing that he's not hurting me, the shifter doesn't hold back. He picks up speed until he's fucking into me hard and fast, his hands gripping my ass tightly.

The next time I look at Nate, he's staring at me with complete awe on his face, and I swear my heart nearly stops in that moment. "You really are mine, aren't you gorgeous?" he growls low, and I swallow, unable to find the words to respond.

Reaching to the sides, I grab Dante's cock again, and this time, I grab Mason's as well. I stroke the pair of them as Nate fucks me, slamming into me hard, his hands holding me tightly, and when Prince Callan comes up behind me again, his hands stroking along my wings, the orgasm rips through me. It's even more forceful than the last one, and stars burst behind my eyes as tingles race along my skin. Nate growls, his face strained as his muscles tighten, and he finds his own release, spilling into me.

I continue to stroke Mason and Dante, and they come soon after, their muscles bunching as they find their own release.

Nate holds me as my body shudders, his chest heaving, and when I sag in his arms, he looks at me with a bewildered expression. "I lost control," he admits softly. "That's never happened before. Not since I learned how to control my animal side."

I fight to catch my breath, grinning at him. "Well, let's hope next time you can do it on purpose." His cock is still inside me, but I'm surprised that I miss the sensation of his spines. Leaning forward, he brushes a strand of sweaty hair away from my eyes, and his touch is gentle as his slitted gaze roams over my face. "Next time..." He trails off, and I get the feeling he's testing out how the words sound in his mouth. I wonder if it's because he's not used to being with a single female for a longer period of time. In any case, I try not to read into it.

"Yes," I say slowly. "You're my fated mate, and now that King Celzar isn't trying to kill us, I expect a whole lot more of," I circle my finger in his general direction and grin, "this." I don't explain how I'm no longer worried that I'll accidentally kill him. Telling him that would open up a whole can of worms about Kai and Dante, and the unknown deadly power in Seral, and I feel too good to let myself think about that right now.

There's a flicker of something in the shifter's eyes. Indecision, maybe? I can't tell, but the expression is gone a second later when he winks. "Whenever you wish, gorgeous."

When I've stopped shuddering, Nate lifts me off him and sets me on my feet. His hands are still gripping my waist, but I step from him and walk to where Prince Callan is standing.

My archangel remains dressed, and his eyes darken as he watches me approach. I still feel uncertain about him. I mean, the guy has been a giant asshole since he found out we are mates, but the moment I'm close enough, he reaches out, his hands sliding behind my back as he kisses me deeply, drowning me in him. His lips are cool, soft, and perfect, and my arms wind around his neck as he kisses me like I'm his...everything.

When he pulls back, I'm panting again, and I peer into his eyes. "Never again," he whispers, almost like it's a promise to himself.

"What?"

"I'll never let you come that close to death again," he says, and his words are filled with such conviction that I have no choice but to believe him. I squirm, not used to being treated like...well, like my death would matter. I mean, sure, I always knew Dad would be disappointed if I failed one of his tests and died, but that's because it'd make him look bad. Right now, Prince Callan is speaking like he simply...cares.

"What's changed, Callan?" I ask, wondering how the archangel in front of me, can seem so different to the prince I first met.

His gaze lingers on my lips. "Everything," he murmurs, and then his expression changes, that cold edge making its way back into his eyes. "And also, nothing."

I frown, feeling more confused than ever. "What's that supposed to mean?"

He sighs, and I can't be certain, but I'm pretty sure his gaze finds Nate before settling back on my face. "Let's get you home, Blake. And then I will explain."

A part of me wants to demand that he tells me now, but we've been through so much, and despite the surge of desire that sizzles inside me, I yawn, exhaustion pulling at my limbs. Mason scoops me into his arms, pressing me against his hard chest.

"I can walk, you know," I remind him. And fly, but I didn't point that out.

He only grips me tighter, his callused hands not letting me go. "You will need to learn to let us treasure you, my mate," he replies.

I roll my eyes, admittedly probably because I'm not used to this kind of attention, but I don't fight him. Partly, because it feels too damn good to be pressed against him, and partly, because I get the feeling he needs this. Prince Callan, Nate, and Dante follow behind, and before we exit the room, I scan the dining hall. "Alaric?" I ask, but the assassin isn't there.

TWENTY-THREE

~ Princess Blake ~

Mason holds his scarred hand out to me. "Ready, my mate?"

The portal burns with green fire that flickers and crackles, and Queen Nerelia stands with a handful of guards, watching as my mates and I wait before the gateway. I place my hand in Mason's. "Are you?"

The Perstalian prince peers at his sister, then his gaze travels around the room like he's thinking about the land beyond these walls. But there's no hesitation in his eyes. Only warmth and acceptance. He nods. "Show me your world, Blake."

I smile, and my gaze flicks over to my four other mates.

Nate's lips twist into a grin. "Let's go see dear old Dad, shall we?"

"Please, please promise me you'll call him that when you meet him," Dante drawls with a wry smile.

I shake my head at both of them. "Let's just get to the ruins of Perstalia in case he's searching for us there," I say. "Then we can go on to Seral. We'll move on before Mason is affected by the air on the surface."

Alaric marches forward. "I'm going first. In case there are more surprises," he growls, and without waiting, he strides straight into the portal.

"He has a point," Prince Callan says with a shrug, and the archangel follows after him.

"Ready?" I send to Shade.

She adjusts her perch on my shoulder. *"Let's get out of here."*

Taking a deep breath, I tug on Mason's hand, pulling him with us into the portal, and Nate and Dante follow.

Magic crackles and swirls around us, twisting and winding, and then my feet are on solid ground again. It takes me a moment to reorient myself, but I let go of Mason's hand and straighten as the scent of ash fills my nose.

"Whoa, what the fuck?" Shade squawks in my head.

I draw my blade in an instant, and Prince Callan and Alaric stand a few paces ahead, weapons already in their hands as they take up defensive stances.

"I didn't expect it to look like this," Mason

murmurs, his expression grim as he studies the charred landscape.

Nate and Dante exit the portal behind us, and they're quick to grab their own weapons. "Where did you take us, Mason?" Nate growls, his slitted gaze searching for threats though it remains silent around us.

Dropping into a squat, Mason digs his fingers into the ash beneath our boots, then he lifts his hand, rubbing the powder between his fingers. "To the surface," he confirms. "Specifically, the center of the city as requested."

Dante curses, and I gape at the smouldering rubble around me. Where there had been rows of ancient Perstalian houses made of crumbling stone and cobbled streets, now there's simply...nothing. Nothing but blackened earth and piles of rubble on the ground. I walk forward, my brow creased as I stare at the wreckage.

"This can't be good," Nate mutters, then he cocks his head abruptly as if he's listening to something in the distance. I'm about to ask him what he's detected, when Prince Callan shoots into the air, his powerful wings sending a gust of wind over us and stirring the ash on the ground. The archangel returns a short while later, his boots slamming onto the ground as he lands with a demon soldier in his grasp.

Prince Callan releases the soldier, and Nate growls as my mates start to form up around me. I wiggle through their hastily made perimeter. "Relax, it's

Sebastian," I say quickly in the hopes they'll stop acting like a pack of territorial wolf shifters. "He's one of Dad's trusted soldiers."

Relief floods Sebastian's filthy face when he spots me. His hair is a mess, and his armor is covered in ash and blood, and I wonder just how long he's been out here.

"Your highness," the soldier barks, making a fist and placing his arm on his chest as he bows his head and drops a knee to the ground.

"Admit it, you missed this, didn't you?" Shade teases when a satisfied smirk forms on my face.

"Missed what? Being respected and not cuffed and imprisoned in an underground land? Yeah, I guess you could say that," I reply.

Her laughter fills my head.

"To your feet, Sebastian," I tell the soldier. "Explain what happened here."

My mates are all standing on either side of me now, and as the soldier stands, they size up the demon like they're just waiting for him to make one wrong move so they can kill him. Well, they all do except Dante, who appears merely intrigued by the soldier's presence.

Sebastian trains his gaze on me, and he knows better than to make me ask again.

"I'm here for you, princess," he says, dipping his head again.

Dante and I share a look before I turn back to Sebastian. "Me?"

The soldier nods. "His highness, King Dalton, came looking for you days ago. He was quite upset when you failed to return home following the bonding challenge."

"Right," I say slowly. Dad was most likely disappointed that I hadn't followed his plans and returned home as he intended. That I hadn't completed the competition to his satisfaction.

"He made us search the ruins in the hopes we would locate you," Sebastian goes on.

"Okay," I say. "But that doesn't explain, well," I stretch my arms wide indicating to the charred rubble around us, "this."

The soldier's face hardens. "It was during our search that we discovered a small coven of witches who had been hiding in the ruins. It didn't look like they'd been here long, but from what we could gather, they'd been abducting alphas in Perstalia with the help of a few individuals from the other realms. His highness gave orders for us to engage them."

My brows rise in surprise. "And this all happened because of a few witches?"

"There were more in hiding than we had originally calculated, and they were quick to retaliate. We lost a few good soldiers, and a handful of the witches escaped," Sebastian explains solemnly.

My jaw tightens. "And King Dalton?"

"He wasn't harmed, but he feared you may have been taken by the witches. We managed to capture two witches, and we kept them alive for interrogation.

They lasted some time, but when they still refused to confess to your capture, they were executed, and the king ordered me and a handful of others to remain here in case you returned. We later received word from a few alphas that they last saw you with multiple males, assumed to be your mates. His highness believed you may have been missing because you wanted, uh," he clears his throat, "private time with your mates."

Nate smirks, and Dante gives me a sensual smile. Just having them look at me like that makes my body heat, but I force my gaze away. Now is not the time.

"Okay," I say to Sebastian. "Well, I guess you'd better gather the others, and let's get home. May as well tell Dad the truth of what happened to us."

An uneasy expression crosses Sebastian's face, and his gaze darts to Prince Callan, and then back to me. My gut twists as I get the unmistakable feeling that something is wrong. "What is it?" I demand.

The soldier takes a steadying breath. "King Dalton isn't in Seral."

"What?" I step closer to the guard, and my hand shoots out. I grip the soldier by the front of his breastplate. "Where did he go?"

"The witches we interrogated," Sebastian explains. "They didn't divulge anything about your whereabouts, but they did confess to a plan involving Toralyn."

"The angels?" My heart sinks.

Prince Callan is close to the soldier in less than a

second, a severe expression on his face. "What of Toralyn?" he commands.

"S-something about a planned attack. King Dalton went personally with a regiment of soldiers to warn them. But that was days ago, and he hasn't returned to Perstalia since."

My head reels, and I release Sebastian, stepping back.

"We know there are witches already infiltrating Seral," I say to my mates. "What if this was simply a ploy to lure the king away from the demon realm?"

"From what this soldier has told us, I doubt the witches planned their capture and interrogation," Mason replies. "But there's no way to know for sure."

Prince Callan turns toward me, and his face is the picture of wrath. "I must return to Toralyn immediately." It's not a question; it's a statement.

His gaze bores into me, and I'm sure he already knows what I'm going to say before the words pass my lips. "We're going with you."

WANT MORE?

Thank you so much for reading Ruthless Monsters! The story will continue in book 3: Tortured Royals. If you enjoyed reading the latest instalment of Blake's story, it would mean the world to me if you could leave a review on Amazon or Goodreads! Honest reviews help other readers decide if a series is worth their time, and it helps out indies so much. Thank you!

If you'd like to read an exclusive bonus chapter and find out where Alaric goes after walking from the room in chapter 22, sign up to Mia Hartson's mailing list via her website:
www.miahartson.com/gameofpsychossignup

ALSO BY MIA HARTSON

HER CURSED PROTECTORS

Shadow Shifter (prequel)

The Blood of Monsters

The Cries of Monsters

The Curse of Monsters

The Wars of Monsters

Blurb for The Blood of Monsters:

Every decade, twelve young women from my island are gifted to the monsters.

This year, I'm in the line-up. But unlike the others, I want to be taken. Correction, I *need* to be taken—for my sister's sake. It's my fault she was chosen during the last offering, and I have to find out if she's alive.

I thought I was ready, but nothing could have prepared me for the four monsters who claim me. A vampire, wolf shifter, demon, and siren. They're terrifying, powerful, and infuriatingly arrogant...and now these alphas are fixated on me.

Turns out, finding my sister won't be as easy as I'd hoped. Now that I'm in their world, the monsters think I'll become one of them. I'm in their monster trials, and they're going to play with me until I turn.

These assholes think it'll be easy to break me, but they

picked the wrong girl. Because I'm already a monster. They just don't know it yet.

*This is a fun reverse harem fantasy novel for audiences aged 18 years and older. **Language warning **Slow burn romance **Multiple POV*

About the Author

Mia Hartson is a fantasy and paranormal romance author who enjoys writing about strong heroines who aren't afraid to get their hands dirty (or bloody), and hunky, misunderstood heroes who would do anything to protect their girl.

Mia lives in Adelaide with her husband, two girls, and her fur baby. When she's not writing, she's devouring another book, binging the latest fantasy TV series, or going on adventures with her family.

For more information about Mia Hartson, her books, and upcoming releases visit:

Website: www.miahartson.com
Newsletter:
www.miahartson.com/gameofpsychossignup
Facebook page:
www.facebook.com/AuthorMiaHartson
Facebook reader group (Mia's Mischievious Monsters):
www.facebook.com/groups/miahartsonsmischievousmonsters

Goodreads: www.goodreads.com/author/show/22415741.Mia_Hartson
Instagram: www.instagram.com/authormiahartson
Bookbub: www.bookbub.com/authors/mia-hartson
TikTok: www.tiktok.com/@miahartsonauthor